The Eternal Flame
and Other Stories

The Eternal Flame
and Other Stories

by
Michel Corday

translated, annotated and introduced by
Brian Stableford

A Black Coat Press Book

ISBN 978-1-61227-189-7. First Printing. July 2013. Published by Black Coat Press, an imprint of Hollywood Comics.com, LLC, P.O. Box 17270, Encino, CA 91416. All rights reserved. Except for review purposes, no part of this book may be reproduced or transmitted in any form or by any means, electronic or mechanical, including photocopying, recording, or by any information storage and retrieval system, without permission in writing from the publisher. The stories and characters depicted in this novel are entirely fictional. Printed in the United States of America.

TABLE OF CONTENTS

Introduction

La Flamme éternelle by Michel Corday, here translated as "The Eternal Flame," was originally published
in Paris in 1931 by Ernest Flammarion. Its sequel, *Ciel
Rose*, here translated as "Pink Sky," was issued by the
same publisher in 1933. The story making up the collection, "Les Ailes de Flamme," here translated as "Wings
of Flame," belongs to a much earlier period of the author's career, having appeared in the September 1909
issue of the periodical *Je Sais Tout*.

In addition to the two novellas included in the present volume, Corday wrote two other significant items of
speculative fiction. The novelette "Le Mysterieuse
Dajan-Phinn" was first published in the April and May
1908 issues of *Je Sais Tout* and translated into English as
"The Mysterious Dajan-Phinn" in the Black Coat Press
anthology *The World Above the World*.[1] The novel *Le
Lynx*, one of two novels the Corday wrote in collaboration with André Couvreur—a much more prolific writer
of speculative fiction—was published by Lafitte et Cie
in 1911; an English translation was published in America by Dillingham in 1913 as *The Inner Man*. Corday's
satire *En Tricogne, un an chez les Tricons, roman très
contemporain* [In Tricogne, a Year among the Tricons:
An Exceedingly Contemporary Novel] (1926) also has
an inevitable fantastic element.

According to the Bibliothèque Nationale catalogue,
Michel Corday was born in 1869, although other sources

---

[1] Black Coat Press, ISBN 978-1-61227-002-9.

record the date as 1870. He was educated at the Collège Chaptal and the École Polytechnique. He recorded few other details about himself in his entry in *Qui êtes-vous?*, the short-lived French version of *Who's Who*, except for a selective list of his books, the fact that he was an Officer of the Légion d'honneur, and that he was fond of motoring and canoeing. His experiences during the Great War, while he was working in Paris as a civil servant—which he recorded in a diary subsequently published in three volumes in the early 1930s—caused him to become an ardent propagandist for pacifism thereafter; *Ciel rose* is his most striking fictional development of that passionate concern.

Corday is best known today because he edited the final collection of works left unpublished at his death by his friend Anatole France, *Pages inédites d'Anatole France* [Unpublished Pages by Anatole France] (1925), and also wrote a memoir of the author, *Anatole France, d'après ses confidences et ses souvenirs* [Anatole France, according to his Confidences and his Memories] (1927). The latter helped pave the way for him to achieve considerable success thereafter with two further biographically-based works, *La Vie amoureuse de Diderot* [Diderot's Love Life] (1928), focusing on the private life of the great Encyclopedist, and *Charlotte Corday* (1929), about his most famous namesake, the assassin who stabbed the Revolutionary leader Marat in his bath. Prior to that late success, however, he had enjoyed a long career when he was known as a writer of light popular fiction, mostly in a sentimental vein, of which "Les Ailes de Flamme" would be a typical example were it not for the uncommonly baroque nature of its melodramatic component.

Corday's first novel was *Le Cancer* [Cancer] (1894), written when the diagnosis was still relatively young and the mere word first began to engender a quasi-superstitious terror, thus afflicting the luckless protagonist with the status of a modern leper. *Intérieurs d'officiers* [Officers' Home Lives] (1894) set a pattern that was to become more typical of his endeavors, however, and was followed by *Femmes d'officiers* [Officers' Wives] (1895), *Jeunes mariés* [Young Couples] (1896) and *Coeurs de soldats* [Soldiers' Hearts] (1897).

1897 was a particularly prolific year, in which he also published the autobiographical *Confessions d'un enfant du siège* [Confessions of a Child of the Siege (i.e. the 1870 Siege of Paris)] (1897), dedicated to Jules Verne, which credits Verne with changing the consciousness of a generation, *Misères secrètes* [Secret Miseries] (1897) and the one-act play *La Croix* (published 1897). *Mon petit mari, Ma petite femme* (1899) was probably his most successful novel, and in the early years of the 20th century, before the Great War, he became a regular contributor to the new generation of middlebrow magazines that sprang up in that period, including *Touche à Tout*, which serialized several of his novels and numerous shorter pieces, as well as *Je Sais Tout*. He continued to publish steadily after the war until his death in 1937, but his fiction never recovered the large audience it had previously had, and his non-fiction was much more successful, critically as well as commercially.

Although his interest in science *per se* was limited, Corday was inevitably interested in the manner in which technological developments had transformed the nature of warfare, and the consequent augmentation of the threat of future conflicts. *Ciel rose* is one of numerous novels produced in the interbellum period elaborating that sense of threat, although it differs from most of the others in refusing to develop its scenario as a horror story, preferring instead to develop, in far more intimate detail, a rare narrative strategy previously employed by Gustave Guitton and Gustave Le Rouge in their first part-work endeavor, launched with *La Conspiration des milliardaires* (1899) and translated into English in four volumes as *The Dominion of the World*.[2]

La Flamme éternelle is even more unusual, in being one of the few novels about scientific discovery to focus on the economic implications of discovery, including publicity, capitalization and the contest of vested interests. It was a pioneering work in its development of those themes, especially with regard to the harnessing of atomic energy, and is also original in the manner in which it poses the question of the ultimate objectives of scientific and social progress. Its linkage with *Ciel rose* helps to round out the latter argument, and enables the two novellas to form a whole that is greater than the sum of their parts.

Although that whole invites comparison with slightly earlier accounts of the threat of future war that are far more elaborate such as Ernest Perochon's *Les Hommes frénétiques* (1925)[3] and Léon Daudet's *La Napus, fléau de l'an 2227* (1927)[4], it offers a striking contrast with them in attempting to oppose their dour cynicism and

---

[2] Black Coat Press: 1. *The Plutocratic Plot*, ISBN 978-1-61227-095-1; 2. *The Transatlantic Threat*, ISBN 978-1-61227-096-8; 3. *The Psychic Spies*, ISBN 978-1-61227-097-5; 4. *The Victims Victorious*, ISBN 978-1-61227-098-2.

[3] tr. as *The Frenetic People*, Black Coat Press, ISBN 978-1-61227-118-7.

[4] tr. as *The Napus: The Great Plague of 2227.*

pessimistic resignation. The opposition in question is certainly deliberate; it seems likely that Corday was familiar with both those earlier works, and was reacting against them, thus making a significant and distinctive contribution to the whole nexus of thought.

The following translations of *La Flamme éternelle* and *Ciel Rose* were taken from copies of the Flammarion editions. The translation of "Les Ailes de Flamme" was taken from the version of the relevant volume of *Je Sais Tout* reproduced on the Bibliothèque Nationale's *gallica* website.

Brian Stableford

THE ETERNAL FLAME

"Never has such a vast hope been
given to the world... The Earth will
no longer die... Nor the human race...
Its genius will burn like an eternal flame."

I

"No trouble at home? Your wife? Your kids? No? Oh, that's good. You had me worried, you know. When I arrived that the paper I was told that you'd telephoned, that you wanted to see me here, today, at four o'clock. I thought..."

"Good old Laronce…just like you, immediately imagining catastrophes. No, no. Don't worry. No trouble. On the contrary."

On the flowery terrace of Bellevue, in front of the Center for Studies in Physics, the young scientist François Thibault patted his friend, the journalist Laronce, on the shoulder to calm him down.

In the sumptuous June sunlight, the contrast between the two men seemed comical. Tall and solidly built, his face forceful and tender beneath the unkempt hedge of his bushy chestnut-brown hair, François Thibault was the image of placid and cheerful strength. Laronce had a puny build, red hair and a tormented expression. He was forever picking at his ragged beard or readjusting his old-fashioned pince-nez with three fin-gers.

"So," said the journalist, "why did you call me?"

"To show you my discovery. It's finished. No one has seen it. You'll be the first."

"Oh! Your wife must know..."

"Of course! Naturally, she knows—and my bosses know too. But it's a first, even so!"

"Well, what is it? I know that for seven years you've been working on matter, on the atom, but that's all. You've never wanted to tell me anymore."

"That's true. I owe you an apology, old chap. It was me that I didn't trust. I wasn't sure of success."

"So, the invention…?"

"I'll show it to you right away.

He plucked a rose from one of the bushes on the terrace and preceded Laronce into the main building of the Center. The two men passed rapidly through a white-walled vestibule as vast and sonorous as a chapel, where a monumental global map of the world stood on a pedes-tal.

The laboratory where François Thibault worked overlooked the terrace via tall bay windows similar to those of an orangery. The walls were lined with display cabinets in which glassware, measuring instruments and bottles of chemical products gleamed.

On a small table, brightly illuminated by a window, there was a kind of microscope. François Thibault de-tached a rose petal and, after rubbing it slightly, placed it on a slide. He carefully positioned the slide and turned a knob. Immediately, an electric motor fixed to the ground next to the table began to hum.

Laronce started. "What's happening? What does that signify?"

Smiling, the young inventor said in an unemotional voice: "The rose petal is dissociating. The energy that it's releasing will animate the motor for days. Just think—the dissociation of a gram of matter furnishes as much energy as the combustion of three hundred thousand kilos of coal!"

"I don't understand," Laronce confessed, bitterly.

"You must have heard mention of the dissociation of matter?"

"Like everyone else—which is to say that I don't know anything about it."

"Would you like me to try to give you're a rapid lesson? It wouldn't annoy you?"

"Agreed. Just a second—with your permission?" Laronce took a notepad and pencil from his pocket and sat down at the long table that occupied the middle of the laboratory. "I wouldn't be sorry to put together the elements of an article to appear when the time is ripe. I'm listening—but don't forget that you're talking to the public."

"Yes. Well, this is it. It's necessary to think of space—all space—as a kind of fluid: animate, quivering and vital, traversed by vibrant waves, radiations, like light, electricity and many others that are being discovered every day. In brief, the universe is energy. Sometimes, that energy becomes concentrated, agglomerates, and condenses into matter. Thus, a nebula appears; it becomes a giant star, then a star; a world is born—and in that world, every atom is a whirlpool of energy in stable equilibrium."

The journalist stopped writing and raised his head. "Pardon me, but how can that energy, with which you're populating space, become something weighty—matter?"

"You can explain it to your readers by analogy. Can't an electric current, which is energy that is invisible, give rise to a spark, which has form and color? Doesn't lightning sometimes accumulate into a ball of fire?"

"Let's admit that. So what?"

"Then you can imagine how, by virtue of an inverse process, the atom can restore the energy that's concentrated within in, like a lightly-wound spiral spring unwinding. Having come from space, the energy returns to space. It's been known for a long time that so-called radioactive substances emit parcels of the energy of which they're a temporarily condensed form, but all substances can dissociate. By provoking that dissociation by an easy and reliable method, therefore, one could procure unlimited energy, effortlessly, inexpensively and endlessly."

"And you've found this method?"

"Yes—but thanks to many pioneers, whose work I've merely carried forward. A discovery is always a conclusion. All those who are trying to reach the same goal make up a ladder, like gymnasts in a human pyramid; the only who arrives at the top is supported by all the others."

Laronce was pensive. He murmured, in a sigh: "Extraordinary..."

"Then again, I was lucky, and helped by a memory. Do you remember the story of Archimedes setting fire, from the ramparts of Syracuse, to the Roman ships blockading the city with his ardent mirrors? That solar ardor concentrated at the focus of a curved mirror or lens—what a beam of light! The sun doesn't only emit calorific radiation. It emits others, like cathode rays. To be sure, they're not as easy to concentrate at a focal point, but it can be done. And matter dissociates at their focal point in the same way that matter at the focal point of ardent rays catches fire.

"Of course, I had to render that dissociation progressive, in order to remain in control of it. Take note too that I'd be able to use a pebble as easily as a rose petal. Anything will do—but vegetable matter seems to me to be preferable, because it represents an inexhaustible substance. Finally, I employ the liberated energy in the form of electricity because the present world is electrically equipped."

Laronce scribbled rapid notes on the paper. Nothing was visible but his red hair, in short frizzy curls, so well-nourished with pomade that it looked like varnished mahogany. Without raising his head he said: "And then? The results?"

François Thibault smiled softly, and in a simple and proud tone he said: "I think this profusion of energy will change the conditions of life completely." Then, becoming gradually more excited, he went on: "Think about it. It's the end of coal, oil, all the combustibles whose extraction is so difficult, so perilous and so barbaric, and of which the Earth only contains limited quantities—reserves that will be rapidly exhausted. It's the end of hydroelectric power, which depends on bad weather and demands titanic earthworks. Energy—infinite energy—for nothing! It will permit all hopes, it will permit all daring. I glimpse repercussions so profound, so far-reaching…if I told you…"

He was interrupted by the entrance of his wife. Petite and brunette, simultaneously slim and plump, Marianne Thibault had large dark eyes, a fresh and natural mouth, and restrained gestures. They lived in a small detached house near the Center where François worked, so she often came to the laboratory. She knew that Laronce would be there that day.

"Bonjour, Laronce," she said, offering him her hand. "Has François brought you up to date?"

The journalist had risen to his feet. François was familiar with his comrade's anxious personality, but he was astonished to see his expression so troubled. His forehead was furrowed by deep wrinkles: a strange manner of celebrating the great event.

"Yes, I've heard the bad news," Laronce replied, hoarsely.

"What do you mean?" the young woman asked.

"Knowing about his invention, you're going to let him spread it around?"

"Of course."

"But don't you see that it will get him into terrible trouble, and that, what's more, it will come to nothing?"

"Why?"

"You haven't thought about the formidable adversaries who are going to bar the way? But he's just named them himself. The coal magnates and the hydroelectric men, and most of all the oil men—all those terrible antagonists, ready to do anything: in brief, all the merchants of energy." He turned to François. "It's necessary to add to the list the manufacturers of explosives, munitions, war materials in general—for they'll be frustrated. In fact, your invention will doubtless permit the realization of electrical war: war by comparison with which chemical warfare and microbial warfare will merely be innocent trifles, petty jigs; war in which the planet can be systematically blasted with lightning—war, in short, that will render all other means of attack futile and vain."

"Certainly," François agreed, forcefully. "War the mere dread of which, the mere threat of which, will in fact lead to the suppression of war. That's how I conceive it."

"Yes. Well, those people won't permit your discovery to see the light of day. They'll begin by stifling it, by denying it."

With a strong and supple hand, François caressed the cast-iron casing of the enormous motor that was still purring. Tranquilly, he said: "It can't be denied, since it exists."

These forebodings did not trouble him very much. Obviously, the journalist was exaggerating. Since the distant times when they had been neighbors, as children, in their home town, Francois had been familiar with Laronce's two-sided character, both envious and devoted; his friendship was suggesting a fear that delighted his jealousy.

The young inventor had to admit, however, that although he had devoted himself to his discovery for a long time, often thinking about the benefits that it might bring, he had not thought sufficiently about the means of delivering it to the world. He would have to begin a new apprenticeship—and when he had called Laronce, he had strongly suspected that his comrade would point out all the difficulties to him.

"Your invention will be suppressed," the latter went on, furiously. "The newspapers won't talk about it. Oh, you don't know about the conspiracy of silence. It was born with the big press, the one that manufactures opinion. The conspiracy of silence is the most formidable weapon ever discovered. If one wants to prevent a project from bearing fruit, one keeps quiet about it. That's sufficient. It dies. You see, old chap, all the great wealthy corporations are connected, whether they like it or not; they all share the same fear of an upheaval. All their coffers are bound together, like the bricks in a wall—and what a wall! If one of them is threatened, the others defend it, instinctively. You're going to threaten the interests of the oil men, the coal producers, the armaments manufacturers? They'll sound the rallying cry, and the entire horde will be in league against you. And as the big press is in their hands, your fate is certain. A simple order: *shh!* And you're erased from the world."

François, who did not want to believe in such a black outlook, remarked softly: "But you, my dear Laronce, will talk about my research, when the time comes?"

Laronce was the news editor of the *Bonjour*.

"Me? I can only talk about it if the boss authorizes me to do so. If he imposes a veto, my paper jumps to it. Even the advertising industry—paid advertising, you understand—will refuse yours insertion if it receives the order. Even if you found a major backer, and arrived with a wad of bills, the advertising industry would slam the door in your face, if the big men have decided that it should."

"There's still an independent press, though."

"Nobody reads it."

"There are specialized journals; there are communications to Academies, scientific societies; there are lectures, the radio…what do I know?"

"Well, yes," Laronce admitted. "The rumor of your discovery will spread no matter what. Then there'll be a change of tactics. You'll be denigrated, doomed in the public mind. You'll be held up to ridicule. It will be insinuated that it's a fake, a confidence trick, a hoax. Or it'll be presented as a laboratory experiment without any practical application, and full of dangers. Or, in the end, after having tried to wear down your patience, you'll be granted the privilege of expert reports, which will be secretly sabotaged..."

"You're exaggerating, Laronce."

"Me? Come on! You know better than I do how all those who have proposed fuels less costly or less flammable than gasoline have been discouraged. What became of their trials? What became of the light accumulator discovered by a Spanish priest? In another field of research, what became of the methods of bread-manufacture that went directly from wheat to bread, free from the all-powerful mill?"

"Perhaps those inventions weren't workable?"

"That's what will be said about yours. Any means is good to crush the intruder. I've been told that the tire-manufacturers buy up all the patents that could supersede their tires, in order to bury them at the bottom of a drawer. And they might not be content to attack your invention—sometimes, they pick on the inventor. Do you remember Thimonnier, the inventor of the sewing machine, whom the tailors tried to drown?[5] And Lebon, the inventor of gas lighting, murdered in the Champs-Élysées on the eve of Napoléon's coronation? It was obviously the work of merchants of Argand lamps.[6] And many others...

---

[5] Barthélemy Thimonnier (1793-1867) obtained a patent for a sewing machine in 1830 and founded a manufacturing company to exploit it, initially by providing military uniforms; it was burned down repeatedly by manual workers fearful for their future, and by the time the machine finally took off commercially Thimonnier had died in poverty.

[6] This is pure conjecture; as François observes, the murder of Philippe le Bon, or Lebon (1767-1804), who industrialized the production of flammable gas from wood, remained stubbornly mysterious.

"Of course, the invention doesn't disappear with the inventor—but it's held back. The murderers have gained time. That's the great drama of technology: an industry becomes ferocious as soon as a new invention threatens its existence, or even threatens merely to change its equipment."

"Come, let's not be dramatic," said François, cheerfully. "The Lebon case was never clarified. And on the other hand, I can cite you numerous inventors who lived, as they say, laden with years and honors: Bessemer, who revolutionized metallurgy; Edison, whose little incandescent bulb put all other light-sources in the shade."

Laronce became exasperated. "The battle was less intense then than it is today. Think about the adversaries you'll have against you. You cited the oil men yourself. You know full well that those fellows, when they're fighting one another for supremacy, are ever-ready to transform their conflicts of interest into world wars—to throw the two halves of the globe against one another. Of what will they be capable the day when they unite against you!"

He took a large silver watch out of his waistcoat. "Time for the paper to go to press! I have to run." He paused in the vestibule, however, beneath the gigantic globe. "Adieu, Marianne. Excuse me for having spoken in front of you, but it was necessary that those things be said, and it's better that you heard them."

He shook François' hand, and added: "You too, old chap, forgive me. You understand—you're flying at a high altitude in your dreams, as if in the clouds, and it needs an obscure little journalist like me to warn you about the dangers of landing. Believe me—don't divulge your invention. Don't start a fight that really is too unequal. Think about it. Take advice. Consult your nearest and dearest—and keep me up to date."

He fled.

"What a character," François murmured.

He did not feel shaken. How little they counted, these risks—problematic, in any case—before the total certainty of alleviating suffering, spreading well-being, ameliorating the lot of human beings; before the hope of meriting their approval, their gratitude and their praise; before the pride of changing the face and fate of the world...

He was still resolved to divulge his discovery. On that point, at least, he would not consult his relatives, as Laronce advised. His parents? He was their pride, their reason for living, their god. They lit up with joy every time he was able to visit them in the dear old Burgundian estate. Since his decision was made, and firm, what was the point of worrying them needlessly? What was the point of consulting Marianne's father, Pierre Contal, since the famous author of *Génie antique*, passionately attached to the past, deplored science and denied progress?

In the shadow of the enormous globe, Marianne had drawn closer to her husband. She did not say much. François called her his "silent darling." To be sure, no one can exteriorize their most tender sentiments; it is one of the infirmities of the human creature; everyone keeps the best of themselves to themselves—but Marianne was subject to that strange modesty in the extreme, even though she had realized the most tender union and loving family with François. She looked up at him with her magnificent gaze and simply said: "What he said isn't true, is it?"

He hugged her to him, burying her in the hollow of his solid shoulder. "No, it's not true. You know that. He sees everything in black. But I had to consult him. If he hadn't been informed first, he would have been deeply hurt."

They went outside. The terrace was their garden. On a lawn, their two children were playing, watched by a young maidservant. They came running. Lise arrived first. She was seven. Because of her pretty face, her happy smile and her perfect little body, François called her "the majorette." Two-year-old Claude followed her. His arms swinging, his hands waving, he threw his rounded belly and his awkward feet forward like a little Silenus drunk on life. He was at the gracious age that precedes the ingrate age.

François lifted him high into the air and advanced to the edge of the terrace. In a great silence compounded from a thousand rumors, the ocean of Paris extended in the evening mist. And from the stone balcony, where so many ambitious dreamers must have invoked or cursed or challenged the enormous city, François, in his turn, spoke to the child he was holding in his arms.

"No, my little Claude, it isn't true, what that wretch Laronce says. No, no, now that energy will no longer cost anything, great things can be done. It's necessary that in this great Paris, people can see as clearly by night as by day. It's necessary that the whole world—the whole world, you hear—will be warm in winter and cool in summer. You'll see that, my little Claude.

"You'll see the sky become clear, because we'll no longer be expelling the smoke of coal fires into it. You'll see the city extend, further and further, becoming, for thirty or forty kilometers around, an immense park of greenery, flowers and villas. As electricity, which can do anything, won't cost anything, all that vegetation will be able to grow, thick and fast; rain or sunshine will be summoned to it according to its needs.

"People will be able to live further away because they'll be able to travel faster. After a day's work, which will be made much easier, simpler and shorter, everyone will disperse in all directions, in lightning-fast cars. It will be the reign of guided projectiles, rockets, propeller-driven torpedoes. Yes, my little Claude, you'll see that magnificent culmination: projectiles that will finally be useful for something!

"And because life will already have become a little easier, people will become a little better. You'll see all those things, my little Claude. And you'll be able to glimpse so many others..."

II

François took his entire family by road to the family house in Briolle where his parents lived. He brought them the great news. He imagined their pride, their excitement. He would certainly keep quiet about Laronce's stupid warnings. They would seek the best means of spreading the discovery together.

He enjoyed consulting them. With them, he became a child again. He still called them "Papa" and "Maman," like a good child. They had, to be sure, kept him to themselves for a long time. His mother had given him his elementary education. His father had opened broad views on simple lines in the various directions of knowledge. Both had watched out for the awakening of a predilection, and as soon as they had noticed his liking for the physical sciences, they had encouraged and served it. He owed the intoxication of the first revelatory readings and the first small home experiments to them. At fifteen, he had left for Paris, where a family friend had adopted him during his external examinations at the college and his early years in the laboratory.

No, truly, at Briolle he could not succeed in persuading himself that he was thirty years old. He rediscovered the enthusiasm, the exuberance and the gaiety of being fifteen in the family house where, beneath the patina of care and age, the wax and the fruit flourished. For him, it was like a tender museum in which a story or a memory was attached to every item of furniture, portrait or trinket. And he found it touching that the old dwelling had opened itself to young inventions, that electricity accomplished many household tasks there, that one could hear the purr of an automobile engine, that the telephone rang and the wireless sang.

Impatient to arrive in Briolle, to proclaim his complete success joyfully, François drove at high speed. Finally, the familiar locations surged forth where he felt at home. Papa and Maman were waiting at the gate. She was strong and placid; he was tall and smiling; they both wore their vigorous fifties well. François was so accustomed to finding them immutable that he was ingenuously astonished to find slight signs of age in them: wrinkles deepening, hairs going gray.

He yielded immediately to the pleasure of telling them the great news. During the first effusion, amid the awkward kisses of the arrival, he declared: "It's finished. It's complete. It's done."

There was no real discussion, however, until after the evening meal and the children had gone to bed. François rediscovered the old family custom of lingering momentarily around the cleared table, his elbows on the cloth. He called that meeting "the Elbow Club."

What was the best way of spreading his discovery? He knew, vaguely, that it was customary to set up a joint stock company, but there his knowledge ended. They perceived very rapidly that all four of them were equally ignorant of the world and practice of business.

The contrary would have been surprising. Monsieur Thibault, after a short stint in the Navy, had devoted himself to the estate that he had inherited from his parents. His wife belonged to a family of academics. Marianne had been brought up by a father who was illustrious, to be sure, but a worshipper of the past. François has lived primarily in the atmosphere of the laboratory.

The young inventor was amused by their communal ingenuousness. Putting all their intelligence together, they would not have been able to distinguish a share from a debenture.

"To think that in school they load our memories with so much superfluity and leave us ignorant of such useful things! We don't learn the vocabulary of Finance, or that of the Law; we're not even given the means to defend ourselves in life. We aren't taught how the political machine functions, or the human machine. In brief, we're ignorant of the mechanism of everything that surrounds us, from the doorbell to the progress of the stars...but all that can be sorted out."

Madame Thibault was unworried by their temporary embarrassment. She had such faith in her son that she was certain of his eventual triumph. One way or another, he would succeed. She had always taken her child's side, fiercely—a true lioness. By the way she pronounced "my" when she talked about him, one sensed that, for her, other people's children did not exist.

Her husband did not share her serenity, however. He bit his fingernails and blinked his eyes—certain signs, in him, of emotion or anxiety. He confessed his fears. One heard stories of inventors dispossessed of their discoveries, robbed as in a wood. He sensed that his son needed a guide who was not only very well-informed but also very reliable and very honest. To whom should he entrust himself? He had no friends or relatives in the world of business.

Marianne, who had remained silent until then, as was her habit, said discreetly: "Papa knows Chérance quite well."

Chérance! Although François remained a stranger to the world of finance, its language and customs, he was too keenly interested in the times in which he lived to be entirely ignorant of Chérance. He was haloed by a legend of delicate splendor, lucid audacity and proud honesty. The newspapers related that he maintained a squadron of aircraft, always ready to take off at a moment's notice, either to take him to one of the sumptuous dwellings he had acquired throughout Europe, or to carry correspondence promptly, or even to supply his table with some rare and distantly-originated delicacy. In brief, he seemed be a head taller than the rest of the aristocrats of industrial banking, the new barons who ruled the world.

He also had a reputation as a passionate bibliophile, the most fervent lover of sought-after books and rare manuscripts. Doubtless he cultivated the friendship of Pierre Contal out of admiration for that marvelous evoker of the past, the author of *Laïs*, *Cadmus* and *Génie antique*, but also in the hope of occasionally gleaning a few original manuscripts in his home. In that spirit of fervor, he could not refuse to welcome and aid the writer's own son-in-law.

Yes, Marianne the Silent was right.

Thus, Pierre Contal would favor, indirectly, the diffusion of the great discovery. That collaboration had been quite unexpected, for the progress of science had no more furious adversary that the author of *Génie antique*. François knew something about that. He could not forget a certain historic scene, by which the fresh romance of his engagement had almost been interrupted.

At that time, he had usually observed a sage discretion in Pierre Contal's presence, imposing silence on his own opinions, as much out of respect for the Master as for love of his daughter. Then, one day, even so, he had yielded to a foolish temptation to convert him, to win him to his own views. He had proclaimed his faith in human progress, in the best of times, and had perceived too late, to his horror, that his future father-in-law could not tolerate contradiction, at least on that terrain. He had seen that man—ordinarily mild, polite and timid—bound and bristle, and then attack like a crazed wild boar. But for Marianne's delicate patience, their marriage plans might have foundered that day.

Now, that diehard disparager of progress was about to serve the cause of science, whether he liked it or not—for even in the unlikely event that he refused to give his son-in-law an introduction to Chérance, the young inventor would only have to present himself to the financier in the name of his father-in-law to be assured of a good welcome. And once again, François tasted the salt of the irony that gives life its authentic flavor.

Except in winter, when he was resident in the house in Passy with which all his friends in the world of letters were familiar, Pierre Contal lived on the estate of Clos-Mussy, which he had acquired ten years before, two leagues from Briolle. Monsieur Thibault, who had a taste for writing, like most mariners, had hastened to show him his travel notes on the ruins of Easter Island as soon as he became aware of that illustrious neighborhood. A relationship had been formed. It was thus that, on his subsequent vacation, François had met Marianne. How many times he had traveled those two leagues, at all hours, by all means, in all weathers! He knew every tree on the route by heart.

The day after the Elbow Club had recognized its ignorance, François, accompanied by Marianne, went by car from Briolle to Clos-Mussy. He went too rapidly to count the trees on the way, but he smiled at the memories with which the road was strewn.

Pierre Contal was expecting his daughter that morning. A letter from Marianne had notified him that she would arrive in Briolle the previous evening—for, although he had always refused to acquire a telephone, he consented to read his mail almost regularly, even though letters had to make use of modern means of transport: trains, automobiles and airplanes.

The newspapers and magazines had often reproduced the features of Pierre Contal, for the suffrage of connoisseurs had brought him to the height of renown. The crowd followed him. His gifts as an evocative writer, his infallible erudition, and most of all his style, endowed with a Hellenic grace, were celebrated. *Génie antique* was unanimously considered as a perfect masterpiece.

Marianne and François found themselves in his library, where books filled the walls, crushed the tables and inundated the floor.

Of medium height, solidly built, gray-haired, with a fleshy nose and a bristling moustache, but a soft and kindly gaze, he was dressed without ostentation in brown flannel suit with a red kerchief at his neck and a skullcap planted on top of his head in the fashion of a zouave.

He immediately inquired about Lise and Claude. He had a marked fondness for Lise, the majorette. The mysterious law of heredity often give children the features of their grandparents; Lise reminded him of his wife, who had died prematurely in the epidemic of influenza unleashed by the world war. His wife reappeared in that little girl; such resemblances are the smiles of shades.

Marianne promised to bring the two children to see him that afternoon, and while he was rejoicing she said, without transition: "Don't you know Chérance, Papa?"

He was sitting at his work-table, where beautiful vestiges of old marbles served as paperweights on thick piles of papers. He raised his arms and, his gaze mischievous and his mouth rounded beneath his bristling moustache, he cried: "I should think so! Oh, I don't know anyone else who's such a slave to his passion. You only have to wave a page of manuscript in front of him to make him fly around the world. In Paris, I've seen that demigod on his knees in front of my waste-paper basket, searching it for crumpled or torn fragments."

By virtue of a discreet modesty, he did not confess that Chérance was desperately covetous of the manuscript of *Génie antique*. Contal, who wanted to keep it in the family, was deaf to the all-powerful financier's allusions, sighs, and expansive and pressing offers. Lowering his head, however, and peering over his spectacles suspiciously, he said: "Why the devil are you interested in Chérance?"

"François has need of him."

In order to avoid the return of a perilous discussion, the young inventor got straight to the point. "Yes. My research is concluded. The advice and support of a financier would be useful to me. I'd be glad to have a letter of introduction to Monsieur Chérance."

Pierre Contal had a confused awareness of the nature of the work that his son-in-law's had been doing for the last seven years, but he detested all the fruits of science. Far from applauding, he raised his arms again, waving his hands like a drowning man.

"Don't we have enough of these waves, vibrations, rays and radiations yet, in which we're struggling like flies in a spider's web?"

François made no reply. What point was there is running the risk of irritating him needlessly? What point was there in exchanging once again the eternal arguments that the partisans and adversaries of progress threw at one another's heads without ever convincing anyone? What was the point of reopening a trial in which the future would be the only judge?

Standing in front of her father, Marianne leaned over him. "You have to write the letter, Father. Anyway, it's very important for Monsieur Chérance too."

Contal murmured: "Nothing's important."

However, he picked a sheet of paper out of a sheaf. He thought for a few moments, while caressing his lip with the end of his goose-quill. Then he started writing. Marianne and François exchanged triumphant glances.

When he had finished, he said: "There. I've asked him to help you as he would help me, if I were mad enough to want to change the world."

With the edge of his hand he pressed the letter down on the blotting-pad, and he repeated, obstinately: "For it *is* madness."

François could not help himself. "But Father, many people will have less difficulty..."

Certainly, in pronouncing that sentence he had no intention of opening a debate. Not at all. He knew full well that Pierre Contal had written to Chérance in spite of his convictions—and in a surge of gratitude, he had wanted to associate him with his work, to show him the benevolent consequences of that letter.

But the great man misunderstood; he thought he was being challenged to a duel. Putting his spectacles down on the table, he fixed François with a hard stare. Keeping the letter in his extended hand, he said: "You'll never recognize the definitive vanity of your efforts? I don't believe your discoveries in science constitute progress. I don't even believe in progress. But even admitting momentarily that it exists, don't you feel that it will be as limited and restricted as the fate of the human species itself? Your science has taken care to warn us about that. It informs us that life will disappear from the frozen Earth. Even before the planet becomes a dead world, an icy bolide, humanity will have died out. Even if it were capable of improvement, which I don't believe, there wouldn't be time. I repeat, it would be madness to found hope in a future whose limits we already perceive."

Pierre Contal could not have suspected the effect of his words. He had just struck the inventor at his most sensitive spot, in his most secret and radiant hope. François choked, his heart congested. He could no longer contain himself. He was going to turn back on Pierre Control the very argument with which he adversary had tried to crush him. He would never again have such a chance to convince him, to show him the infinite possibilities of science. He would reveal to him the reckless anticipations that he had scarcely mentioned even to Marianne. At the risk of seeing the letter to Chérance torn up in spite, he would speak.

"But how do you know that the human race will disappear?" he said. "With the infinite energy that it will have at its disposal, humans will be able to do anything. When solar energy declines, how do you know that they won't move the Earth out of its orbit, and launch it into the zone of attraction of another of those suns that star our night, which will pour light, heat and life upon them in its turn? Thus, moving from sun to sun, the Earth will be assured of an eternal youth. The human race will no longer disappear, and it will never cease to improve itself."

But Pierre Contal, his eyes round, showed so much surprise, and even anxiety, that François put out his hands in a gesture of appeasement.

"Naturally, it's only an intellectual anticipation, a mere possibility. The time for such an attempt hasn't yet come. But to know what is possible, to know that one has the energy necessary to do it—isn't that something? From now on, isn't such an assurance capable of sustaining people? Can't they extract some comfort from the conviction that their race will live forever, that their efforts are permanent, that their progress will accumulate endlessly, toward perfection? Never has such a vast hope been made to gleam in their eyes. Doesn't such a view explain the intuition of the divine that's in all souls, the promise of eternity that's in all religions? Might not this faith in human destiny become the supreme creed?"

Pierre Contal shook his head. "You said it yourself: it's only a dream. I don't believe that it's capable of affecting people, influencing their actions, reacting upon their lives. They'll make fun of it. There's no proof, in any case, that if they had an eternal future ahead of them, they'd employ it to improve themselves. You know my opinion on that point. And if your anticipation obtains any consistency, it might, on the contrary, plunge them into a tragic despair, because they'll perceive the perpetuity of their wretched condition."

Then, as if secretly satisfied to have snuffed out François' enthusiasm with the final word, he handed the young inventor the letter to Chérance.

III

François was introduced into a drawing-room the size of a museum, with the elegance of a boudoir. He was waiting for Chérance. The financier, who lived in a Louis XV mansion in the vicinity of the Bois de Boulogne, had the whim of only accommodating furniture of that period—and before those fine marvels, François felt the satisfaction one experiences in caressing a pearly, finished, perfect work of art with one's gaze or one's fingers.

Sensitive to consideration and small attentions, he congratulated himself on Chérance's methods. The financier could have given him an appointment, without any urgency, in his offices in the Champs-Élysées. On the contrary, scarcely had he received Pierre Contal's letter than he had offered François, by telephone, a meeting at his home that same afternoon. And yet, great barons of his sort hardly were ever their own masters.

He smiled at an impish thought. It haunted him every time he had to approach some highly-placed person. He thought he had found a means of not being intimidated. It was sufficient for him to remember deliberately that the great man had been a little baby like everyone else: a chubby babe in arms lavished with caresses babbling adorable nonsense; a baby who had no other concern but to sleep, eat, drink and excrete. Then, the severe

features and the prestigious mask were no longer imposing. One simply thought: *this is what age has made of a
plump bonny baby...*

A door opened, revealing Chérance. He was short,
slim, bald and elegant. He had a small black moustache,
a firm gaze and an imperious chin. He looked to be
about fifty. Frank and cordial, he held out his hands to
François. "I have the greatest admiration for your father-
in-law. I'd do anything to oblige him. Oh, I envy you,
young man, living in the intimacy of such a genius..."

François remembered Chérance's passion. For him,
living in the intimacy of Pierre Contal would be to have
the ability to glean at his ease the slightest scraps of
handwriting, even from the waste-paper basket.

The financier continued: "Let's see—I believe it's a
matter of a discovery. Come and tell me about it." His
voice, a trifle hoarse, was alert and seductive. François
forgot to imagine Chérance as a little baby. Immediately,
he felt conquered, and he was happy to be subjugated.

He followed the charmer into his study. The financier had resisted contemporary fashion, which demanded
a cold, surgical sobriety, the nudity of an operating theater. On the contrary, here, once again, everything bore
the charming imprint of the eighteenth century. And
Chérance, sitting behind his desk, his features delicate
and his expression proud, evoked some minister of the
ancien régime just as faithfully. Without a doubt, however, his power was more extensive than that of a Choi-
seul or a Necker, for one could be certain that the aris-
tocracy of industrial finance governed governments.

François summarized his invention as clearly as
possible. Chérance, his forearms leaning on the desk and
his hands linked, seemed extremely attentive. He not
only had the gift of comprehension, but the even rarer

one of listening. He refrained from interrupting the brief speech. Perhaps, entrenched in the hard struggle of business affairs behind his mask, he was even exaggerating his impassivity.

When François indicated the industrial consequences of his discovery, however, the financier betrayed his emotion. A surge of blood reddened his forehead, inflating the temporal vein. In a casual voice, however, he said, simply: "In brief, you're offering us an inexhaustible and gratuitous source of electricity?"

"For the moment," François agreed, "that is indeed the best formulation."

Rapidly and precisely, the financier elucidated the points that seemed to him to be essential. "Will your apparatus be expensive, difficult to construct?"

"No dearer or more difficult to construct than a simple microscope.."

"And the operation? Complicated? Dangerous?"

"Neither."

"You have your patents, of course?"

"An agent at the Center for Studies in Physics is taking care of it."

"You have a working model?"

"Of course," said François. "If you have a spare moment, I'd be happy to show it to you right away. I had the intention of making the proposal. Bellevue is five minutes away by car."

Chérance rang for his chauffeur and rose to his feet. "Agreed."

As they went through the drawing room, François complimented its perfection.

"Yes," agreed the financier. "It's necessary for an era to be already remote in the past before one can really collect its flower. It's only then that one can choose the excellence that it has produced, which has stood the test of time and taste."

Scarcely were they in the car, however, than he returned to François Thibault's invention.

"Is Thuilier still the director of the Center?"

"And Lavolige the deputy director."

"Both members of the Institut, aren't they?"

François nodded his head, smiling. "Both of them."

It seemed to him to be improbable that Chérance was fetishistic about official titles, but the financier doubtless judged it prudent to have the discovery certified by orthodox scientists before launching it into the world. He wanted the testimony of two members of the Institut. Discreetly as he had revealed it, his desire was evident.

François wanted to show him that he had anticipated that. "This morning, I told the gentlemen in question that I was coming to see you this afternoon, and that you might perhaps come to my laboratory, so I think they'll both be there."

He was mistaken. Thuilier, the director, was indeed present at the rose-petal experiment, but the deputy director, Lavolige, did not put in an appearance. "Monsieur Lavolige must have forgotten," François explained to Chérance. "You must excuse him—he's very distracted."

Lavolige was, indeed, distracted by nature—but, far from seeking to vanquish it, he cultivated his weakness. He knew that Ampère had used the back of a cab as a blackboard, that Henri Poincaré took a bed sheet traveling instead of a nightshirt. He had, therefore, unbridled his own distraction in order to bear a stronger resemblance to a great scientist. He missed meetings and engagements, and broke his promises. Then, mild, disheveled, wheedling, desolate and almost sincere, he begged forgiveness, blaming a life overburdened with work and a brain overladen with thought.

To tell the truth, the little eccentric steered his boat very cleverly; his thoughtlessness served his interests and his passions. In forgetting Chérance's probable visit, he was satisfying both his jealousy and his prudence. He was avoiding praising a discovery of which he was enraged not to have been the author, and he was also avoiding adding his patronage to it, perhaps prematurely, in the presence of an important individual.

By contrast, Thuilier warmly celebrated François Thibault's invention. Stern and dark, perfectly handsome, he had the air of sad disdain and cruel gentleness that is attributed to Asiatic princes. Rich and laborious, he was ravaged by ambition. He had hesitated over his vocation for a long time, taken several different paths, always searching for the one that would lead him most rapidly to the top. Finally, he had devoted himself to the Center for Studies in Physics. He had given it his time, his effort and his money. He had expected, in exchange, influence, titles and honors.

He was certainly excited, at present, by the prodigious discovery and its infinite consequences, but he wanted to claim the merit and the glory of it for the Center, and, in consequence, its Director.

François was as cheerful about Thuilier's panegyric as Lavolige's absence. "Everyone has his line. It's human nature." He watched Chérance carefully. Standing up straight, elegant and businesslike, his hands clasped behind his back, the latter was meditating before the apparatus.

Evidently, the man, sated with money but still avoid for power, must see it as the most formidable instrument of domination. Soon he would have the fate of the kings of energy—those of oil, coal and explosives—at his mercy. He would be the master of those masters of the world. In his eyes, that simple metal tube must shine like the emblem of unlimited power, the scepter of an unparalleled empire.

Only the redness of his forehead and the throbbing of his temples betrayed that feverish pressure of avarice. Suddenly, he seemed to wake up, spun on his heel, congratulated Thuilier in a few well-chosen words on the glory that would soon illuminate the Center. Then, leaving the director pale and swooning with pride, he took François by the arm and drew him on to the terrace, where he strode back and forth with a sustained stride.

"Well," he said, "it's extremely interesting. To exploit your patents, we're going to form a little company. I'll have associates. We'll make an appeal to the public. It's necessary to be among friends to conserve the independence of the enterprise, to remain the masters. You'll be assured of the technical directorship, a seat on the board, dividend-paying shares. In sum, we'll give you the lion's share. You can count on me."

François stammered thanks. Chérance cut him off. "Ah! By the way, what shall we call your apparatus? That's quite important. Have you given it a name?"

The inventor smiled. "When my wife and I talk about it—which is today, nearly every day—we call it the press. You get it? It liberates and spreads the energy stored in grains of matter, as a press liberates and spreads wine, the energy contained in the grapes. But the term might be confusing..."

"I fear so."

"Yes. It's a little pet name. For the public, I'd prefer to call it the Starter: that which provides impetus; which releases concentrated and constrained energies that are ready to surge forth."

"Excellent!" exclaimed Chérance. "The Starter—very good. And it's an English word that has become French, already international, which will be immediately understood by all those who speak either of the two languages—five hundred million inhabitants, a third of the planet." Still holding his companion by the arm, he continued to draw him along the terrace, indifferent to the horizon of Paris, blurred by heat-haze and the smoke of factories. "And for the Company, do you have a name? That's also very important. You must have given it some thought..."

"Not so much. In sum, we're liberating universal energy. That ought to be the name of the Company."

"No, no," the financier protested, sharply. "It's weak, banal, trite. It might be the name of a bank."

"There's also cosmic energy—the meaning is identical, but the tern's more elevated."

"Yes, yes, obviously," Chérance acquiesced, unenthusiastically.

"I've also thought about Sidereal Energy. The name isn't exact, because it seems to indicate recourse to the stars, when I'm using certain solar rays. It's much later, in millions of years, when the sun deteriorates, that people will have recourse to the rays of the other suns that are the stars. Already, their astonishing power has been recognized. What are called penetrating rays..."

Chérance interrupted him. "Sidereal Energy...that's perfect. Let's not seek any further. It's sonorous, musical, and a little mysterious—in sum, as you say, it has the implication of the future. Perfect, perfect." He stopped beside his car. Before getting into it, he said: "Time's pressing. Very soon—tomorrow, no doubt—

you'll hear from me. *Au revoir*, my friend. I needn't stand on ceremony with you, need I? Give my regards to Pierre Contal. Tell him that he can be proud of you, that he has a son-in-law worthy of him."

IV

In the curve that the Seine describes level with Mantes, opposite Vétheuil, at Fraicourt, factories had grown apace, like a crop. In the course of the work, the young inventor had certainly encountered ill will, stupidity and even knavery from time to time, but his faith in his definitive success was so robust that he had supported these minor hitches lightly.

Convinced that Paris would rapidly expand over thirty or forty kilometers around, in great spaces of verdure and stone, he had proposed that they install themselves right away beyond the reach of the future city. Then again, he was pleased to be on the waterway, on the great stream that ran toward the sea and the New World.

In accordance with the custom established since the development of aerial transport, the inscription *Sidereal Energy* was raised in large white letters on the vermilion of the tiled roofs. Henceforth, the ground would be "read" as maps had once been read. The architect had even risked an objection: in case of conflict, the factory would be marked out as an enemy target—but François had replied, laughing, that aerial warfare would soon be impossible, for the infinite energy that would be disposable would make it possible to prohibit the sky to any aircraft whatsoever.

Chérance had strongly advised the inventor, when he published his discovery, only to point out the immediate and practical effects, and not to indicate the distant repercussions—those that he called "the philosophical consequences."

The financier had given him that advice one day when they were both traveling by car toward Fraicourt in order to visit the factory site. Francois, in a surge of confidence, had confessed to him the supreme hope that he founded on his invention: the possibility of being able, when the time came—doubtless millions of years in the future—to move the Earth out of its orbit and incorporate it into another solar system, and then another, thus to ensure, in a voyage toward infinity, a literally eternal life. For him, that glimpse of possibility truly crowned his work. It opened limitless perspectives to human destiny. He repeated that such a vast hope had never been given to the Earth."

The financier, however, had put a hand on his sleeve and raised the other index finger.

"Beware of being misunderstood. Incomprehension is the great reef. It's necessary to avoid it. The man in the street can't grasp these long range views. They surpass him and frighten him. He'd prefer to doubt your lucidity than his own intelligence. Count yourself lucky if he understands and appreciates the tangible benefits that you're bringing him."

François, thoroughly conquered by Chérance, was glad to take him as a guide. He therefore followed the financier's advice when he drafted a report of his invention for the Académie des Sciences, and abstained from listing "the philosophical consequences."

Chérance had similarly recommended that he refrain from publishing his discovery until the factory was finished. On that point too his advice was taken. François asked his boss, Thuilier, who was a member of the Institut, to read his communication to the Académie des Sciences. The director of the Center accepted enthusiastically; it was a presentation that would attract the attention of the worldwide elite to the establishment at Bellevue and himself.

In spite of his authority, and the number and importance of his titles, his reading did not meet with unanimous assent. Thuilier encountered resistance. Some members of his scientific audience remained incredulous, reserved or skeptical. François was not surprised by that. He had expected it. A curious spirit of hierarchy, caste and tradition, a mistrustful humor and the fear of being duped rendered official science particularly suspicious of any novelty. But all those obstinate individuals, in François' view, would quickly be obliged to yield to the evidence.

The day after the communication, the majority of the newspapers reproduced it or summarized it, contrary to Laronce's prediction. To be sure, they did not give it the privileged place that was then reserved for major crimes, sporting exploits and scandals. They even abstained from commenting on it or discussing it. The news did not explode. It diffused, discreetly.

That is because science does not interest the crowd—or, rather, does not excite it. People are untouched by science; it does not speak to their hearts. They profit from it, but are not moved by it. While certain sanctuaries disappear beneath ex-votos, no mother ever decorates a statue of Pasteur with flowers.

Certainly, François was not expecting the idolatrous fervor that was then afforded to the heroes of tennis or boxing. Nor was he expecting the drawing-room glory founded on audacious advertising and human respect, which socialites lavish most willingly on those they understand the least. The day after Thuilier's lecture, however, he knew the signs of petty notoriety.

Photographers asked him to pose before their lenses. In order that his face would clear at the moment the snap was taken, one of them told him: "I admire your discovery." That was his method. He said to painters or writers, "I admire your paintings" or "I admire your books." Another, having been told that Francois Thibault was a father, asked him at the same time, with the same intention, the names of his children.

Other photographers presented themselves at Bellevue, at the Center, in order to take picture of the Starter for the illustrated papers. The majority were received by Thuilier, who employed himself with indefatigable zeal in demonstrations of the apparatus.

The deputy director, Lavolige, still disorganized and fluttering had tried to lend him a hand, but the impish little fellow was so distracted that he always feared that he might forget some detail of the set-up and function. He had been obliged to renounce supporting his superior.

Journalists begged the young inventor for interviews. Some, encouraged by his good manners, confided to him that they were not suited to that profession, and told him their troubles and their hopes rather than interrogating him about his discovery. Others, treating his home as if it were their own, were stiff, surly and demanding, as if they were doing him a great favor.

All these articles appeared without difficulty. Contrary to his prophecies, Laronce was able to celebrate his childhood friend in the *Bonjour* at his ease. The journalist was simultaneously delighted and disappointed by that, because he loved and envied François at the same time. The article, well-nourished, was both agreeable and lively, for the bitter man was overflowing with talent.

Laronce was the son of a Briolle cooper. The Thibaults, his neighbors, had opened their house freely to the preciously intelligent red-haired boy that their François had adopted as a companion. It was, therefore, sufficient for the journalist to draw upon his memories in order to depict François, his happy, healthy and pampered childhood, his adolescence rich in enthusiasm and scientific projects, and also his simple cheerfulness and seductive tenderness.

He related the future inventor's first experiments, the time when he had autopsied all his electric toys, when he had blown all the fuses in the house. Discreetly, he evoked François Thibault, married to the daughter of the great Pierre Contal, his loving household, his two lovely children. Then Laronce wrote about his visit to Bellevue and the miracle of the rose petal. He concluded by showing his friend animated since his early childhood by an optimistic confidence in better times, for knowledge and for human beings, by virtue of a robust faith that never ceased to fortify him and expand within him, which sustained him like the framework of his life.

That article delighted François. Laronce was decidedly an exquisite friend, when bile did not drown his heart. He hastened to the *Bonjour* to give him the accolade.

"I can't tell you how much pleasure you've given me, old chap. Words fail me."

The journalist, however, had recovered his habitual bitterness. "Yes, I hurried to sing your praises while we're still permitted to do so—for it won't last. Anyway, you're happy?"

"I think so."

"Well, that's the main thing."

Certainly he was happy. For seven years he had lived huddled over his research and its results. Now, he was entering a new phase, He was about to distribute his discovery and its benefits. He embarked upon that crusade cheerfully.

He would have liked to get carried away, to collect approval frankly. When a popular science magazine asked him to write an article about his discovery, when a radio company asked him to explain it before the microphone, he experienced a sort of disappointment in addressing himself to unknown readers and invisible listeners. He would have liked to communicate directly with all of them, to have them before him and lean toward them, to convince them by means of all the force of his presence.

He only savored that full satisfaction at his lecture at the Sorbonne under the auspices of the Center. It was organized and chaired by Thuilier. For François, it was a revelation. He discovered that he had a gift for public speaking, a necessary condition of the apostolate. He was astonished to feel quite at ease, mentally free and sure of himself. While speaking, he could make out the detail of every face. Impishly, he was tempted to wake a member of the audience whose eyelids were dropping. On the other hand, all the attentive and fervent gazes sustained him. And in his great need for sympathy and approval, he would have preferred, at the end of the lecture, that the gentle applause might ring more loudly, and never end.

In sum, Laronce's blackest predictions were unrealized.

François thought that it was necessary, contrary to his custom, to observe the good as well as the bad. He therefore congratulated himself in Chérance's presence for the broad welcome of the newspapers. All doors were opening before him.

The financier replied, with a wry smile beneath his small moustache: "They've been greased."

In fact, the publicity campaign was beginning. It was conducted by the commercial director of the Company, Dutrait, a young protégé of Chérance's. Very spirited and very capable, he admired the financier so much that he had taken him for a model. He imitated his brisk elegance, his casual courtesy, his prompt decisiveness and his imperious bearing. On one point alone he did not succeed in resembling him. While Chérance always observed a regal punctuality, Dutrait always arrived late. Impotent to correct his vice, he spent most of his time repairing its deplorable effects.

Dutrait had employed a powerful agency to distribute photographs and information that were to imprint the name and merits of Sidereal Energy in all articles. The initial success was rapid. The example was provided by the electricity supply companies that still used coal to produce light and power, and which resolutely adopted the Starter. They were imitated by two rail networks that had been planning to use hydroelectric power for their electrification and were thus able to install the costly installation works. A few electrochemical and electrometallurgical factories followed suit.

The directors of the Company were delighted with these early results, full of promise. They met at the headquarters of Sidereal Energy in the Avenue Victor Hugo. Chérance, who had accepted the chairmanship of the board, directed them with a light but firm hand, giving them a free rein, and was able in that role to savor the sportive joys that the drivers of mail-coaches once had.

At board meetings, François never succeeded in remembering the names of his associates. He got them confused. To be sure, they differed in appearance and mannerisms. Thus, in session, some remained silent, smiling at some pleasant dream or filling their blotters with complicated and puerile drawings. Others, by contrast, spoke with voluptuous abundance, sucking their words like boiled sweets. And yet, there was a family atmosphere about them; they had the ease that habit confers.

They were all, in fact, hardened in the profession. Each of them sat on several boards. It was always the same men that one found around all the green tables. In the country, one tiny phalanx administered the work of everyone else.

With François they were courteous, benevolent and protective. They consented to assure him of the success of his invention. Far from taking offense at their attitude, he was glad of it. He observed the feudal lords that fate had given him as allies in his crusade—the society of money, the customs and people of which were new to him—with a keen curiosity.

In the evenings, he gave Marianne amusing sketches of his day, as well as reporting the first signs of success. They continued to live in the small detached house at Bellevue what was annexed to the Center for Studies in Physics. Already, they could have moved to a larger dwelling, for Chérance had kept his word; François' own situation followed the successful trajectory of Sidereal Energy—but the sudden surge of fortune did not intoxicate either of them.

Perhaps because his needs were not great, perhaps because, thanks to his family, he had never known hardship, François was not subject to the fetishism of money. He knew, of course, that in his era, money was a form of power, that it played the role in society that blood plays in the living body, that it brought ease and security to life, but he denied forcefully that only money counts and that anything can be bought.

He had always thought that if, one day, he had a veritable superfluity at his disposal, he would first of all offer himself the pleasure of giving pleasure: of making those around him happy, fulfilling desires, effacing worries, realizing dreams, paying delicate and tender attentions, seeing faces light up with joy, and even with gratitude; in brief, plucking the charming flower of the egotism that is known as altruism. Already, his wish had been granted.

If François was happy to offer his silent darling those beginnings of success, he was perhaps even happier to bring them to the house of his childhood, in his rapid escapes to Briolle. Oh, it was then that Maman straightened up, as powerful and placid as an allegorical statue. Of course, had she not always said that *her* son would succeed? And it was then too that Papa, in order to straighten his face and hide his emotion, bit his fingernails and blinked.

He owed his father so much; he had lived in close proximity with him until he was sixteen. The former mariner returned to the land had seen a great deal and meditated a great deal. François had inherited his humane morality from him, his faith in better times, whose advent his discovery was about to hasten and whose perspectives it would extend endlessly.

It is necessary to admit that a discordant voice sometimes mingled with the concert of familial praise. When François went to his little house in Clos-Mussy, Marianne told her father in a few prudent but proud words about the launching of Sidereal Energy. Then, Pierre Contal raised his eyes to the ceiling, shook his head, clicked his tongue against his teeth and murmured: "It will all end badly."

François was untroubled, however. He repeated to himself that a great law of equilibrium guides the universe, that good and bad, eulogy and criticism, compensate one another. Those somber prophecies, whether they came from the obscure Laronce or the illustrious Pierre Contal, were the inevitable ransom of his radiant hope.

And it was, in fact, in his visits to his childhood home that he felt most warmly enveloped, comforted by that human sympathy, that approval, for which he had a liking, and perhaps a need.

As the warm days of summer were returning, it amused him to imagine that the garden itself, as a friend of his past youth, was celebrating on his behalf. The trees extended their braches toward him, the leaves applauded like tiny hands, and the flowers bloomed for him like fireworks, saluting him with their silent explosions.

V

At Fraicourt, on the threshold of the factory, François was watching out for Dutrait's airplane. He had to show he commercial director the results of his latest experiments. The driver of an electric car would have no more need to carry a source of power, piles or accumulators; it would be sufficient for him to capture a radiation, like the users of radiophony. The problem, resolved long ago in theory, could be solved in practice now that there was a profusion, a superabundance of energy available. Soon, in a vehicle, one would no longer have to do anything but "pick up" a wave, as one had, for many centuries, picked up the wind aboard a boat.

Dutrait had encouraged him strongly to pursue that research. Now that it was concluded, radio-propulsion companies would doubtless spring up, just as radio broadcasting companies had. Naturally, they would employ the Starter, thus giving a further boost to Sidereal Energy.

According to Dutrait, that boost was needed. The hopes authorized by the initial successes had not been realized. At recent board meetings, François thought he had detected a discreet reproach in the limited welcome of his associates. They were resentful of his disappointment of their impatience. Still courteous and polite, however, they avoided insisting on that weakening of success and openly seeking its causes.

On the contrary, Dutrait, in his conversations with François, formally put the blame on the change of attitude by the press. As commercial director, he kept close track of it. The doors that had initially opened had closed. Newspapers that had graciously accepted favorable articles to begin with now refused even paid insertions. Evidently, a few magnates had commanded the measure. They were, after all, defending their skins. Some had already been wounded. Shares in coal-mining had fallen noticeably since the launch of the Starter, and many other enterprises must be sensing that they were under threat.

The information that Dutrait gave him only served to confirm what Laronce had said—for the journalist, for his part, had not failed to alert his friend as soon as he caught wind of the conspiracy. His predictions were realized. The famous conspiracy of silence was being woven around the discovery.

A singular fellow, Laronce; after the publication of his charming article about François, he had disappeared. He had stopped visiting the house in Bellevue during the enchanted months when everything seemed to be smiling on the young invention. The sight of the happiness of others rendered him truly unhappy. He had only reappeared to tell his friend, with a sincere indignation and a secret jubilation, the names of the first papers whose publicity was closed to Sidereal Energy.

"It had to happen, you know," he explained. "If the order wasn't given sooner, it's because the Manitous hadn't realized the danger immediately. They were taken by surprise. You benefited from that. People were able to talk about your invention. But they understood, in the end. Now you've been erased. It's as if you no longer existed."

When François argued that the exclusion was not general, Laronce had demonstrated to him harshly that all the papers would enter the conspiracy.

The *Bonjour* hadn't done so yet, but it would. Evidently, there were different kinds of papers in the major press. Some, like the *Bonjour*, were family concerns that had been handed down from father to son. Some, in the hands of one man, were instruments of defense or ambition. Other opinion-factories were run by companies. Some affirmed their publicity, some managed it discreetly—but those were just shades; fundamentally, they all obeyed the same interests, the same power of money and, when the need arose, the same command.

He was right. Gradually, all the newspapers were closed to Sidereal Energy—but the truth got out and sprang forth even so. The lucid and prestigious Chérance did not appear to be greatly alarmed by this trickery. Every time he was notified of another setback, she swept dread aside with a brief gesture as if her were chasing away an importunate fly.

"Bah! It's temporary..."

And, as if to demonstrate his calmness with regard to the business that was dearest to his heart and crowned his life, he set off for India in an airplane.

Dutrait, who had become a bibliophile in imitation of his boss, told François that Chérance hoped to discover the oldest manuscripts in the world in Tibetan monasteries. He added, half seriously and half in jest, that the financier wanted to bury himself in the search in order to forget his great failure as a collector, his chagrin at not being the possessor of the much more desirable rare pearl that Pierre Contal obstinately refused him: the manuscript of *Génie antique*.

The time set for the meeting was long past, however, and Dutrait had not appeared. Francois was irritated by that. There is no time more stupidly lost than that spent waiting. In addition, a Swedish mission was due to inspect the Starter that afternoon at the Center for Studies in Physics. Thuilier would certainly do the honors, but now that attempts were being made to stifle his discovery, it would have pleased the young inventor to explain it himself to the foreigners, to convince them and win them over.

He consulted his watch. Dutrait had never been able to cure himself of his infirmity and become punctual. Like the convicts of old, he dragged around a cannonball attached to his ankle, which slowed him down, diminished him and whose chain he could not saw through.

With his eyes on the dial, François thought: *One can put right a watch that loses time, but a man who is slow can't correct himself. Oh, we're still in the infancy of humankind.*

In front of him stretched the workers' village. The houses, cheerfully graceful in the Dutch style, were varied in design and painted in bright colors. Although spring had scarcely begun, they were already tufted with verdure. That was because François, free to dispense energy without counting the cost, had applied electricity to cultivation, just as he had applied it to all kinds of domestic labor. He had thus been able to realize, under every roof, the material wellbeing that appeared to him to be the necessary base, the trampoline, of moral wellbeing. In another domain, too, he had been able to bring his actions and doctrines into accord, by applying the regime of profit-sharing, which ought to succeed wage-earning as the latter had succeeded serfdom.

He had been able to remain faithful to his principles in this respect thanks to Chérance, who had deliberately covered him in these attempts and had allocated him generous credit. Was the financier acting out of a kind of natural elegance? Did he want to demonstrate his faith in the discovery of the Starter? Or was he, as an impenitent bibliophile, attempting indirectly to please the author of *Génie antique*? He was doubtless obedient to all these various motives; all our actions have complex causes.

Dutrait did not arrive. François despaired of meeting the Swedish mission at Bellevue. He decided to telephone the Company offices, where the commercial director was based, in order to find out whether he was at least on his way, and went back into his office. At that precise moment, the phone rang—doubtless Dutrait, about to offer ingenious reasons for his delay, politely request forgiveness and "do the repentance dance."

Smiling, François picked up the receiver.

Suddenly, a sledgehammer blow descended upon his head. An awkward and troubled voice was telephoning from Bellevue. He seized scraps of sentence: "Explosion of a Starter…at the Center for Studies…during a demonstration…façade collapsed…"

Two thoughts went through him, with a double impact. One was for Marianne, Lise and Claude; their house was next door to the Center. The other was paltry and absurd: but for Dutrait's lateness, he would have been demonstrating the Starter to the Swedes himself, and the explosion would not have occurred. He dared not confess his mortal dread openly. He said, obliquely: "Was anyone hurt?"

No. When the explosion occurred, the foreign mission had been visiting the Museum Hall. Resuscitated, Francois breathed more easily. Already, he had recovered his valor. One of his favorite maxims came to mind: Everything is reparable except death.

His faith in the destiny of his apparatus was so robust that he had not reflected, at first, on the potential repercussions of the accident. It was a severe blow, however. It was capable of seriously hurting the business, already weak and anemic because of the conspiracy of silence. The dangers of the Starter! François could imagine the value that his adversaries would be able to extract from some such formula. Oh, why did Chérance, that decisive and reliable leader, have to be absent at such a moment?

Firstly, however, it was necessary to take stock of the damage, and its cause. François raced to the service aircraft, whose pilot was always ready to take off. On the way, the explosion haunted him. What could have caused it? What imbecile, what clumsy oaf...or what criminal? With a shrug of his shoulders he rejected the suspicion of sabotage. "Come on, let's not be dramatic."

When he landed at Bellevue, his first glance was at the Center for Studies. He dreaded finding it in ruins—but only the laboratory windows had been broken. A small group of people was standing in front of the façade. François recognized one of his laboratory assistants, and interrogated him rapidly while they made their way to the laboratory. The shock had broken the glass in the display-cases, smashed apparatus. The Starter no longer existed. They walked over shards of glass and lumps of plaster detached from the ceiling.

"How did it happen?"

Monsieur Thuilier, the director, had been delayed at a conference in Paris. In his absence, the deputy director, Monsieur Lavolige, had carried out the customary demonstration for the Swedish mission—but he had left the motor running when he had taken the visitors to the museum. It was then that the explosion had occurred, abrupt and brutal, "like a thunderbolt."

"Where is Monsieur Lavolige?"

"He's gone to Paris with the Swedes."

Lavolige! Of course. The fool had neglected the regulator—perfectly simple—that rendered the dissociation progressive. Or, rather, he had allowed the Starter to deregulate of its own accord. Had he done so out of pure inadvertence? Had he pretended to be distracted? Had he, at the last moment, given a flick of the thumb, yielded to some diabolical temptation surging from the unconscious? How could one know? No man ever descends to the bottom of the sewers of his own mind. All the more reason why no one can fathom the heart of another.

He put Lavolige out of his mind, as one expels a
rogue with a kick up the backside in order to send him to
be hanged somewhere else. He murmured to himself:
"Let there be no more question of that imbecile."

He left the laboratory. When he went past the big
globe in the vestibule he was tempted to murmur: "Don't
worry—we're going to continue busying ourselves with
you."

He was in haste to see his family. How precious
their existence had seemed to him during that brief ordeal...

He hugged them wordlessly, however, for we keep
our greatest tenderness to ourselves. Everyone in the
house had recovered from the alarm. Lise had found her
lovely smile again, as clear and pure as the tinkle of a
bell. Claude repeated his story to every new arrival; he
had already fixed the words and inflections with sure
theatrical instinct that operates at all ages but which
childhood displays ingenuously. There had been a bang!
Maman was all pale. She had hugged Lise and him very
tightly.

"My poor darlings," said François, "you've had a
fright. In fact, the accident was more stupid than serious."

"It was Monsieur Lavolige, wasn't it?" asked Marianne.

"Yes. He made a mistake of which only he was capable. A child wouldn't have made it. That's what it's
necessary to make clear without delay—the exceptional,
unique character of the error. I have to go see Laronce.
He'll advise me. He won't be displeased to see me in an
embarrassing situation, and he'll be delighted to get me

out of it. He's a poor weather friend. I'm counting on the *Bonjour* to publish an explanation."

"What about the other papers?"

"Oh, naturally, those who've shut up will talk. They'll wax lyrical about the accident. We've had the conspiracy of silence; we're about to have the alarm call. It's inevitable. In truth, I think I prefer the second campaign to the first. I was stifling. It seemed to me that I'd been buried alive—whereas now, I think we're going to be able to defend ourselves."

On the threshold, he looked back. "Would you be kind enough to phone Briolle. It's best to avoid my parents finding out about the explosion via the papers. They'd think that we've all been killed. They can send a message to your father, since he's just taken up residence at Clos-Mussy again. Oh, this time Pierre Contal can declare: 'All this will end badly'—but no, no, all this will end well. Or rather, all this will never end."

A quarter of an hour later, François climbed the stairs at the *Bonjour* in the Place de la Madeleine and went into Laronce's office. Very small and extremely cluttered with files, it resembled the cavities that rats hollow out in bales of old papers.

François understood, by the journalist's firm and warm handshake, that he already knew about the accident at Bellevue. In fact, Laronce handed him the dispatch from the agency that he had just received.

An explosion that might have had the most serious consequences has just occurred at the Center for Studies in Physics at Bellevue. It was provoked by a "Starter." It will be recalled that the apparatus in question, according to its partisans, was to represent an inexhaustible and gratuitous source of energy. A few industries have even adopted it. The cause of the explosion, which fortu-nately only caused material damage, is as yet unknown.

Having read the dispatch, François said: "Yes, it's neutral, but it permits the incrimination of the apparatus itself. You see, old chap, I want to ask you the favor of explaining that the explosion resulted from a stupid mis-take, and unparalleled and unrepeatable inadvertence—unrepeatable, you hear."

"You don't believe that it was malevolence?" Laronce insinuated.

The inventor had decided to spare Lavolige, how-ever. After all, by dint of feigning distraction, confusion and overwork, he might perhaps have become truly dis-tracted, confused and overworked. "No, no," he said. "It was inimitable clumsiness, but it was clumsiness. Obvi-ously, the papers that have undertaken the conspiracy of silence against the Starter will make the most of the ac-cident..."

"Of that you can be sure," Laronce said, sardonical-ly.

"Well, it's necessary to seize the initiative. It's nec-essary to employ the preventive method, to immunize minds, to put them on their guard against that poison. Firstly, I repeat, the explosion is absolutely exceptional in nature. Secondly, it's necessary to remember that the employment of energy, in any form whatsoever, always involves risks. There are short-circuits, gas explosions and boiler explosions, but one doesn't renounce elec-tricity, gas or steam. All the forces in play around us have their traitors. Gravity itself can be murderous; a mere fall will suffice.

Laronce was jotting down notes on a scrap of paper.

François continued: "The Starter is harmless in it-self. Suppose a child were playing with a lens. If, instead of innocently setting fire to a shoelace, he set fire to a barrel of gunpowder and blew up the neighborhood, should one blame the lens? Should people declare it dangerous? Obviously not. You realize that I'm giving you these arguments as they occur to me. You'll find others.

Laronce was jostled by disparate sentiments. He was triumphant in seeing his predictions come true; after having tried to stifle the invention, its danger would now be denounced. He savored the dark satisfaction of having got the better of his friend, of seeing him wounded while he, in his obscurity, escaped the blows of fate. A journalist without glory, he was proud of helping out the inventor of genius—and at the same time, he was frankly glad to be of service to François, to support him, to assist him. He would truly have liked to free him from an unjust concern, whose weight he felt on his own heart. That secret jubilation and sincere compassion lit a small flame in his gaze, behind his steel-rimmed pince-nez.

Cordially warmly, almost affectionately, he declared: "You can count on me. You know that the *Bonjour* hasn't entered into the conspiracy against your company thus far. I don't know what attitude the big boss, old Butat, will adopt after today's accident, but I'll write my article anyway. We'll see whether it gets through."

VI

The *Bonjour*'s antechamber was bare and dismal. The dirt on the doors, the rips and ink-stains in the wallpaper and the dust on the ledges testified to the fact that the building did not have a woman's touch.

Behind a small table, a fat and morose usher in a blue uniform with silver buttons was reading a newspaper. From time to time, people came in, headed toward him, and tried to interest him in their requests, leaning over and confiding their destiny to him. Sated with power, he maintained the impassivity of an idol. Miserly with his gestures, he merely entered a name in a list or confided a brief word to an internal telephone system. Then he resumed his reading.

Sitting on the bench, François envied that serenity. Early that morning he had scrutinized the daily issue of *Le Bonjour*; he had not discovered the anticipated article. Immediately, he had come in search information, but the impassive usher, having listened to a voice on the telephone, had rendered his verdict. Monsieur Laronce was opening his mail and begged Monsieur Thibault to wait momentarily.

François was impatient to know why Laronce's article had not appeared. Had it not been written? Had it been suppressed? He remembered the care, the fever, with which he had searched the paper column by column. There was something comical about it. He had been unable to abandon the search of the pages; an article can so easily hide. Don't we sometimes read a headline and then find ourselves unable to find it again?

A door opened. Laronce showed his mahogany hair, his darkly wrinkled forehead, his steel-rimmed pince-nez and his copper-filing beard. He drew François into his den, which seemed to be hollowed out of stacks of paper.

"So, you've seen? My paper didn't print it. I was written, and even set up in type. Look, here are the proofs. When I left the office yesterday evening, I was convinced that it wouldn't be spiked—then, this morning, I saw, as you did, that it hadn't appeared. I haven't had time to find out why, but I'll demand explanations. I'll insist..."

"I forbid it!" exclaimed François. "Above all, I don't want to make enemies. Above all, you hear. I've simply come to find out what happened. I thought you'd know..."

"What happened?" said Laronce, sarcastically. "Oh, it's quite simple. I can tell you that without fear of error. The editor must have read my article late in the evening and submitted it to the bosses, who vetoed it. Just like that. The *Bonjour*, you understand, is one of the rare papers that remained neutral in the Sidereal Energy affair. It even accepted paid advertisements—except that, in wanting to defend you the day after the accident, we forced it to choose a side. There was a change of mind."

"That's strange," François murmured. "The Butats aren't threatened personally. Are they really entering the conspiracy for the sake of solidarity?"

"Obviously, your invention is no threat to them. Their fortune is mostly based on forests in Scandinavia, but I repeat, all these people support one another. They're connected. Look, there's René Foucard, Butat's son-in-law, who takes a high hand with the editing—'the black on white,' as he calls it. Well, René Foucard's father is a born administrator; he sits on twenty-five boards. He must have interests in coal, oil, explosives and armaments manufacture. There's the link. He must have been consulted. I can hear his verdict from here. The astonishing thing is that the Butat clan hasn't taken note of his hostility earlier, and taken a harder line."

Sincerely irritated by not having been able to help his friend he wanted to show, in his defense, that his paper could have done even less. "After all," he said, hoarsely, "*Le Bonjour* has only abstained. Not all the newspapers have done likewise. Have you seen this morning's press?"

"No. I read *Le Bonjour* and got out my car."

"Well, you'll see. Many papers have commented on the accident."

He must have read the papers himself and then thrown them away without folding them up, because the flood surrounded his armchair. He picked one up.

"Here—read this."

It was one of the serious and sententious papers that Laronce called "the heavy press." The sentences filed before François' eyes in solemn procession.

In time, perhaps it will be possible to liberate intra-atomic energy safely. Yesterday's accident demonstrates that that time has not yet come. The event has revealed that the invention is not yet perfected, that its usage is still dangerous. People should only make use of the energies that can be unleashed once they have been properly mastered. It seemed that, in this case, nature has rebelled. Sometimes, it gives these warnings to the reckless individuals who strive to extract its secrets. It puts us on our guard against the pretended progress of a science whose excesses end up rendering it hateful. Nature wants us to pause, to cast a glance toward the peaceful times when our forefathers wisely obeyed its laws. Never has the myth of Prometheus appeared so just or so profound: woe betides the man who aspires to steal the fire of heaven.

"That's idiotic," said François, softly, putting the paper down.

Laronce handed him another paper. "Read this one."

It was a paper whose proprietor had wit, so all his editors were constrained to be witty. They tried. This time, the sentences fluttered, assuming the light step off ballerinas.

We have been promised miracles. It was all over for the laborious work of coal mines. The shafts were going to be filled in, and the oil-wells too. People would dance on them as on the ruins of the Bastille. No more hard work, no more effort. Better still: no more war. We were assured of comfort for all and a perpetual spring. In brief, the Age of Happiness. Alas! Why did the mediocre inventor of the Starter not meditate upon fables and their wisdom? The adventure of Perrette and the jug of milk would have deterred him from promising so much.[7] Today, the jug is in pieces. Goodbye calf, cow, pig, brood. And he would also remember that in wanting to emulate the ox, the frog inflated himself so much that he burst.

Miraculously—it is the only miracle in this affair—the explosion at Bellevue did not claim any victims. Let us rejoice that it has only provoked outbursts of laughter.

"Do you want more?" Laronce asked. "Here. Look at the headlines. *The End of a Dream. Alarm Signal. The Final Point. The Coup de Grâce. The Firework.* Here's one that takes the form of a road sign: *Warning: Dangerous Corner.* Another that of electricity substations: *Danger of Death.* Do you want to read them?"

François pushed them away with his hand. He smiled palely. "No thanks. That's enough."

He needed to be outside, free and alone. He was short of breath, his chest constricted. He rapidly took

---

[7] The reference is to a fable by Jean de La Fontaine, known in English as "the Milkmaid and the Pot of Milk."

leave of his friend. His car was parked in a discreet side street behind the Madeleine. He sat down at the steering wheel and remained pensive.

For the first time since he had published his discovery, he felt sorely hurt. He had dreamed of approval, gratitude, the fervor of the crowd. His strong and tender nature had hungered and thirsted for it. He was been wounded in the most sensitive part of his being.

The bite of hatred had always plunged him into a sort of depression. It stupefied him. It acted on him like a venom that induced paralysis and provoked delirium. For a while, he had refused to believe it, and denied the evidence. One might have thought that the human being of the future already existed in him, a human being who would have discarded abject sentiments, in the same way that the useless and baleful appendix had been discarded. For baseness is not necessary.

At the time of his initial success as a student, he had already experienced that strange incredulity. One of his masters had shown him an anonymous letter that had attempted to harm him, to hinder his career. It was an accumulation of filthy calumnies. Francois thought he had recognized the handwriting of an envious comrade, Bloch-Hébert. He was a sad monster, as unhealthy as a boil and as pretentious as a turkey. Because he had a hideous smile, he thought he was already Voltaire. With the proof in his hand, François had refused to believe it. He had denied it, repressed it. His mind had not been able to take it aboard, to absorb it. It was too gross, too dirty.

Today, ten years later, before the wave of slurs, a part of him again refused to accept the evidence. Although he was suffering from it, he was tempted to deny it. To what were they obedient, the journalists who had written these venomous or perfidious articles? Obviously, they wanted above all to earn their living by serving the designs of their masters. But some of them must be sincere: those oppressed by all superiority; those who experienced, like dogs, the need to relieve themselves at the base of al pedestals; those who enjoyed the satisfaction of a natural malevolence; those who genuinely hated science and novelty; those, finally, who were truly convinced of the danger of the Starter.

It was necessary, without delay, to face up to the mob, to break it, to drown out its clamor. Supporting himself on the steering-wheel, François straightened up. His weakness dissipated. He breathed deeply, and shrugged his strong shoulders. It was time to go back to Bellevue. He pulled away.

"I'll defend myself."

But how? The newspapers? He could no longer knock on any door. He had seen them successively slammed in his face. Now, in each of them, a judas-hole was open in which a weapon gleamed. How could he proclaim the truth? How could he explain the stupid injustice of those accusations? How could he persuade people that the Starter was no more dangerous than gas, steam or electricity? Certainly, there were means of propaganda other than the press: circulars, posters, cinema, the radio. But which should he choose? Obviously, he would be able to consult the administrators of Sidereal Energy, buy without their chairman, they would not exist. Then again, he was afraid of their courteous reproof, more certain than ever the day after the accident. Of, how he missed Chérance! He would surely have guided him through this difficult pass.

But time was pressing—and suddenly, his decision was made. He would speak. That same morning, just as

67

he was about to set out for Paris, Mariette Lizeray had called him on the telephone. He was aware of the reputation of her well-intentioned enterprise, *Le Franc-Parler*. She devoted her resources and her life to it. As soon as current events brought any personality into the light, she brought him by means of subtle urbanity to the platform she had founded. Authors explained their theses, politicians their doctrines, aviators their exploits, industrialists their methods and scientists their research. Those speeches were followed by a faithful, ardent and liberal public, and the microphone disseminated them all over the world.

That morning, the moving spirit of the *Franc-Parler* had offered him her pulpit. Persuasive and pressing, she had shown him the med to clarify opinion, to underline the fortuitous nature of the accident. Anxious to see Laronce before anything else, he had put off his reply. Now he was determined to accept.

As soon as he returned to Bellevue he called Mariette Lizeray. Immediately, they fell into accord on the necessity of acting quickly. They agreed that he would speak the following evening.

The *Franc-Parler*'s base of operations was a converted theater in the European quarter. When François went on to the stage, the auditorium was packed. Mariette Lizeray took her place beside him, behind the green-topped table. She was a petite woman, pale and brunette, energetic and fragile, devoid of coquetry and ageless. She whispered to him: "It's a full house. You have the honors of the stairway—there are people on the steps."

Spectators were indeed, for want of space, sitting on the steps of the two lateral staircases that linked the stage to the hall. Such an influx astonished him.

Immediately, he found the same mental liberty as in his lecture at the Sorbonne. He amused himself by examining all the faces in the crowd. In the front row, Marianne and Lise were smiling at him. Papa and Maman had come from Briolle. Even Pierre Contal had accompanied them.

The illustrious writer must be more convinced than ever that "it would all end badly," but he was good beneath his violent fanaticism; he was quite capable of taking a malicious pleasure in seeing François in difficulty and, at the same time, of wanting to bring him the comfort and authority of his presence.

That educated audience did in fact, appreciate the glory of Pierre Contal. And when Mariette Lizeray, in a brief introductory speech, congratulated herself on seeing the author of *Génie antique* at the *Franc-Parler*, the entire hall welcomed him with a fervent ovation.

François took the floor. First he depicted the energy scattered everywhere, sometimes accumulating in matter and then returning to space "like those vortices of dust that the wind lifts over the road like phantoms, which then evaporate again." He explained his discovery in its entirety in the accessible terms he had employed to reveal it to Laronce on the day when he had introduced "the miracle of the rose petal" for the first time.

Without further delay, he explained the accident at Bellevue. He affirmed that the explosion had been caused by clumsiness, an unprecedented and certainly unrepeatable error of stupidity. His plea for the defense was profound and abundant, developing all the arguments he had wanted to spread via the *Bonjour*. In order to make a mental impression he repeated the analogy of the glass lens. Was it not inoffensive in itself? However, one could accuse it of being dangerous since it could by setting fire to a powder-keg, provoke a catastrophe.

While he spoke, he watched the faces. They expressed a taut attention. Only one member of the audience seemed distracted. He was sitting at the journalists' table, at the foot of the stage to the right. He was visibly irritated. Perhaps he was simply annoyed at being sent to the *Franc-Parler* that evening in order to write a report. A total absence of chin further emphasized his bad-tempered expression. While his colleagues were taking notes, he was daydreaming bitterly, his nose and pencil in the air.

From then on, for François, the rest of the audience no longer existed: not Marianne, not Lise, nor Papa, nor Maman, nor the illustrious Pierre Contal, nor the countless, invisible radio listeners. For him, it was uniquely a matter of interesting, seducing and possessing the man without a chin.

With broad strokes, he indicated the imminent miracles that could be expected from that limitless and cost-free energy: the hard labors abolished, the others lightened, the comfort spread, the intemperate weather mastered. He delighted in evoking as an example the happy metamorphosis of the capital, such as he had shown it, playfully, to little Claude on the terrace at Bellevue.

But the surly journalist was no more moved by that than the two-year-old Claude had been.

Then François talked about war. Such a profusion of energy would permit the conception of electrical warfare. Henceforth, at any distance, it would be possible to flatten an entire country, without a single person or stone remaining standing. It would be possible to cause all the powder in projectile or ammunition dumps to explode. It would be possible to stop all the engines on land and at sea, in the air or underwater. The mere threat of such a war would be equivalent to the suppression of war. For the deadly and sacrilegious formula "the inevitable war" it would be possible to substitute the comforting device "the impossible war."

A burst of applause saluted that great experiment, but the man without a chin was trimming his fingernails. Gradually, François became irritated, and raised the stakes. When the audience had calmed down, he resumed in a more aggressive tone, when seemed to be addressed to that recalcitrant listener.

"Oh, I know that it's fashionable, these days, to denigrate science. Celebrating its discoveries smacks of the distribution of prizes, schoolmasters' lectures, democratic banquets. Away with all that! It's fashionable, on the contrary to deplore discoveries, to proclaim that, far from constituting progress, they constitute a backward step, a return to barbarity. By using such language, one earns a badge of distinction. And note that the detractors of science are the first to call on its help and assistance. Does the most backward country squire see his child fall ill? Then, by telephone, even by wireless telegraph, he begs for a train, and automobile or an airplane to bring him the saving serum."

That sally appealed to the audience, who approved it with an amused purr—but the man without a chin, lowering his nose over his fascinating task, continued trimming his fingernails. François felt an imperious need rising within him to move the fellow. Then, while deploring the excesses of a technology still in its infancy— what is a century in human history?—he proclaimed his faith in the miracles of knowledge, in human destiny.

"But it requires time for humans to improve their lot. Not seeing them evolve before our eyes, we believe them to be immutable. That is because the notion of duration, of long duration, is not yet familiar to us. Place yourself on a beach in front of a cliff. Think about the time that it required for those successive layers of sediment, of rolled flint, to be deposited in the bosom of the waters, to harden there, before forming the surface of continents. Well, to modify human beings, perhaps it will require as many centuries as to edify a cliff. But the human species will have all the time at its disposal that it needs to improve itself, precisely because of the unlimited energy of which it will henceforth be the master."

This time, the sulky journalist raised his head slowly and directed a dead gaze at the lecturer. Then, in order to retain that attention, to clarify that gaze, François understood that he was going to cut loose, that he was about to go all the way, that he was about to cross the frontier at which Chérance had advised him so forcefully to stop. In that man's face he spat his secret thought, as one spits blood. Avid to convince him, he repeated the words that he had allowed to slip out when he had attempted to convince the great Pierre Contal.

Yes, in millions of years, when the ardor of the sun weakened, humans would be able to move the Earth into other systems, toward the other suns that we call the stars, and which, successively, would pour out life. Thus they would be assured of a literally endless existence...and the human race would never disappear. Human genius would shone like an eternal flame. Humans would become godlike. Thus would be realized the promise of immortality that is in all religions, the intuition of the divine that is in all souls...never would a vaster hope be offered on Earth...

But the man without a chin sniggered, and nudged his neighbor's ribs with his elbow.

VII

The explosion at Bellevue had one consequence that François had not foreseen. In one day, it brought him into the light more than his discovery had in two years. Certainly, he was attacked, he was derided, he was called into question—but he was no longer ignored. On the contrary, he was hoisted into the glare of publicity.

That is because a singular law governs the press of the current era. Every event of note enjoys favorable treatment. There is no admitted right to keep quiet about it. Better still, it is prominently displayed. All explosions merit column space. The mistrustful publicity that ordinarily does not allow anything to be celebrated gratuitously abandons its prerogatives as soon as there is a question, near or distant, of scandal. And the all-powerful barons who direct the press from a distance bow down before that privilege.

The vogue then lifts its man up, like a tidal bore that overturns all the obstacles in its path. The *Bonjour*, after a brief hesitation, was obliged to obey that irresistible law. Laronce's article appeared, twenty-four hours late.

It is necessary to admit that the man with the pince-nez, although experienced in his profession, had not anticipated that turnaround. That is because he was short-sighted. Overexcited by the immediate difficulties that his friend had encountered, he had looked no further.

Simultaneously annoyed and delighted to have lacked clairvoyance, he explained to François in an angry tone: "Obviously, I ought to have suspected it. It's the aviator's feat all over again. You remember the story of the pilot who beat the altitude record—he was the man who had been further from the Earth than anyone

73

else. Thirteen kilometers...what a pedestal! What a unique glory! Well, no one talked about it. No one knew anything about him, even his name. You could have asked anyone in the world: "Who holds the altitude record?" and no one would have answered. One day, however, the rumor went around that his altimeter was faulty, and that he had never surpassed four thousand meters—and immediately, it was all over the press. For weeks on end his portrait was on the front page of every paper."

"Thanks for the comparison," François said, cheerfully.

"I know that the two cases aren't identical," Laronce admitted, acidly, "but you'll agree that they present some analogy. On the one hand, an exploit unknown until it became debatable; on the other, an apparatus left in the shadows until it explodes."

François smiled at the gibe indulgently. Evidently, the explosion had attracted attention to him, and to his apparatus. That was what had led him to speak at the *Franc-Parler*. That was what had launched him, spread his lecture far and wide, as a charge propels a projectile.

Oh, when Mariette Lizeray had telephoned him so early, on the day after the accident, he had not suspected that she was simply the first, that hers would be followed by so many other requests, that she was the harbinger of the vogue.

The vogue...

It flattered his great need for encouragement, for fervor. At the same time, he was aware of the spice of irony when he remembered how it had come to him.

Was it not comical to see his portrait, which had appeared discreetly on the inside pages of a few publications when his discovery was announced, now displayed on the front pages of all the dailies and all the magazines? That portrait had even escaped the newspapers to leap on to the cinema screen. Better still: henceforth, it spoke. A film with sound had been made of the inventor in his laboratory. He had even been obliged to learn a brief speech by heart, in order to appear to be improvising it in front of the camera.

He said: "The limitless and cost-free energy that we shall have at our disposal henceforth will suppress the hardest labor, lighten others and make them more flexible, ameliorate agriculture, regularize the seasons, spread wellbeing and finally render war impossible. And it will undoubtedly permit the planet to prolong its existence indefinitely, and human progress to continue indefinitely, to shine like an eternal flame."

He had never discovered so many friends as since the accident. Childhood companions, comrades of the college or the laboratory, felt admiration for him because they saw his portrait everywhere. The remembered him, wanted to see him again, ingenuously displayed their pride in knowing him and in being able to say: "I know him." That too was both comical and touching.

Even in that candid search by his former comrades, François savored the sympathy and the assent. He savored them again in the gaze, suddenly shining with curiosity, that women now darted at him when he was introduced in a drawing room. He savored them at the mere thought that his name was henceforth inserted in all memories, present in all minds, that he this occupied a small place of his own in all those lives.

One evening, he confessed to Marianne, while laughing, the great need for approval that he satisfied in the vogue. And he said to her: "That must be a vice, for no virtue has ever marked a character so profoundly."

He congratulated himself most of all on seeing that the accident and the lecture, the one driving the other, had launched and spread his ideas. They had penetrated as far as the crowd. The voyage of the Earth through infinite space, from solar system to solar system, seemed finally to have made an impact on minds. Caricatures made allusion to it, even in the popular press. Evidently, the artists who drew them and the editors who accepted them both assumed that they would be understood by the great public.

One represented a pale sun shedding tears, and it was saying to the fickle Earth, which was running away toward a new destiny: "Coward..."

In another, two old men were sitting on a bench, shivering under the same cooled sun, and one was saying to the other: "Ah! Long live Sirius or Aldebaran."

One of those caricatures indicated that only the inferior races were unworthy of taking an interest in these audacious anticipations. It represented two black men in a desert. One was saying: "The Earth will never die, you now." And the other was replying, with a bleak, indifferent expression: "Oh..."

There was more. In a well-patronized Music Hall revue, a new scene was inspired by the Earth's voyage among the suns that are the stars. Groups of actresses represented the principal constellations, recognizable by the emblems with which the pretty girls were ornamented: the Lyre, the Swan, the Chariot and so on. The Earth, the prima ballerina, danced amid all these stars. Solicited by each of them, she hesitated, and swayed. She did not know to which she ought to entrust her fate, which one to rotate around.

The most certain sign of the vogue, however, was the assault of the journalists. In the expansive days of

June, Bellevue became a place of pilgrimage. They no longer wanted cold and brief technical interviews with François, as they had when his discovery had been made. They interrogated him about everything. He was asked, in the name of publicity, to name his favorite perfume, his preferred tobacco, his brilliantine and his razor. In that era, such questions represented the decisive sign of notoriety, the supreme consecration.

In reality, the majority of reporters consulted him about the possibility of prolonging the life of the Earth and human progress. Some of them felt obliged to affect a bantering, or even ironic tone, as if to emphasize that they did not take such reveries seriously, but what did it matter? Even the mockers proved by their questions that they had deemed the problem interesting, if not to them, at least to their readers.

Usually, objections were raised at first. That did not surprise him. In fact, as soon as a new idea is presented to us, our minds initially seek to oppose it, to discover its weak point. That is what François called, "the directorial spirit." He claimed that a theater director, when an author reads him a script, has only one thing on his mind: the grounds for turning it down.

Delighted that people were interested in his ideas, François refuted every objection with smiling patience. One journalist even had the idea of reproducing that conversation in the form of a dialogue between the inventor and himself. The reader witnessed an inoffensive duel in which ideas were crosses instead of swords.

"To launch the Earth out of its trajectory it would be necessary to have a point of support, as in the case of the rocket, the autopropulsive projectile. Then the terrestrial crust, which is as thin as a rind, would be dislocated."

"No one knows the thickness of the terrestrial crust. No one even knows whether there is a central fire. Then again, it will not necessarily require a propulsive force. One might have recourse to an attractive force, akin to terrestrial magnetism or universal gravitation. Since it's a matter of an attempt to be undertaken in millions of years, what's the point of determining today a launch project on which our descendants will certainly improve? I've only envisaged the principle of the enterprise, the possibility of successive escapes, indefinitely renewed—in brief, an assurance against the death of the Earth."

"The atmosphere enveloping the planet would be ripped, torn away, in such a voyage."

"Why? The Earth is traveling around the sun at more than twenty kilometers a second, and yet the atmosphere remains stable."

"What collisions the Earth would risk in such a voyage!"

"Even now, one could calculate its trajectory in such a way as not to collide with any heavenly body in its course. What will be the case after thousands of years of progress in astronomy? The problem is of the same order as that of establishing the timetable of a special train among the regular traffic of a network."

"But what if the new sun is too bright, and renders life on Earth impossible?"

"Astronomy is still in its infancy. Three centuries ago, its laws were still unknown. In millions of years, when human attempt the adventure, they will be much more familiar with the heavens and their worlds. They will choose their star carefully."

"All right. But the year won't be the same in duration. Life will suffer no less perturbation than the Earth."

"It won't be the first time. Didn't glaciers once cover regions that are temperate today? Humans have incredible faculties of adaptation. They will make a new home. That will be less serious than freezing to death for lack of solar heat."

"But if solar ardor weakens, your Starter will no longer work, since it depends on it—but humans will need it in order to escape."

"They'll utilize different radiations, emitted by other suns. Even now extraordinary penetrating radiations coming to us from the regions of Andromeda and Hercules are been studied, which can go through lead walls five meters thick."

"In one way or another, isn't the human species bound to disappear? Even if such an attempt were crowned with success, it wouldn't save it?

"Why should the human species disappear? Other species, animal and vegetable, are defenseless in the face of natural law. They're passive. By contrast, the human species, that happy accident, has never ceased to struggle against nature. It has always tried to tame nature, whether by checking its variations or utilizing its forces. To avert the perils that threaten the species, it will combat them. It will not allow itself to die."

"One last objection. If humans will have limitless energy at their disposal when the sun weakens, why not employ it directly to create the heat and light that they lack, rather than launching themselves into a reckless enterprise?"

"That's one view, in fact, that it's not necessary to oppose. In the same spirit, one could envisage a temporary solution, which would consist of moving the Earth nearer to the sun, in order to delay the moment when it could no longer pour out life. But the interastral voyage remains the supreme means of salvation, the one that humans will employ as a last resort. It is, I repeat, an assurance against death for the planet and for the race, the prospect of eternal duration. It leaves the future open to infinity."

The journalists who came to Bellevue did not only present objections to the inventor. They interrogated him about all aspects of the future of which he had become the prophet. They believed, or pretended to believe, that he had penetrated its secrets. He took great care to warn them, however, that it was a matter of long-range anticipations, and that it was necessary to have a sense of duration to comprehend them.

Thus, humans would end up adopting a morality founded on knowledge, in accord with the great laws of harmony, equilibrium and interdependence that regulate the universe. But all those notions, which we owe primarily to astronomy, are still so recent that they have not yet penetrated minds. It would be necessary to wait. In the same way, from the politically viewpoint, the Earth would be gradually be organized in the image of the animal organism, in which all the cells are simultaneously free and integral. Humans would be the cells of the terrestrial organism. In order to elaborate the marvelous model of aggregation that an organism represents, however, nature has taken millions of years. Humans would require a similar time to imitate it. There too, it would be necessary to wait. And in order to obtain consciousness of duration, Francois advised the journalists, like the audience at the *Franc-Parler*, to "look at a cliff."

He was often asked whether his discovery would permit the realization of the transmutation of metals. Would people be able to change lead into gold? Would they have the alchemists' famous philosopher's stone?

He replied that such a transformation would, indeed, become possible, but that it was of no great interest. The value of gold depended on its rarity. When it could be produced in abundance without any expense, it would not be worth any more than zinc or iron. The transmutation offered only one advantage: it would cause people to stop representing public wealth by means of ingots buried in a cellar—a barbaric custom unworthy of a modern state, a last reminiscence of our rude ancestors' spoils of war.

François added, in the same order of ideas, that the formidable and gratuitous energy that would be available would permit the wholesale manufacture of precious stones identical to natural gems. They would be valueless, but at least all women would be able to enjoy the gleaming stream of beautiful adornment. That would be emblematic of the future, which would tend toward luxury for all, toward leveling by elevation.

One reporter asked François, as was able to read the future accurately: "Will people nourish themselves on chemical pills?"

He protested, raising his arms to the Heavens. Obviously, humankind devoted an enormous amount of time and effort to the production of food. How much labor the ensemble of cultivated field and plantations of the world represented! How many risks sea-fishermen ran! But that labor and those perils would diminish. Electrical cultivation would provide more abundant and more frequent harvests. As for long-distance fishing, it would gradually be substituted by pisciculture and the employment of giant tanks. For all animal-breeding, our descendants would enjoy an age of vast reserves and parks. But it would be sacrilege to deprive people of the table, of the honest, delicate and charming joys of the meals that remained the true communion between individuals seeking society and pleasure.

And when he was asked whether future humankind would abolish sleep, as some people would like to do, he protested just as vigorously. That would be another folly, to deprive creatures not only of a repose useful in itself but also the luxury of taking refuge there, of burying oneself and huddling up after a well-spent day.

With the same insistence, finally, he opposed the doctrine of necessary suffering. Get away! Is it necessary to be ill to appreciate health? Is it necessary to eat vile things to savor delicious food? It is claimed that we would weary of a sky that was always clear; that is false. The islands where a perpetual spring reigns are the fortunate isles. We do not weary of happiness, which is life's reason for being. Should we not, at every opportunity, suppress pain? Is that not the primordial instinct of the most primitive creature? By what aberration can we still permit women to suffer in order to give life?

That life, it is necessary without cease to render gentler, more pleasant and richer. It is necessary to ornament it with new pleasures instead of taking them away. For, by dint of pruning it and stripping it, one arrives at the concept of the fakir, the living mummy. Why not the grave right away?

It was on the subject of that increase, that embellishment of life that the expanded most willingly before his visitors. None was dearer to him. He bore it within him; it communicated its own warmth to him—and he experienced a physical pleasure in liberating it, in proclaiming his infinite confidence in human possibility. Besides which, it summarized, in a sort of *Credo*, his faith in the future of humankind.

The day after the accident, the magazine *Terra* had pressed him to write an article for it. It was a polyglot magazine, the most influential in the world: a veritable symbol of the international spirit born in that epoch, with offices in New York, Paris, Buenos Aires and Berlin. François had chosen his favorite theme, "The Better Life," and he smiled as he compared the opulent periodical that was about to spread his thought throughout the world with the cold technical journals that had accorded him their severe hospitality at the moment of his discovery.

Although he had gathered together there, as in a bouquet, all the reasons for his confidence in human destiny, he distributed fragments of the spray every day to those who came to consult him. Delighted to be heard, to be understood, he was radiant with hope. He surrendered himself, and blossomed. He felt at one with the world, in the beautiful surge of summer when the flowers burst forth and open their hearts.

It was in that intoxication of enthusiasm that he received a visit from Chérance.

The financier had returned from his trip to India. François had only caught a glimpse of him, two days earlier, when he descended from the airplane. Assailed by accolades and handshakes, Chérance had only managed to call to him, hoarsely: "Soon, no?"

Certainly, François was in a hurry to tell him about everything that had happened since his departure, to fill the absence, to recover his advice, so firm and so reliable, but he waited until the financier had settled before going to see him in Boulogne. "He needs time to think," he said to Marianne.

But Chérance got in ahead of him, and came to surprise him at the laboratory at Bellevue, like a mere reporter.

"As you can see," François told him, "the disaster has been repaired."

Indeed, the damage caused by the Starter's "thunderbolt" had vanished; the windows had been replaced, the ceiling replastered, the instruments set straight.

With regard to the accident, François explained the singular character of Lavolige, the man who, by virtue of affecting an air of distraction, overwork and confusion, like a fly in a bottle, had probable ended up contracting those ills, and retained a kind of good intention even in his villainy.

Chérance shrugged his shoulders. "I've seen many imbeciles in my life, but never one of that species." As François offered him a seat, he added: "No, I'd rather walk a little."

They walked back and forth on the terrace, as on the day when Chérance had witnessed the miracle of the rose-petal—but he did not seem as well-disposed as he had on that first visit. He did not have those warm and cordial impulses that had initially seduced François. He seemed preoccupied and constrained.

He seemed to shake off his malaise, however.

"The explosion isn't important," he declared. "There are accidents on the railways, on the roads, in aviation, but they've never prevented anyone from getting into a train, an automobile or an airplane. You said the same yourself in your lecture at the *Franc-Parler*, of which I've been shown extracts."

He stopped, with a familiar gesture, he placed his hand on François' sleeve. "Oh, my friend if only you had limited yourself to those arguments!"

François thought that he understood. He had infringed Chérance's advice. He had revealed the "philosophical consequences" of his discovery in public. That explained the financier's muted chagrin.

"Yes," he continued, "you haven't been understood. Do you remember what I said to you, one day when we went to visit the works at Fraicourt together—that people would rather doubt your lucidity than their own intelligence?"

François started, traversed by a sharp and precise anxiety. "What do you mean?" he exclaimed.

Chérance raised his head. He radiated such authority that, although François was considerably taller, he seemed to be talking to him from on high. At the same time, he resumed his warm and cordial manner, a trifle brusquely.

"You know that I consider your mind to be the most magnificent, the most well-balanced and the sanest there is in the world. I place it as high as that of Pierre Contal—which, for me, is saying a great deal. But it's not a matter of me. It's a matter of our adversaries, of those with an interest in depreciating your discovery. Oh, they know full well that they'll be beaten in the end—but they want to gain time, to hold back the moment of their defeat. Those men were lying in wait for you. They hoped to hurt your invention through you, throw suspicion on it and you at the same time. You've opened yourself up, exposed your flank. Oh, they haven't hung around. They haven't missed the opportunity. I've only been back for two days and I've already heard the imbecilic rumors that are circulating about you. They're confided in whispers—it only requires a word. Less than that—a gesture."

Chérance touched his forehead.

Mad! So, they wanted to pass you him as a lunatic. They wouldn't succeed in making the monstrous accusation stick, in having it taken seriously. It was so excessive as to be unthinkable.

"Comical," he murmured.

In reporting these rumors to him, was Chérance offering himself the paltry satisfaction of demonstrating that he had seen clearly, that François had been wrong not to follow his advice? No, no. He was not so petty. If he was speaking, it was doubtless because he thought it useful.

"You're right," he continued. "It's comical. But at the same time, it's troublesome. Very troublesome. These sorts of rumors are the sort of irritant that can't be combated—for to do so immediately gives them importance. And note that the newspapers haven't entertained them as yet. But the petty press, which lives on gossip, slander, scraps and leftovers—the rags—will certainly take it up. Oh, I preferred the conspiracy of silence or the cries of alarm after the accident."

He linked arms with François and resumed walking. "I apologize, my friend, for having been the echo of these stupid rumors, but that's because we can take a lesson from them, all the same—belated, it's true. If you'll take my advice you'll stop exposing your distant hopes to poor devils short of copy, who deform them out of malice or stupidity. Remain reserved. Contain yourself—at least while we're still in the launch period. Oh, when we hold the world in our hands, you can cradle it at your leisure—but we're not there yet. On the contrary; we need all our strength, more than ever."

"Why?"

Chérance had stopped beside his car, whose chauffeur was holding the door open.

"Because a serious squall is threatening us. The conspiracy of silence made a sensible impact on Sidereal Energy, but, by an irony that won't escape you, the explosion at Bellevue brought the Starter back into the news. Everyone making electricity is inclined to use your apparatus. The success of experiments in radio-propulsion, in particular, has opened the eyes of the big oil men, stirred up their fears. You know that two rival groups can march together. In the face of peril they'll unite against us. The competition will be fierce. We need to win."

And Chérance leapt nimbly into his vehicle.

Two years before, François had been left alone in the same fashion, on the edge of the terrace, after having accompanied Chérance to his car, but then the financier had left him full of hope. Today, he had put the most anxious doubt that can haunt a human being into his mind.

His fingernails digging into his palms, however, he stiffened himself against the vertigo. No, no, he would not vacillate. He had his invention to defend, his work to realize. Proudly, he envisaged his task. It was unique. No human being had ever assumed one like it. The planet was running through space on its invisible rail, and he was its compass. Was he going to leave it to rotate piteously until it perished of cold around a cool sun? Or was he going to permit it to launch itself into infinite space one day, toward eternal life? He really did hold human destiny in his hands, as one holds a lever.

It was up to him, and him alone, to ignite that vast hope, that promise of immortality. He no longer belonged to himself. He no longer had the right to weaken, to let go, before accomplishing his destiny. Oh, how beautiful it seemed to him, at that moment. Founders of religions had appeared on Earth to say to humans: "I am God." Was his role not more marvelous still, having come to say to humans: "You shall be gods."

VIII

Sitting by the window open to the summer, in the small room in which he had lived until his fifteenth year, Francois remained pensive. On the table, the proofs of his article, "The Better Life," were spread out. They had arrived that morning at Briolle, and he was wondering whether he should send them back to *Terra*.

Immediately after Chérance's visit and that brief meditation in which he had envisaged the unique grandeur of his task, when he had stiffened himself against vertigo, he had decided to leave for Briolle. It was the best means of following the financier's advice, of escaping the journalists for whom an excursion to Bellevue had become a kind of fashionable sport.

Should he hide the odious rumor that constrained him to flee from Marianne? He had been very tempted to do so. The imminent vacation would have been sufficient to justify the departure for the country. He would thus avoid causing his wife unnecessary anxiety. Neither of them was completely free of the unjust prejudice that weighs upon the mentally ill, as it weighs upon suicides, which gives them a shameful, inadmissible character.

On the other hand, he would not be able to prevent the absurd rumor from reaching Marianne. As soon as the gutter press got hold of it, Laronce would come running, his pockets stuffed with newspapers, with a little gleam ignited behind his steel-rimmed pince-nez. He always appeared on such occasions. He was even capable of bounding as far as Briolle, his birthplace.

In the end, François felt so solid and secure, and the rumor appeared to him to be so incredible, that he would be able to report it to Marianne without troubling her, and he had given in to the relief of entrusting himself to his wife.

The "silent darling" had retained her beautiful tranquility. She had scarcely been indignant. She had understood immediately that it was a matter of denigrating the inventor in order to denigrate the invention. It was a desperate attempt by adversaries who could not resign themselves to admitting that they were beaten, who would retreat one step at a time, seeking to delay the moment of their defeat.

They had both simply resolved to leave their parents in ignorance of the stupid calumny. What was the point of troubling the joy of the Thibaults, so radiant every time their grown-up son, their god, returned to them? As for Pierre Contal, it would have been truly superfluous to furnish him with a further opportunity to raise his arms and eyes to the heavens and repeat that "it would all end badly"—especially given that he was fundamentally good and generous, and it would have pained him to be excessively triumphant.

How often Francois had congratulated himself on having alerted his wife and taken her for an ally! Since their arrival at Briolle the telephone and the mail had brought them echoes of the gutter press, Marianne would surely have come across them. Forewarned, she helped him to stifle them, to prevent them from reaching the Thibaults.

And then, this morning, the proofs of "The Better Life" had arrived at Briolle—and just as he prepared to correct them, the enormous irony of fate had become apparent to him. Was he about to proclaim his faith in humankind at the very moment when humankind was about to reveal its baseness so vilely? And he hesitated before the sheets spread out on his writing-pad.

Save for the small bed transformed into a divan, nothing had changed in François' bedroom since his childhood. He continued to reside there gladly every time he visited Briolle. It served him as a study. Brightly-colored English engravings and framed photographs stood out against the pale blue walls: a portrait of Monsieur Thibault in his naval uniform, commanding an entire squadron; pictures of little Francois, from François in his first short trousers to François on his first bicycle, via all sorts of little François, costumed as a Norman peasant, a hunter or a clown.

A glazed pitch-pine display-case fitted to the wall contained his treasures, the souvenirs that his father had brought back from his voyages when he was a small boy: ash from Vesuvius, stuffed hummingbirds from Brazil, Malayan madrepores, uncut rubies from Laos, Polynesian corals, fossils found in Tunisian phosphates. Perhaps it was in collecting those specimens of the planet that he had acquired a sympathy for it. While very young, he had looked at his collection with the same loving gaze with which he was later to envelop the giant globe at the Center for Studies.

His scientific toys were dormant in a cupboard: the first microscope, the first induction coil, the first electric motor, the internal telephone, the little radio set, He had been so frequently hypnotized by them in shop windows, had desired them so strongly, had experienced so much joy in possessing them, that he had sometimes thought, in their midst, that he was living a dream in an enchanted world. They were his magic wands.

A small Louis XVI secretaire served as his desk. It was there that, for years, for half an hour a day, his father had given him a broad view of all important knowledge in simple outlines. Monsieur Thibault had always tried to make his lessons as interesting as anecdotes, so effectively that young François, condemning an entire pedagogical system off-hand without knowing it, said: "But it isn't work, since it isn't boring."

Twenty years had passed. Now on his little school desk, proofs from the most influential periodical in the world were waiting for him. It was offering him the chance to be heard throughout the world. His corrected text would be immediately translated into English, German and Spanish for printing in four languages. But he could not bring himself to start work. He feared, in that confrontation with his written thoughts, no longer being in agreement with himself; for he had to confess that the base attacks had succeed in disturbing him. They had not caused him any serious and continuous anxiety as to his reason—obviously, he did not doubt his lucidity—but he had begun to doubt his faith, his mission.

Nevertheless he began to reread his text. He had first inveighed against the grievances that it was fashionable to heap upon scientific progress, even though its worst detractors, those privileged by fortune, were the most prompt to take advantage of it in all its forms. Not only did they deny it, that unfortunate progress, but even reproached it for being a regression, a reversion to barbarity.

Evidently, François recognized in his article, technology has created a new slavery, that of the wage-earning factory worker. Evidently, the production-line and mechanization are shocking in their cruel rigor. Evidently, the reign of speed, arrogant and brutal, encourages and multiplies coarseness. Evidently, capital cities, with their congested arteries, their toxic atmosphere, their blazing signs, enfever life more than they embellish it. But so what? The machine age is less than a hundred years old. What is that? It is taking its first steps. And we know that infancy is excessive in its cries, its gestures, and all its manifestations. We are therefore subject to the excess of technology before acquiring all its advantages. One the ingrate age is over, and the first frenzy has past, it will become moderate, flexible, and disciplined.

Then again, the adversaries of scientific progress really did leave too many benefits in the shade. There were, however, evident truths, truths to warrant the distribution of prizes, as François put it, apologizing for recalling them. That same technology, so decried, has reduced the working day from twelve hours to eight in fifty years. It has brought comfort into zones that are increasing incessantly. Medical discoveries have extended average life-expectancy by ten years in a single generation. Rapid transport and instantaneous communication, by permitting the planet to be better known, have done more in the same interval to bring individuals dear to one another together more often, and to allow help to be brought more quickly to others, have rendered life fuller, more sensitive and more concentrated. If the telephone bill were calculated honestly, in terms of what has been realized thanks to its existence, and what would not have been realized without it, it would be recognized that it has changed the conditions of life. And has not radio broadcasting modified it as much? Are not household tasks, like couture and cuisine, lightened when they are accompanied by music? When the speaker brings news of the entire world into every hearth, does it not seem to enlarge rooms and minds?

Then François came to the real, the great problem. Having attempted to establish that material progress exists, he asked whether moral progress exists: progress in conduct. In his view, the two questions were linked. He saw material wellbeing as the necessary condition of moral wellbeing. Only a people materially favored could improve morally. It was only on the solid platform of material progress that moral progress could be edified. But would it be edified? And François gave his reasons for hope.

First of all, he measured the road already traveled. Had not life been morally improved since the age of cave-dwellers? Was there not a difference between the rude and bestial ancestor and the scientist who dissects the atom and weighs the stars? Had not humans, along the way, distributed treasures of art and beauty sprung from their fingers and minds? Had the creatures themselves not been enriched, in making their way? Were they still primitive brutes? Had they not shown that they knew how to ornament themselves with charm and grace, elegance and nobility, that they were capable of altruism and generosity, of courage and rectitude, of so many kind or affectionate impulses, so many spiritual or chivalrous actions, that we can glimpse a gleam of a better humankind within them?

And François envisaged another reason for hope:

"The mass of information that we owe to science has not yet penetrated minds profoundly. That is logical, for the notions are recent; they are only a few centuries old. But the time will come when they are finally familiar to the crowd. Then they will react on morality in a favorable direction."

And he clarified that view with an example:

"Astronomy ought to be the first of the sciences, because it is narrowly involved in our lives. It regulates the clock and dictates the calendar; it determines day and night, rain and good weather, leads the cycle of the seasons and explains all the celestial miracles suspended over our heads. Well, when astronomy has penetrated minds, it will deposit there the notion of interdependence. Everything in the universe is connected. The worlds are united by sensible bonds. The impact that disturbs one of them id felt by the others. Moreover, just as the worlds are connected in space, so the cells are connected in the body; when one of them overheats, the entire body is feverish. Thus, at the extremities of the microscope and the telescope, one finds the same law.

"Now, that notion of solidarity in the infinitely large and the infinitely small has not yet struck minds forcefully. Thus, humans are poorly defended against contagion, which is the maleficent aspect of the interdependence of beings, and they are in no hurry to reap the benefits of that solidarity. The tenants in the same house, the readers of the same newspaper, the users of the same network, are not yet associated. When they do unite, however, they dictate their law. A time will come when human beings, better enlightened by science, will finally perceive that they are dependent on one another, like the cells of an organism or heavenly bodies. Then they will understand that it is in their interest to unite, to help one another, that altruism is only the prolonged flowering of egotism. Then they will conform to the great laws of solidarity, of harmony, of equilibrium that govern the universe, and will finally create a morality inspired by science."

No, human beings have not yet attained the limit of mental possibilities—and François suggested proofs of that.

"Everyone has been able to observe in himself that the imagination is richer in dreams than in the waking state. One is amazed by its fantasies, and its ingenuity, its boldness in sleep. One exclaims: 'How was I able to find all that?' That signifies clearly that we have not yet caused all the notes of the human keyboard to resonate in everyday life. Why should humans not spread out in the light all the treasures that are only enjoyed thus far in the dark? That will come."

Another proof. The most innocent gulp of champagne, the slightest stimulant, enables us to see life through rose-tinted lenses, not painted in black. All intoxication teds toward lightness. Does that not signify that when our faculties are exalted, expended, they show us life as it ought to be, as it might be: the better life; the life to come?

He proclaimed once again:

"How can one despair of moral progress when one discovers the improvement that physical being can achieve? Think about the prodigies realized by the heart, by hearing, sight, and most of all, the human brain. The same beings that bear those marvels within them simultaneously show themselves to be so coarse, so crudely hewn. Is there not a shocking anomaly there, that must slowly disappear? Doubtless it required millions of years to bring the physical being to that level of perfection. Why should mental being, in further millions of years, not attain the same summit? Why should human beings, anatomical marvels, not become as perfect mentally as they already are physically?"

From line to line, his enthusiasm and his confidence increased.

"There are two beautiful human types. Why should all humans not become beautiful? There are intelligent individuals. Why should all individuals not become intelligent? Yes, these questions might appear naïve, but reflect on them. Selection, which we practice on animal and vegetable species, realizes that miracle every day. All the individuals of the same species can attain perfection. Only the reproduction of the human species is left to chance—but that aberration will be renounced. Has not the important influence of internal glands on human faculties already been established? Can we not envisage from now on a mental orthopedics founded on that discovery? There is no doubt about it: the future holds the promise of happiness."

And he had decided to conclude his article with an allusion to the infinite destiny of the Earth.

"Alas, morose minds might think, if it existed, progress would be limited. What is the point of so much effort, since the human race must disappear on the day when the Sun will no longer warm the Earth? Well, no. The human race will not necessarily disappear. We now know that our descendants will have an inexhaustible energy-source at their disposal. Let us imagine, boldly, that they will be able to modify the orbit of the planet, launch it toward other suns that will pour new youth into it. Then, a literally-eternal humankind will be able to nourish the hope of infinite progress."

François pushed the proofs away. He smiled bitterly. He remembered the recent times in which he had surrendered himself to the journalists who had hastened to Bellevue, with so much confidence, joy, abandonment and radiant enthusiasm; when he had preached his faith in the infinite destiny of the Earth; when he had showed them human genius hurling its eternal flame into space.

Oh, he had not suspected then that he was exposing his flank to his adversaries, Chérance had been right. The press that the financier called "the rags" had soon gone to work. A strange trade! It picked up scraps, scrapings, dust and excreta everywhere that the residues of life were evacuated. It transformed them, dressed them up, and sold them on, like those enterprises that process household waste, drawing motive force, fertilizer and bricks therefrom.

Every day the post brought him those petty infamies, or the telephone notified him of them. One never remains ignorant of a disagreeable echo. Some friend, out of zeal or malice, will always send you the poisonous cuttings.

The majority of the articles worked by insinuation. They were concierges' whispers: "It's said that..." "I don't know whether it's true, but..." Sometimes they were hypocritically deplored, with a sigh. Some, on the other hand, lied brazenly. They cited the asylums or sanitaria in which the inventor was confined. Others affected a bantering tone, joking about his nurses, his straitjacket, his cold showers, his padded cell.

Obviously, the same motives animated those who were crying madness and those who had previously spread alarm after the explosion. They were obeying orders by virtue of monetary need, or the hatred of science and progress, or envy, or even simple cruelty, but this time, the attack was more perfidious, viler, and also more efficacious.

François rapidly felt its effects; there was no doubt that many people were avoiding him. In adversity we have very sensitive antennae, which reveal desertions, treasons and the sound of retreating footsteps.

The comrades of childhood, college and the laboratory, who had shown themselves so proud to know François when the vogue had put him in the spotlight, who had sought every opportunity to issue invitations to him or to remember themselves to him, were no longer showing any signs of life. They were stealing away in alarm, disappearing, scuttling like rats into their holes.

Official science no longer knew him. Even Thuilier, who has supported him so stubbornly so long as his discovery made the Center for Studies illustrious, had abandoned him as soon as he promised the planet an infinite destiny, especially since journalists began pretending to doubt his sanity. When François called him from Briolle by telephone, he was curt and reticent, or avoided taking the call personally. When reporters came to the Center in search of news of the inventor, Thuilier refused to be interviewed. Deep down, he and his peers were afraid of appearing to take such far-reaching anticipations seriously. They were afraid of appearing to have enthusiasm, imagination, audacity and courage. They were afraid of compromising themselves. They turned their backs on him out of cowardice.

But the petty journalists, in crying madness, had not only created a void around him. They had not only injured him in his great need for approval and sympathy. They had hurt him more profoundly. They had succeeded in making him anxious, even though he felt that he was in full possession of his faculties. From time to time, in retreat at Briolle, a doubt traversed him like a dart, a stabbing pain: "What if it's true?"

Precisely because he knew the human machine well, because he saw it palpitating as one sees a clockwork mechanism beating under glass, he had a sense of its fragility. He knew that a blood clot, trapped in a narrow cerebral vein, was sufficient to stop that admirable marvel.

Was he sure that he was still lucid? How could he know? When one loses one's reason, one is not aware of it.

When he was assailed by doubt, he scrutinized the faces of his relatives. The splendid serenity of Maman, always so proud and so sure of him, calmed him down. His father's brow, always slightly furrowed by care, revived his own anxieties. But what was he imagining? His parents did not know anything. Sometimes, as when one leans over the crystal of a spring, he saw his own reflection in the limpid and profound eyes of his two children. They would doubtless betray their surprise, ingenuously, if they found him changed. And when Marianne asked him to take her out in the car with the children, he congratulated himself because she let him take the wheel, entrusting their lives to him. Was that not proof that she was not afraid?

So, cowardice, envy, hatred and cruelty had been unleashed against him. Was it not derisory, was it not an excessive irony, to announce the apotheosis, the divinity of humankind at the very moment when he was experiencing its villainy? And as yet, he had not touched the bottom of that baseness, he had not fathomed the abyss.

Then, with his elbow on the top of his little childhood desk, his forehead in his hand, he wanted to lean over that sewer and, in spite of its pestilence, measure its depth.

How many stupid voices rose from the gulf! Hypocrisies, lies, vanities, prejudices, superstitions, fanaticisms...the custom that it is necessary to observe because it is the custom, the fashion that it is necessary to follow because it is the fashion...

The blockheads who want both to honor maternity and dishonor the unwed mother...

The nationalisms choking in the corsets of customs duties, which want to sell everything to foreigners and not buy anything from them. The orators who, having outlawed war, glorify the warriors...

What barbaric or shocking spectacles glimpsed in the shadows!

The housewife who calmly shakes the dirty residues of her hearth over the heads of passers-by...

The early morning crowd that hurls itself into suburban trains, is engulfed like a tidal wave in the subterranean passages of the Metro, rushing to assault the carriages in order to be crushed and faint therein...

Everywhere, the insolent triumph of cynics and, even more deplorable, of mediocrities...

The condition of domestic servants....

The decadence of prostitutes...

The imbecilic escalation of armaments, applauded by chauvinists, stimulated by rich merchants...

And social iniquity. Yes, it's true, one no longer hears its old complaint, by virtue of hearing it all the time. But is injustice any less insupportable because it is evident? Because it is accepted, is the contrast any less revolting between the excess of luxury and the excess of hardship, between the businessman who makes a fortune with a signature and the worker literally condemned to forced labor in order to prolong his life until the following day?

Lower down, beneath social crime, crimes of violence are outlined, those unchained brutes, those semi-madmen, those mental defectives whom society permits to commit murder on condition of murdering them thereafter, rather than preventing them from being born or from doing harm. Further down, executions, tortures and their incredible refinements, Then massacres, pogroms, even more inhuman and cruel: the father forced by the soldiery to lick his son's blood from the ground; the mother constrained to hold on her knees her own child, about to be decapitated...

Lower still, War, the great Collector of all stupidities and all crimes, all lies and all savageries.

Finally, the mire at the bottom of the drain: all the perversions, all the debauchery, all the aberrations, all the turpitudes; the base reality that no book has every dared to depict, the unspeakable life...

François raised his head.

Well, no, in spite of everything, he would not despair. He retained his faith in the future, in a more beautiful life, indefinitely more beautiful. From the depths of the execrable gulf, humans would be able gradually to raise themselves up. They would slowly hoist themselves toward the light, step by step, millennium by millennium. A few were already showing them the example, the road. And when they emerged into the light, freed of their stains, they would appear in divine perfection.

François collected the pages of his article, "The Better Life." He sent it to the magazine, unchanged. And it spread his message throughout the world.

IX

One afternoon in September, at Briolle, François was summoned to the telephone by Chérance.

"Hello...? Monsieur Chérance here... Ah, it's you, my friend. Is everyone there is good health? Good. Here it is: Sandler—yes, the great Sandler of Mondial Oil—has just arrived by plane from America. He wants to see us. He's invited us to diner tomorrow evening at his hotel, the Imperial. Is that all right with you…? Agreed. Come to find me at Boulogne, then, about midday. That way, we can chat before the meeting and arrive together."

He concluded, as was his custom, with polite formulas. He sent his best wishes to Marianne, and he never forgot to be asked to be remembered to "the worthy master" Pierre Contal. Was the tenacious bibliophile not desperate to obtain the manuscript of *Génie antique*?

Chérance had always been perfectly obliging since François' departure for Briolle, He kept him up to date by telephone with the progress of Sidereal Energy, which the absurd rumors spread about the inventor did not appear to be affecting. He had also given signs of life while taking the waters at a health spa and then during a sojourn by the sea. And as it was easier to perceive his interlocutor's true intentions over the telephone than face to face, François had been able to convince himself that Chérance was not manifesting any anxiety regarding his mental condition. More sensitive than ever to sympathy, he was truly grateful to the financier for marching by his side and supporting him in that difficult pass.

François left by himself. Marianne and the children would take advantage of a few more of the beautiful amber-tinted days of the Burgundian autumn.

He congratulated himself for resuming contact with the world, for confronting its gaze. He would be able to demonstrate that he was lucid, but he would have preferred a less sensational reentry. He was apprehensive of the meeting with the president of Mondial Oil. Doubtless it would be rich in consequences.

Once again Chérance had anticipated correctly; the big oil men were coming on to the stage—and the journey by air was evidence of Sandler's haste. Such crossings were certainly becoming frequent; in the high atmosphere, at a thousand kilometers an hour, it took no more than six hours to cross from one shore to the other—but was Sandler still of an age to tolerate the trip without fatigue? He must be in a hurry to arrive.

François realized that he knew very little about the individual whose name was known all over the world. He did not know what he looked like. He only knew that he had repeated the endeavors of Rockefeller on a larger scale, that he had aggregated half the oil companies in the world. For François, however, he was more a symbol than a living being: one of those men as rich as a nation, who considered themselves more as the custodians than the possessors of their fortune. They only accumulated it in order to spread it. They were rich in money as the heart is rich in blood.

But what did Sandler want, exactly? François hastened to ask that question of Chérance in the car that took them to the Imperia. The financier appeared to be in an excellent humor. Comfortably slumped in the front of the car, with his wrist passed through the arm-rest, he mimed his ignorance, arching his eyebrows and making his little moustache bristle with a grimace.

No, truly, he did not known, exactly. Apparently, Sandler, whom he had met at a conference in the United States, was bringing a proposition for the chairman of Sidereal Energy in the name of two English and American groups, united in the face of the peril. But what proposition? Chérance was incapable of guessing.

The certain thing was that Sandler must feel threatened in his sovereignty. And, not without self-satisfaction, the financier reminded François of the primary role played by oil at the moment when the Starter was about to dethrone it. Oil? One not only obtained the gasoline necessary for all automobiles therefrom, but also the heavy fuel-oil that would soon be necessary for all ships. In brief, it animated all the engines in the world. It haunted all peace negotiators, all the great international conferences. Wars were fought over it. An oil consortium was ready to do anything to obtain a concession. Was it refused? It had been seen to foment troubles, assassinations, even revolutions, in order that the refractory government might be replaced by a more accommodating one. One of its potentates, furious that a major nation had refused him the concession of its oil, had been known to attempt to isolate it, to asphyxiate it, to sever its diplomatic and mercantile relations with the rest of the planet.

Oh, such fellows had tusks. They did not give in without striking a blow.

But Chérance seemed to be enjoying himself, like a lover of fencing smiling at the thought of a hard-fought match.

The president of Mondial Oil had an apartment at the Imperial furnished like a luxury liner. Sandler was quite different from the image that Francois had formed of him: short, gray-haired and solicitous, he had a face and complexion that were almost Japanese, a modest expression, gold-rimmed spectacles and child-like hands. His smile uncovered upper teeth that were powerful and jutting.

He excused himself for not speaking French very well. Alas, François had completely forgotten English. For want of aptitude in languages, he had not obtained any benefit from his college lessons, or even from a holiday in Derbyshire.

Sandler took his meals in his apartment. Waiters hastened about, as rapid, invisible and mute as a flock of bats. They served a rich parfait and authentic wines. The American tried to congratulate the young inventor on his discovery in French. François understood him imperfectly, but he was not tempted to smile. He thought, humbly: *If only I spoke English as he speaks French...* He was always irritated to see his compatriots mocking foreign accents. *We, of course, have found the best means of having no accent—we don't speak foreign languages!*

Chérance, a great cosmopolitan, spoke English admirably. He offered to serve as interpreter. Thanks to that improvisation, Sandler was able to interrogate François about his family, his children. He manifested a veritable adoration for his own daughter. Having thus sacrificed to courtesy, however, the American gradually renounced a difficult conversation, and the two potentates, becoming animated, were soon only speaking English.

Undoubtedly they had broached the debate: the Starter versus oil. Oh, how Francois regretted then not having taken his first invention, a translation machine, any further. It was no more complicated than a calculating machine not a television set. The speaker sat before a microphone; each word "sounded" the corresponding word, and all the listeners received a literal translation through their earphones. Until everyone learned a second language in the cradle, how useful that machine would have been in international conferences! How many misunderstandings it might have avoided!

From time to time, Chérance kept François up to date with a brief word: "We're discussing Sidereal Energy" or "We're not entirely in accord." His gaze attentive, his nostrils pinched, he maintained a firm and flexible jaw, without ever interrupting. Sandler rubbed his little hands, and showed his teeth in sickly smiles.

The battle seemed to François to be hard-fought.

As the American rose to his feet he said to him, pointing at Chérance: "Terrible man."

What had they decided?

When they were back beside the financier's car, François said: "Well?" That is the question that summarizes all questions.

Instead of replying, Chérance asked him to go with him. François agreed.

"Lechartreux's" ordered the financier.

The chauffeur must often have taken his boss to Lechartreux's because he pulled away without asking for the address.

"Here it is," said Chérance, when they were on the way. "We haven't been able to reach an agreement. That's very unfortunate—but accord is impossible."

"What did Sandler ask for?"

"First he showed me the enormous losses that the generalization of the Starter will impose on the oil concessionaries. You know that he represents them all. The losses are evident. But so what? It's a fatal law. Every industry installs itself on the ruins of those it replaces. Besides which, oil deposits are limited. They aren't renewable. They'll have dried up in the near future, so we're only going to hasten the moment when the petrol companies will be obliged to cease their exploitation. It's also necessary to add that oil, so long as it gushes, won't lose all its value. Its by-products are useful, notably lubricating oils and greases. You've told me yourself that engines will rotate faster and faster, so lubricants will become increasingly precious."

François was pleased that he had remembered that glimpse of the future. "That's true," he confirmed.

"Those were the arguments I tried to get across to Sandler. Naturally, he didn't yield to them. To compensate for the loss that the oil cartel will suffer, he asked, quite simply, to buy Sidereal Energy on their behalf."

"That's very serious," said François.

"I should think so! I must say that he offered a high price, and I sensed that he was ready to double, or even triple it—but I refused so frankly that he didn't persist Given that the shares of our company aren't in circulation, but all in friendly hands, Sandler can't play his habitual game of buying them up clandestinely, worming his way in and taking over. On the other hand, as our business is irreproachable, it's impossible to use the classic method of ruining it by means of a lawsuit or a political scandal."

"So?"

"Sandler hasn't admitted defeat. He made me another proposition, equally intended in his mind to attenuate the threat. I thought I understood that it would also ensure his neutrality. At that price, he'd leave us in peace. He asked me for a partnership."

"What does that mean?"

"An alliance. Sidereal Energy would become a Franco-American company."

"What!" François exclaimed. "And you didn't accept that?"

"Never in this world!"

Since he had been obliged to watch the debate between Sandler and Chérance, in which the fate of his discovery was at stake, as an outsider, Francois sensed a muted rebellion rising with him. As highly as he rated Chérance, he thought that the financier ought to have consulted him on each important point, instead of keeping him faintly up to date with the conversation. Now, he had to learn after the fact that Chérance had made a decision...

Decidedly, whether it is a matter of a newspaper, a magazine or an industry, those who administer an enterprise always tend to eliminate what they have created. They seem to obey a cruel instinct of nature, in which the male is often sacrificed once having accomplished his work of fecundation.

Finally, François protested: "Why," he said, "did you take it upon yourself to refuse?"

"Why?" cried Chérance, imperiously. "To begin with, I could reply that I have the right, that Sidereal Energy has entrusted the helm of its direction to me, that the Board has given me full authority to negotiate with Sandler. But that would be a paltry argument, unworthy of the two of us. No, the true, the real reason, is that we must, at all costs, remain the masters of the situation. I admit that we'll issue licenses, at our discretion, but we must guard our privilege, our supremacy, our power jealously."

"I don't agree," said François. He pronounced the sentence so curtly that he was surprised by the sound of his own voice.

Chérance was bare-headed. His forehead was red. His temporal vein was near to bursting. Dryly, he said: "What does that mean?"

"I want my discovery to serve the whole world. I don't want it to become an instrument of discord. More precisely, I'm a supporter of an American alliance. I always have been. When we were building our factories at

Fraicourt, on the banks of the Seine, I took pleasure in the thought that we were on a road that led toward the sea, toward the New World. It was childish, perhaps, but that was how I felt..."

"But you don't know the Americans!" exclaimed Chérance. "You've never been there. I've dealt with them, myself. I don't deny their great qualities, but good God, they're awkward company: puerile, pretentious..."

"I don't really believe in racial characteristics," François admitted. "One race is much the same as any other. I can't imagine that the hundred and twenty million inhabitants of the United States all have the same faults."

"You know full well, my friend, that in these matters it's always a matter of a majority. If I say that the Nordic type is blond with blue eyes, it's because the majority of Norsemen have blue eyes and blond hair."

"Oh, I agree with you with regard to physical characteristics," François agreed. "At least while the races aren't mixed—and from now on, they'll be mixed very rapidly; remember that rapid locomotion is less than a hundred years old. But relative to mental traits, I have strong reservations. Appearance is variable—and it's not important. A face is never anything but a small tumult of flesh on a bone structure. On the other hand, I believe that there's very little fundamental difference between one people and another. It's a question of skin. Have you ever looked in the window of a food shop? It's astonishing how much one skinned rabbit resembles another..."

Chérance cut him off with a hint of aggravation. "Where is this going?"

François was in full flow. He continued straight ahead. "There are a lot of questions that you understand thoroughly and about which I know nothing. You've seen that I gladly defer to your experience—but I've meditated problems that might never have caught your attention. So, I can prove to you, with scientific certainty, that civilization, in the most radiant sense of the word, is heading toward America, which will be its promised land for a long time."

"That is indeed a demonstration that I'd be interested to hear."

"I'll come to it. I've reflected a great deal on the question of America. The New World has been alternately exalted and denigrated. It's the well-known phenomenon of the pendulum, which moves to the right and then to the left before finding its equilibrium. Oh, I don't admire all Americans—or rather, I don't understand them all. Some verdicts of their judges, their official continence, their scorn for the negro race, which they nevertheless freed at the cost of their blood—all of that disconcerts me...but they realize material well-being, and that's the most important thing. For it's only on that solid platform that moral wellbeing can be edified. They're on the right path. It's said that they're not ideal. What a joke! Between us, what ideal have we built in the workshop of Europe? President Wilson was the greatest idealist of modern times. Besides which, America's detractors fail to recognize, more or less consciously, all sorts of artistic, spiritual and intellectual merits that one already sees sprouting in that new land, and whose flowering will astonish the world. I don't attribute racial traits to Americans. I say that their continent has youth in its favor, with its excesses and its immense promise."

"And the demonstration?"

"It's not mine. One finds the elements of it in any summary of astronomy. In reality, the hearth of civilization is always installed in the most temperate region of the globe. Now, that zone shifts because the axis of the Earth slowly changes its orientation, like that of a top. That blessed zone describes a curve around the Earth. One can follow its track since the earliest ages of which humans have retained some memory. From Asia it passed to Egypt, and then successively chose for its capitals Athens, Rome and Paris. Presently, it's crossing the Ocean. It will reach land in New York. It will slowly traverse America, pause in Japan, and then return to Asia to complete its circuit and begin again. Its tour of the world takes two hundred and fifty centuries..."

Chérance studied his companion with wide eyes. Was he, too, beginning to believe him mentally unbalanced? François did not have time to ask him. The car stopped in front of the dusty window of an old bookshop.

"We'll talk about this again," the financier said, simply. "Will you come with me?"

He leapt briskly out of the vehicle, brushed the sidewalk and lunged into Lechartreux's bookshop.

The atmosphere of the old bookshop was so singular that, as soon as he had crossed the threshold, Chérance seemed to forget the march of civilization around the world, the future of the United States, the American alliance and even Sidereal Energy. There are isolating walls that defend us against cold, heat and noise; in the same way, walls of old books separate us from the present day.

Any visitor, entering an old bookshop at hazard, immediately feels distanced from the world. But that dry odor of dust and parchment intoxicated Chérance all the more powerfully because of his passion for rare books. It was even certain that he had no others, except for his formidable appetite for administration. He had no love for amour. A bachelor, he had been notoriously linked for years with the most celebrated cantatrice of the Opéra, but she was as careful to preserve her voice as he was reluctant to sacrifice himself to pleasure. It was, in consequence, a liaison of wise children, who held on to one another with their little fingers.

Chérance introduced François to Lechartreux. He did not add that his young friend was the author of the greatest discovery of modern times, for he knew that the bookseller did not live in the present century, that he was utterly ignorant of his own era. He thought, however, that he ought to report that François Thibault was the son-in-law of Pierre Contal.

Naturally, Lechartreux did not manifest any emotion, for the old bookseller seemed immune to admiration, sympathy and the majority of human sentiments. Nevertheless, after a brief absence, Lechartreux slid under the financier's gaze a book that he had just collected from the back room of the shop. It was a first edition of *Cléopâtre*, one of Pierre Contal's most famous works. Still silent, he opened the volume. The bibliophile who had owned the book, whose collection had doubtless been dispersed, had inserted an autograph letter from the author into it.

Evidently, those four pages were not worth as much as the unobtainable manuscript of *Génie antique*, but Chérance pored over the prestigious script. His forehead was scarlet. Again, his temporal vein seemed close to bursting. He was as excited by the sight of that simple letter as he had been a little while ago, in the car, when he had been defending his supremacy, his worldly privilege. François realized that only the passion for rare paper could counterbalance the passion for power in that man.

X

The inauguration of the first Radio-Propulsion Company was a very simple celebration. That day, François felt a new confidence in the future. A few weeks had passed since his argument with Chérance over the American alliance. He hoped that his reasoning had taken hold in the lucid mind of the financier, who had never returned to the discussion. Sandler had left again very quickly, without seeing either of them again. The campaign in the gutter press seemed to have been aborted. The venom had lost its virulence. Francois sometimes caught a glimpse of a sort of malicious curiosity in the gazes that lingered upon him, but he had made his decision. It no longer affected him. And the Starter continued nevertheless to spread into the world.

That first radio-propulsion enterprise involved river transport by barge between Paris and Rouen. Dutrait, the commercial director of Sidereal Energy, was the veritable creator of the new company. The transmitter was installed in the grounds of the factories at Fraicourt, approximately half way between the two extremities of the line.

The inauguration was held on one of those marvelous days that autumn deploys as it declines to a beautiful death. The ceremony was analogous to that of launching a ship. The guests were to witness the departure of the first barge of the regular service. It was moored near the Pont de Tolbiac. It was called the *Marianne*. Its godfather and godmother were Dutrait and little Lise.

Naturally, Dutrait arrived late. The attaché representing the Minister of the Merchant Marine displayed considerable irritation. One cannot imagine what facilities life suddenly offers to such young men. Before them, all doors open, all heads bow down. Drunk on their power, they quickly become jealous of it.

Chérance, brisk and elegant, distributed handshakes with a haughty cordiality. He regretted not finding Pierre Contal there. Although the author of *Génie antique* had left Burgundy and returned to his winter abode at Passy he had refused to dignify with his presence one of the "deplorable conquests of science."

The attaché made the inevitable speech, but fortunately, as he was still sulking, he cut it short. Assisted by Dutrait, little Lise used scissors to cut the symbolic ribbon linking the *Marianne* to the bank. The barge drew away silently, amid the applause of the crowd. It did not consume any fuel. Radiation emitted at Fraicourt animated its engine. The mechanic had only to tune into it, like a radio operator picking up a broadcasting station. "The barge takes to the waves." That mediocre wordplay delighted Dutrait, who repeated it to everyone.

A buffet had been set up in the new company's hangar. Champagne corks popped. Glasses sparkled in fingertips. People have not yet found any better way to hold communion than drinking together. From the royal banquet to the village wedding, people "raise their glasses."

In sum, the event passed almost unnoticed by the general public. The next day, however, oil shares fell noticeably on the New York Stock Exchange. That drop became steeper in the days that followed. Not only did it extend to other exchanges, but to the entire market in each of them. A crisis was beginning, whose violence was unforeseeable.

François was still a layman in banking matters. Alerted by a telephone call from Laronce, he sought information later from Dutrait. He encountered him almost every day at the headquarters of Sidereal Energy, where they supervised the debut of the new transport company together.

Dutrait explained that the success of the enterprise had provoked the fall in oil. The trial on the Paris-Rouen route had a symbolic value, just as the Paris-Saint-Germain railway line had been the embryo of the country-wide network. Radio-Propulsion could and would extend to all rivers, all roads and all oceans.

But why had the drop become general, extending to all shares?

Dutrait buttoned his jacket, with one of his familiar gestures, which he had borrowed from his boss.

"It was inevitable. The big holders of oil shares have suffered a loss. You admit that? Good. It's necessary that they repair it, for the needs of their treasury. What do they do? They sell other shares. Which? The ones they can sell most dearly—which is to say, the most solid, the best. They put them on the market. They fall in their turn, according to the law of supply and demand. Thus, everything goes down."

Like Chérance, he concluded: "It's time." Then, smiling, he added: "Besides which, the misfortune of one is the good fortune of others. I know people who bet on the fall and who will make fortunes from this collapse."

Candidly, Francois asked: "What do you mean?"

"Yes indeed—an example. Having known that oil shares would fall, one of these lascars declares: 'I'm selling a thousand Mondial Oil.'"

"Even if he doesn't have them?"

"That's not important. He sells dear. Before settlement, the shares go down. He buys cheap, and pockets the difference. The trick is worked."

So, unscrupulous people were going enrich themselves in the catastrophe. François' anguished irritation increased. The financial organization of the world seemed to him to be fragile, temporary and artificial. Above all, it was recent. Like technology, it had the defect of extreme youth. Instantaneous communications, especially radio, brand new, gave it an excessive sensitivity. It was subject to the laws of interdependence, but not yet controlled by them. The damages were suffered without the benefits being enjoyed. In brief, the world panicked too easily. It developed fevers too rapidly. But so what? One cannot live outside one's times.

François was not unaware that similar crises not only provoked ruinations and suicides in the ranks of gamblers but that they also had more distant repercussions, that they devastated humble lives all the way to the depths of the crowd. The thought that his discovery might be responsible for such disasters was unbearable. He murmured: "It's not possible."

He remained convinced that Chérance, and Chérance alone, could avert the catastrophe, with a word or a gesture. The financier had just arrived at Sidereal Energy. His hoarse but penetrating voice was audible through the partition wall. François decided to go and see him right away.

Naturally, Chérance was following the development of the crisis very closely. As soon as François began to deplore it, he interrupted him. Sitting behind his desk, he struck it with the palm of his hand.

"What of it? Those people are afraid of their shadow. What have the oil men lost so far? The few tons that the Paris-Rouen barges would have burned. That's nothing by comparison with world-wide consumption. And like us, they have no idea what tomorrow might bring."

François repeated that the trial would doubtless soon be imitated on land and sea. For the holders of shares in oil, it was an alarm signal. Chérance could not deny that—and, for the first time since the lunch at the Imperial, François returned to the subject of the American partnership. He urged the financier to accept Sandler's proposal.

"Oh, to be sure, I'm just a layman, ignorant in these matters, but a sure instinct tells me that such an alliance would reassure the market. Those who fear losing everything would immediately realize that the damage will be limited, that they will be compensated in part by the benefits that they will derive from the Starter."

Chérance made an angry gesture. "Don't ask me to abandon our privilege. I'm twenty years older than you. You'll live longer than I will. Whatever happens, be sure that you'll eventually regret having abandoned that supremacy, that instrument of power."

He got to his feet. Cordially, almost tenderly, he said: "Come on—it's only a crisis. The market's see many others. It will settle down, as all crises settle down."

Casually, he indicated that the matter was closed for the moment, that he did not intend to discuss it further. François was not tempted to pursue the conversation himself. He sensed that Chérance was utterly intoxicated, reveling in being the master of masters. He considered him with an amazement mingled with fear, as if he were one of those monstrous conquerors who, to ensure their glory and their reign, sacrifice thousands of human lives, without realizing that each of those lives, all things considered, is worth as much as his own.

Very early the next morning, Laronce rang the doorbell of the detached house at Bellevue.

Every time he saw his friend appear like that, François felt a constriction in his breast and his life slow down. He thought: *What new catastrophe has he come to tell me about?*

Laronce had a glitter in his eye and a mournful expression.

"I took the first train," he explained, "in order that I can still get to the paper on time. Dispatches arrive at the *Bonjour* yesterday evening that have delayed publication. Yes, the newspapers are censoring themselves now. It's a habit they acquired in the last war and haven't yet been able to shake off. The telegrams will only appear in the *avant-garde* papers, but people won't read the newspapers that prohibit them."

"What do the dispatches say?"

"I don't want to tell you by phone. Serious troubles have broken out in the coalfields of the North and East. In the last few days, the President of the Council, Feuillard, has received delegations from the miners' unions. That information appeared in the papers but passed unnoticed. No one was interested. Yesterday, bands of unemployed men pillaged stores and attacked pitheads. They've cut the telegraph wires and taken over a telephone exchange. They're threatening to march on Paris. It's said that they're armed with machine-guns and grenades. Troops were sent during the night in motorized trucks to bar their route. There's fear of a revolutionary movement.

"It's the final blow," sighed François.

Laronce explained the news. The consumption of coal had diminished since the employment of the Starter. The mining companies, seeing their stocks growing enormously, had first reduced the working day, and then laid off a number of their workers. Sufficiently compensated, the unemployed had remained placid, but a few days ago, agitators had appeared in the region. Adding a leaven of bitterness to the mass, they had unleashed its effervescence.

Laronce, whom François had told about Sandler's check, was inclined to think that the big oil men had stimulated the uprising. The mining companies, in fact, had no interest in provoking mobs that were as dangerous to their equipment as to the lives of their engineers. Thus, in the contest between oil and the Starter, oil had scored a point—for everyone would attribute the responsibility for the troubles in which rumbles of revolution were heard to Sidereal Energy.

Revolution! Francois was horrified. Before anything else, he had respect for human life. He said: "I don't hate anything but hatred." Logical, he detested all wars, civil wars as well as foreign wars. He curses bloody revolution with all his might. It never seemed necessary to him. He recalled that people had been able to change regimes without violence. He contended that even without the revolution of 1789, France would, solely by virtue of the influence of the Voltaires and the Diderots, have ended up with a constitutional monarchy by 1830, exactly as had happened in reality—and would have been spared the Red Terror, the monstrous Napoléonic adventure, the White Terror, and the grotesque recoil of the Restoration. He shivered at the mere thought of a collision between bands of unemployed workers and troops. He had always inveighed against the employment of the army in such tasks. What? Men, because they were wearing uniforms, were going to fire on their friends, their relatives? Perhaps that sacrilegious impact, for which he felt partly responsible, would occur within a matter of hours. It wasn't possible.

He resolved to badger Chérance again, hard. Although he disapproved on the Sandler group's method of intimidation, the American alliance appeared to him to be more necessary than ever, in the direction of the future. More than ever, he was convinced that such a union would instantly calm the troubles and the crisis.

He took Laronce back to Paris by car, pausing momentarily at the *Bonjour*. No fresh news had come in. He left for Boulogne—but Chérance's private secretary told him that the boss had just been summoned urgently to the Ministry of the Interior by the President of the Council, Feuillard. As the financier had declared that he would call in at home immediately after the meeting, François decided to wait for him. He sat down in the large drawing-room into which he had come for the first time two years earlier, full of confidence and joy.

There was no doubt that in the Minister's mind, Sidereal Energy was at least partly responsible for the troubles in the North; that explained the abrupt summoning of Chérance. But what did the government want?

François had met Feuillard in Pierre Contal's house at Passy. He had been painfully surprised by his mocking cynicism, his affectation of taking nothing seriously—neither people nor ideas. He was typical of those parliamentarians whose souls have been withered by politics; in their hearts only two sentiments remained alive: the fear of the opposition and the passion of power. Pierre Contal said of Feuillard: "I don't like him. He's scornful of humankind, without sadness."

Chérance came back at midday. He seemed furious. Striding through the large drawing-room, he tore off his gloves and threw them aside.

"You know about the riots in the North?"

"Yes," said François. "From Laronce, this morning."

It was those troubles that had caused Feuillard to lose his head. He was trembling before the threat of a parliamentary challenge. He was talking about revoking licenses, suspending the manufacture of the Starter, which, by reducing sales of coal, seemed responsible for the riots. He was invoking the national interest, reasons of State. He had gone so far as to cite the example of absinthe, which had been suppressed by decree. Later, perhaps, production might be resumed, at a prudent rate, in measured doses.

"Oh, I defended myself well," said Chérance. "I told Feuillard for coal what I'd told Sandler for oil. We're not suppressing the exploitation of coal mines. There too, the work can continue until the exhaustion of the seams, utilizing the by-products. You know what they are better than I do. Tar, increasingly necessary for maintaining the roads; benzene, naphtha, and above all aniline and its entire spectrum of dyes... Anyway, the decline of coal had begun before the invention of the Starter. Hydroelectric power was gradually replacing coal. It was a film in slow motion. We've only accelerated the process."

Violently, he went on: "Besides which, these riots are artificial. They'll stop as soon as the agitators fomenting them have left the scene. The big oil men are in the wings. They're trying to draw the government into their game with this maneuver. They're making their bite felt. Feuillard, in spite of his gross cynicism and his leaden trickery, doesn't dare admit that openly in my presence. He can't—but there's no doubt about it. It's still the same campaign, continuing patiently. It's a matter of reducing us by threats, forcing us to throw in the sponge, leading us to an alliance—but I haven't given in. I won't surrender."

"Why?" said François. "I've come to see you this morning to beg you once again to sign the treaty of alliance. You agreed yourself just now that it would calm the troubles immediately—and I'm sure, in spite of my ignorance, that it would also resolve the financial crisis. It's so logical, so necessary. Of course Sandler's method is deplorable. I understand that we'll appear to be giving in to the threat. That's annoying—but it would have come to this if we'd reached an understanding at the beginning. Furthermore, there are precedents. Look, just now, while waiting for you, I thought of an example. When electricity replaced gas for lighting, conflicts of the same kind burst forth. Well, in a number of cities, the old company and the new one merged..."

"Yes, and in many others they remained rivals. No, no—it's blackmail. I won't give in to it. That's what I told Feuillard; I repeat it to you."

His resistance had become stronger since he had repelled this new assault. He was no longer solely possessed by the spirit of domination. He was also stiffened and hardened by pride. He was very red in the face, his veins swollen. He was stubborn to the point of apoplexy and sclerosis.

François understood that he was unshakable. One does not try to bend a statue. Frustrated by his impotence, he sensed that he would harm his cause by persisting. He left in despair.

Marianne was watching for him on the threshold of the house at Bellevue. She was beginning to worry. It was long past their usual lunch time. She had fed the children in order to send them for a walk during the sunlit hours of the brief winter day.

François confessed that he was incapable of taking any nourishment. Weight down by weariness, he let himself fall into an armchair. Marianne sat down beside him. He took her hand and pressed it to his forehead.

"I'm in distress, Marianne."

He talked. He had had other moments of doubt, as on the day when he had meditated all alone in his car, behind the Madeleine, after having seen the ferocious commentaries on the explosion at Bellevue. He had doubted at Briolle before the *Terra* proofs, having heard the gutter press calling him a madman. He was in doubt today because he was, in sum, about to provoke bankruptcies, suicides, perhaps mass murder. What immeasurable irony! He, who had wanted a better life and happiness for human beings, was perhaps about to cause their blood to be shed! With every passing hour, he dreaded hearing news of conflict between the unemployed and the soldiers. He could only glimpse one way out, one glimmer of salvation: the reasonable alliance that would calm everything down. But the prideful ambition of one man barred that road to him....

He wanted to seek forgetfulness in work. He headed toward his laboratory. As he crossed the vestibule he avoided looking at the gigantic globe. He turned away from it, as if by virtue of remorse.

The Earth...he had wanted to envelop it in an atmosphere of wellbeing, to ensure it a life of eternally-increasing happiness. And by his doing, it was suffering a fit of panic. Perhaps it would be soiled by civil war. It seemed to him that, if he placed his hand on that globe, he would feel it as hot and feverish as the forehead of a sick person. And he feared that if he looked at it, he would see bloodstains.

He resumed his most recent research: a supremely hard, supremely light alloy that would permit the construction of a flying machine he called the Hybrid. It was, in effect, a fusion of the dirigible and the airplane, where the two conceptions met. Equipped with chambers that would be evacuated, it would be as light as a soap-bubble; it would not be able to fall, and would not be able to burn. It would avoid two risks: that of burning and that of crashing. Its realization would give an incredible boost to aerial navigation.

But he could not work. He was apprehensive of hearing about the conflict he dreaded, from a telephone call, the radio or a visitor. Dusk was falling rapidly. A sound of footsteps resonated in the vestibule.

The open bay framed a silhouette: Marianne...

She was radiant with joy. Her face was shining in the half-light.

"There," she said. "I've been to ask Papa for the manuscript of *Génie antique*. He was keeping it for me. I've given it to Chérance, on condition that he cable Sandler. It's done. We have peace."

Never had the "silent darling" made such a long speech in a single breath. François hugged her to his broad chest, as if he wanted to fuse her with himself. Then, arms linked, welded together at the shoulder and the hip, they went out of the laboratory—but this time as they went through the vestibule, François enveloped the globe of the world with a gaze shining with tenderness and hope.

PINK SKY

PART ONE

Chapter I
(A Tuesday in May 1960)

"To the Élysée."

On emerging from his Ministry, the Justice Minister. Pierre Arnage, gave that order swiftly to his chauffeur, who was holding the car door. Scarcely had he sat down than the Minister reread Marilène's letter. He still wanted to doubt it. Everything was descending upon him at the same time. His mistress was pregnant. And war was threatening to break out...

He searched through the pages for the most significant phrases: *My dear Pierre, last month's fears have been confirmed... Now, it's almost certain... I knew the sacrifice that I was accepting, the risks I was running, in giving myself to you... I was, and still am, so proud of you... How could I not love a little being born of you...? My fate is in your hands... Whatever you decide, I shall not complain...*

No doubt was possible: a child was going to be born.

He was married; she was not. He was entering an era of inextricable difficulties—and at the very moment when the European Union was breaking into two hostile blocs.

Parliament had still been on Easter break. The Minister's life was peaceful, Suddenly, that absurd schism had split the continent. The Head of State, on holiday at Chambord, had returned to Paris by airplane, immediately summoning the Council. Pierre Arnage had been obliged to leave his estate at Briolle at dawn—and, on calling in at the Ministry, where she was accustomed to write to him, he had found that distressing letter, which Marilène had sent from Geneva.

The automobile went under the porch of the Presidential Palace, went around the sandy courtyard and stopped at the perron. Arnage climbed the steps briskly. Directly in front of him, in the half-light of the spacious vestibule, stood a mirror framed by verdure, extending from floor to ceiling. He saw his silhouette, rather short but lithe and loose-limbed. His black hair, brushed backwards, helmeted his forceful forehead and thin face, proud and hollow-cheeked. At forty-seven, he looked no older than thirty. But what good were all those advantages? On seeing himself so seductive, he felt his misfortune all the more keenly.

All his colleagues had preceded him. They were spread out in sparse groups, as animated as those in the wings of a theater on the evening of a dress rehearsal, in the Salon de Cléopâtre and the Salon du Conseil. He was still shaking hands when the Head of State appeared. The Council immediately went into session.

For nearly a hundred years the Republic had alternately chosen a southern President who was always smiling and a northerner who never smiled. Succeeding one another with the same astronomical regularity as day and night, they took turns in leading the country as if in a farandole or as if in an unreal procession. The current President, the austere Crépin, belonged to the funereal genre. One might have thought that his hard features, with long wrinkles, were sculpted in gray stone. Already, he resembled his bust. Sadly, he recalled the events of the previous day.

The European Union, constructed with so much difficulty, on such fragile bases, was crumbling. At the Assembly in Lausanne, the socialist States had proposed the abolition of wage labor. They had won the vote, but the capitalist States had refused to submit to a sentence they considered to be abusive, while their adversaries, proclaiming their right, seemed determined to impose it by force if necessary.

The prime minister, Martory, criticized these declarations. Conscientious, handsome and nonchalant, he was the ornament of the Council. He was its representative of the sum of elegance and Atticism. He recalled that the situation was not new. A century before, in 1861, the American States had similarly come into conflict with one another. The North had demanded the abolition of slavery; the South had refused. The War of Secession had followed. In reality, one side had wanted protectionism, the other free trade. Today, in demanding the abolition of wage labor, the socialist States were trying to break down the capitalist barrier that hemmed them in, and to impose their regime on the rest of Europe for the convenience of their transactions. In a tone of indolent skepticism, he recognized that in all wars, people pushed for material conquests under idealistic colors.

Pierre Arnage, who had similar pretentions to eloquence, judged those arguments superfluous. He reproved them by ceasing to listen to them. Distractedly, he doodled on the pieces of notepaper with the Presidential heading spread out in front of him. He traces capital

Ms, for Marilène. For two years, that had been his superstitious and affectionate habit at the Ministerial Council.

He had known Marilène for two years. At that time, he had just taken on Public Education in a new Ministry. Dormier, a clerk at the Society of Nations, had recommended his daughter to him, and he had taken her on to his staff. One day, when he had to unveil the statue of a local dignitary in Grenoble, he had taken the young woman with him, because she had made the notes for his speech. She had helped him to write it on the journey. Then, when the ceremony was over, they had taken a short trip into the mountains near La Grave, by way of recompense.

At one time, they had got out of the car. It was June; one felt close to the sky and the sun. The ardent and perfumed air was trembling on the Alpine pastures. Knee-deep in the thick grass, they had run gaily down the slopes amid a warm odor of incense and honey. He had understood that she admired his power, his prestige and his oratorical gifts. And he had discovered in Marilène a new face, a winged, scintillating grace. She surged forth before his eyes like an apparition, the fairy of the florid mountain...

Since then, he had kept her with him when he transferred from Public Education to Justice. She had taken up residence in one of those charming little villas that had flowered amid the verdure at Billancourt when the automobile factories had been removed fifty kilometers from Paris. It was there that he met her. A month before, however, she had been obliged to leave for Geneva, in order to spend the holidays with her father.

Meanwhile, Ducros, the Minister of Foreign Affairs, had taken the floor. He was a gnome with a huge gray head. His bulbous eyes were juxtaposed with his pince-nez. He worked relentlessly, but his mole-like labor risked causing the world to collapse. He read diplomatic dispatches. They were murky and labyrinthine, in accordance with to the immemorial habit. They emanated from men stuck in the past, hostile to their own time, disdainful of the masses. With their index-fingers on their noses they continued to hatch ruses and plots behind closed doors, while all around them great currents of covetousness surged through the air, charged with lightning.

The table of ministers needed the truth; they were being served a plateful of petty tricks. Arnage shrugged his shoulders. He listened without comprehending. Gradually, he retreated into himself. He found his torment there.

Oh, if only one could put a stop to the development of pregnancy...what a relief, what a brightening of the horizon...did inoffensive remedies exist? He had heard talk of powders, tisanes—but the names escaped him. One thinks one that knows something, but when one examines it at close range, one realizes that one does not. Besides, such medicines weren't always effective. There remained brutal abortion. But he would be an accomplice. He would be breaking the law—and he could not forget, after all, that he was the Minister of Justice. Finally, such interventions were not without risk. The mere thought of exposing Marilène to suffering, to danger, was intolerable. He started in revolt, as if pricked by a lancet.

The Council was now listening to Barbier, the Minister of National Defense. He was one of those civilians who, utterly confused by commanding generals, became more militant than the military men. They go through life in battle-dress and helmet, hackles raised and cheeks

inflated like a bugler's. Passing prudishly over the resources of electric, chemical and microbial warfare,
Barbier read reassuring statistics prepared by his bureau-
crats. Listening to them, one had the impression of
watching an interminable parade, hearing the cadenced
march of men and horses, the rumble of armored cars
and heavy artillery, beneath a sky black with aircraft.
The procession was never-ending.

Again, Arnage's attention buckled. His gaze paused
on the young face of Queen Victoria—for the portraits of
all the sovereigns who had been the guests of the Élysée
ornamented the Salle du Conseil. The sight of the femi-
nine face reminded him of his distress. If he renounced
the abortion, only one course of action remained: divorce, in order to marry Marilène...

Divorce? But what right did he have to punish Annette, his wife? She had never done anything wrong.
Quite the contrary. Evidently, her humor had deteriorat-
ed with age, but had he not contributed to its souring by
his own frivolity? She had never ceased to be a god wife.
She had never given him any but sage advice. What attentive cares she lavished on him at the first sign of illness! And when he had been beaten in elections, in the
trough of that unlucky streak from which he had thought
he would never recover, how much courage and confidence she had given him...

He went back to earlier memories, to the spring of
their marriage. He recovered the sharp scent of new furniture, and the fresh and fragrant perfume of Annette's
trousseau. Those two odors had been the scent of their
first home, the scent of their youth.

But he tore himself out of the past in order to throw
himself into the discussion. The tedious explanations
were finished. Everyone had said his bit. Some wanted

to submit it to the Society of Nations. Others doubted its means. Some were calculating the impediments that the trades unions and pacifist leagues would inflict of mobilization. Singularly enough, although war had been illegal for more than thirty years, the ministers still admitted it. They did not identify it as murder. They resigned themselves more easily to that scourge manufactured by human beings than to the scourges unleashed by nature. One might have thought that the sovereigns—the Franz-Josefs and the Victor-Emmanuels—whose portraits ornamented the walls and who had revered war as an institution were still presiding over the assembly.

It became confused and tumultuous. In the hubbub, one could no longer discern the words that were hurtling from mouths, as round and black as bowling balls. Only the President, Crépin, and the Prime Minister, Martory, were maintaining, the one his icy sadness, the other his nonchalant grace. They were consulting the double-faced clock that was set between them in the middle of the table. The session had lasted four hours. With common accord, they would resume it the following day.

The Council had decided nothing.

Nor had Arnage.

Chapter II
(Tuesday)

On the afternoon of the day when the Government had suddenly convened, two men were walking slowly side by side on the terrace that overlooks Paris from the heights of Bellevue.

The older of the two, Pierre Contal, the author of *Génie antique*, had determinedly evoked the past in his books, whose incomparable form was admired the world

131

over. With his bushy white beard, jet black eyes and sober stature, he wore his seventy years well. His son-in-law, François Thibault, the famous inventor of the Starter, was with him. Twenty years earlier he had discovered a practical means of dissociating matter, thus endowing humankind with an inexhaustible and gratuitous source of energy. The middle-aged spread padding his tall figure and his forceful but tender features gave him the appearance of a debonair giant.

The brief report circulated after the Council meeting betrayed the confusion of the ministers, their inability to muzzle their appetites, to hold back stupidity. The two strollers were commenting thus in prudent terms, for they were aware of the antagonism of their tendencies and wanted to spare one another. In the thirty years since François Thibault had married Pierre Contal's daughter, the two men had been fencing with blunted foils, equally careful not to wound one another and not to give ground. Their affection matched their tolerance.

François Thibault had been supported throughout his research by his faith in the future. Convinced that humans would never cease to improve their condition, he even believed that the limitless force with which he had endowed them would ensure the planet a literally eternal life. The race would never disappear; it would tend toward the divine...

To tell the truth, that hope of immortality had never made any impression on the crowd. It honored François Thibault as the inventor of the Starter, but, indifferent to the idea that the human species might one day die out, it did not particularly glorify the man who had been the first to promise the Earth eternity.

Pierre Contal, by contrast, was convinced that human beings would never change, that their false progress was merely progressive forms of barbarism, and that they would disappear from the surface of the globe as wretched as they had appeared. To be sure, he was sincerely anxious about the threat of conflict, but he was one of those who professed that "there will always be wars," and he did not hold back from observing that events were justifying his anticipations.

"Alas, my poor friend," he sighed, "destiny is cruelly proving me right. Here we are on the eve of war. You thought you would make people happy by lightening their burden, but as you see, they remain what they were."

François Thibault shrugged his strong shoulders. "I never thought that humans would improve in twenty years. I know full well that evolution is a slow process. I know that the slightest change, for humans as for all of nature, requires thousands of millions of years—but I don't despair of humans, even on the brink of conflict. Besides which, the catastrophe hasn't been unleashed yet."

"What miracle are you expecting?" Pierre Contal interjected. "Can't you see, in the two camps, the disarray of the diplomats and governments, the resignation of the crowds, the calculated madness of the press, the impatience of the armaments-manufacturers, the sly preparations that surpass one another in the dread of being surpassed? Don't you sense that unbearable tension, that atmosphere of firedamp, at the mercy of the slightest flame? I repeat, my friend, that the catastrophe is inevitable..."

"War is never inevitable," François cut in. "It's precisely our sluggishness that renders it fatal. It's necessary to fight it inch by inch, as one fights a fire, a flood or an epidemic. It's necessary to bar the road to it until the last moment, by any means possible. As for me, I'm ready for it..."

"What are you going to do, then?"

"I have a meeting with Arnage. I'm due to see him in an hour. He's in the government. At Briolle, we were good neighbors. I have some influence over him. He'll tell me what the people who matter are planning..."

"But those wretches don't know anything. They only have official information. They'll be carried away by the hurricane, like dead leaves."

"So I'll only interrogate Arnage as a matter of conscience. What I expect from him, primarily, is that he'll give me complete freedom to talk to the microphone."

"What? You want to talk?"

"This very evening. The professional orators have had their turn. It's now that of the men of action, who, by their endeavors, have truly served the cause. Their achievements will give weight to their words. They're the ones who'll make the language of reason heard."

"Too late—no one's listening any longer."

"Well," said François Thibault, forcefully, "I won't abandon the game. I'm going to play my last card."

"What card?"

"I'll tell you later..." He interrupted himself. His powerful and benevolent features brightened. His son Claude had emerged from the Laboratory and was coming toward them. He had his father's tall stature, the same thick hair, like the edge of a forest, the same blue eyes, soft and clear, but he had youthful slimness, a slender figure and a tight abdomen. His calm gestures had the exquisite grace that athletes acquire in slow-motion films.

Claude worked with his father at the Bellevue Centre for Studies in Physics, where the Starter had been born twenty years before. That communal labor was very welcome to François Thibault. It compensated for the absence of his daughter Lise, who, having married an American, now lived in the United States. In addition, at twenty-three, the boy showed signs of an astonishing talent for discovery. His work on the electrification of air promised prodigies.

The time was long past when, in that same spot, François had held three-year-old Claude in his arms and jokingly pretended to explain the changes that the Starter would bring to the physiognomy of Paris. Already, some of those new features had appeared in reality. The city unfurled as far as the eye could see like a verdant park sown with villas. The sky was striated by swift airships, as numerous as flocks of swallows. And to think that over that animation, over that life, over that peace, the threat of death was hovering—the atmosphere of firedamp that Pierre Contal had mentioned. No, no, it wasn't possible. The firedamp would not ignite. He would not permit that to happen...

He questioned his son enthusiastically: "Well, you've made your telephone calls?"

"Yes, Papa," Claude replied, like a good little boy.

"Tomsk, Tokyo, Ottawa?"

"Yes, Papa."

"Your airmails have arrived?"

"Yes, Papa."

Then François Thibault turned to Pierre Contal and rubbed his powerful hands. "Come on—the city isn't at war yet..."

Chapter III
(Tuesday)

The beautiful May dusk was falling over the main square in Briolle. Perhaps it would be the last evening of peace for the little town. The chestnut-trees on the esplanade, whose flowers were still impregnated with brightness, shone for a moment longer in the twilight, like giant candlesticks, Christmas trees strayed into spring. Then they went out.

Noblemain lingered on the threshold of his garage, under the lamp suspended from the lintel. The raw light fell in a flood over his luxuriant curly hair, his powerful shoulders and vast paunch. There was perhaps no one in Briolle more popular than that plump, eloquent, generous, helpful and plain-speaking man, with the honest face. He was also reputed to be highly skilled in his trade. In spite of his obesity, he knew how to roll briskly under a chassis. At the end of his muscular arms there were precise and delicate hands—the hands of a surgeon.

Noblemain was waiting for nightfall. All the shops clustered around the square had been shut for some time. Only the café of the Hôtel Moderne was still illuminated, but its last regulars were coming out. And while their footsteps echoed in the empty streets, the façade went dark. Then the garage-owner put out the lamp over his door and set off slowly beneath the chestnut trees, in the opaque shadows.

He was genuinely generous by nature; he was impulsively drawn toward misfortune and against injustice—but he suffered from a secret vice: envy. The happiness of others distressed him. If he learned of a stroke of good luck it dug into the fat man like a needle into a pincushion. Even when he thought he had forgotten it, he still suffered from it. He asked himself: "Why am I sad? What's bothering me?" He searched—and remembered that the pharmacist had received an award, or that the bookseller's son had passed his baccalaureate, or even that a postman a hundred leagues away had won a million in the lottery—for local gossip and reading the newspapers had the same effect on him.

He envied good luck even in the form of merit. To have merit is still a kind of luck. Every success brought him distress—even that of an actor in the cinema, a singer, a gymnast or a clown. He even envied the talents of which he was scornful.

But the most atrocious things about that unfortunate man was that he had to slake his rancor. He relieved it basely. By night, he wandered around town. Sometimes he went as far as the neighboring vineyards, where the citizens possessed little bottle-taps. Making sure that he was alone, he would slip a folded sheet of paper into a letter-box, or write three lines in pencil on a door. It was always some perfidious slander. Was it true? Was it false? It mattered little to the envious fat man. The essential thing, for him, was to pour his poison. He had, for a time, vented his spleen, purged his bile.

Noblemain advanced slowly through the trees. In addition to the closed shutters, a few windows were still illuminated. He soon identified them, for he knew that square intimately, where the life of Briolle was concentrated, and on the edge of which he dwelt. He judged his neighbors according to his dual nature, alternately compassionate and jealous. He sympathized with those he did not envy. He knew their worries and their dreams, and also their rivalries, their amours, their friendships, their jealousies, their resentments—all the passions that intersected between the four faces of the square, bumping into one another like fish in a pond.

One the first floor of the Hôtel-de-Ville, an open window permitted a glimpse of a ceiling illuminated by a roseate glow. Mademoiselle Surène was still at work. Although she was not yet thirty, the secretary of the Mairie was the real sovereign of the town; she ruled her administrators with a rod of iron. Harsh and bitter, she rebuked them, molested them, and treated them as intruders from behind her desk. She was certainly not unaware of any of the regulations, but she applied them with an inhuman rigor. People trembled at the thought of confronting her. Her injurious manners contrasted with her beauty, for she had soft and delicate features, and large, slightly-veiled eyes, which always seemed to be dreaming behind their tender lids.

Noblemain felt an indulgence toward Jeanne Surène. Perhaps she was avenging herself on the public for private disappointments. She was certainly in love with the mayor, the opulent Marigot, and he found her to his taste. They liked one another; their conversations, longer than the interests of the town necessitated, testified to that. But she was not a girl to give herself away, and he was not a man to marry beneath himself. The idyll seemed hopeless.

A weak light was discernible behind the mayor's closed shutters. It was not evidence of his presence. He left a night-light on all night to inform burglars that the house was occupied. The precaution was wise, for Marigot sometimes kept large sums of money at home. It was said that the cunning rounding out of the fortune he had obtained by heritage was not only assisted by his work as a stockbroker but by loans and commissions.

Even though he had no luxurious tastes, Noblemain envied the rich ferociously. But he did not pause on that threshold; tonight, it was not for the mayor that his venom was reserved.

The transom of Truchard's shop cut out a rectangle of electric blue light in the darkness. Undoubtedly, in spite of the late hour, Truchard was lovingly manning one of these "talking and seeing" machines in which he dealt, which bore the mark of his genius, but from which he always hesitated over separating himself when the time came to sell them. His machines were so sought-after that he could not satisfy the demand, and yet, he was heading for ruination. That was because his wife's health cost him dear; an inexplicable illness was drying her up like an autumn leaf. To save her, he had called upon the aid of everyone from great pontiffs to charlatans. He had tried all the cures: spas, the sea, the sun, altitude, electricity. Remedies and consultations emptied his purse without bringing relief to his wife.

His son Emile ought to have been helping him, but the boy, twenty years old, led a mysterious and incoherent life. He stayed in Paris for weeks on end, and then reappeared in Briolle. At six o'clock, when the regulars came to Truchard's to listen to the latest news and watch the latest projections transmitted by wireless, he could be seen in a corner of the shop, slumped in a chair, his expression dark, gazing into infinity. It was said that he was affiliated to secret societies, that he was involved in obscure conspiracies. In sum, he was no help to his father.

Oh, that one Noblemain pitied with all his heart. How many times, recently, he had furnished him with labor and parts gratuitously, and even slipped him small sums of money. Vain bounty. The poor fellow was deep in debt. His creditors, alarmed by the rumors of war, were going to press him, make him go bankrupt. He was doomed.

Noblemain had reached the extremity of the square opposite his garage. Here there was more light, and only one shadow, one total solitude. That was the corner of the privileged, of the elect, of those who not only had wealth, like Marigot, but also renown or power.

At the back of a garden, to the left, stood the Thibault house. For centuries, the Thibaults had been the lords of the vine—and their dynasty had ended with that François Thibault, whose celebrity surpassed in history those of Pasteurs, Edisons and Einsteins. After his death, a marble plaque on one of the pillars of the gate would identify the house where he was born to passersby. His statue would surely be erected in the center of the square one day—and Noblemain suffered from that glory; it oppressed him; it crushed him as if he could feel the weight of the bronze monument on his shoulders.

To the right, there was a little door discreetly framed in the wall of the park. It permitted the inhabitants of the château direct access to the square. For ten years that estate had belonged to the Arnages. Noblemain hated Pierre Arnage. He detested not only his free and easy, impertinent way of turning on his heel, of sketching protective salutations with his hand. He took umbrage above all at the importance that little man had acquired in the State, the prestige that bowed heads, flattening the crowd in front of him.

But he was about to be shown that he was just a poor human being, as vulnerable as the rest. Why the devil did that Monsieur have a chauffeur? One can find out anything from a chauffeur, especially when one knows how to inspire confidence in him by means of cordiality, good humor and an honest face. The man who drives a closed vehicle hears everything that is said, and sees everything that is happening behind him in his rear-view mirror. Sometimes, he finds a forgotten letter in a glove compartment. No matter how little natural malice he has, he is the ideal informer.

Now, at the end of that afternoon, Jérôme, Arnage's chauffeur, had spent some time with the garage-owner. That very morning, he had been obliged to drive his boss to Paris, where he had been abruptly summoned to a meeting of the Council. During the long wait in the courtyard of the Élysée, he had arranged the papers that the Minister, doubtless troubled by events, had left in disorder. He had even scanned them. A certain letter, sent from Geneva, had astounded the worthy fellow. That comedy of love, so many of whose scenes had been played behind his back for two years, was definitely turning into a drama...

Noblemain stooped in front of the little door. He melted into the shadows. With the gesture of a stage magician, he took a folded piece of paper from his pocket. It comprised a few lines addressed to Madame Arnage, produced on a typewriter. They began with a couplet:

The lady of the house regrets not having a child.

The man of the house would like to be able to say the same.

A few precise details followed.

It was mediocre and it was base—but when he had slipped his piece of paper into the letter-box, Noblemain felt relieved.

Chapter IV
(Wednesday)

"How calm it is!" said Jean Liseray. "How far away we are from everything. How good it is. Don't you think so, Marilène?"

They were sitting side by side in the stern of a ferry-boat that was heading directly from Geneva to Lausanne. A light blonde mist, spangled with sunlight falling from the sky, was blurring the mountains around the lake. Nothing could be heard but the dull and muffled beating of paddle-wheels—the Lac Leman fleet still consisted of paddle-boats—and nothing was breathed in but the keen scent of the stirred-up water.

Marilène was dreaming. He took her by the arm and shook her cheerfully. "Well? Don't you think so?"

She sketched a taut smile and replied, in a patient tone; "Yes, my little old man, I think so."

My little old man: that was what she had called him straight away, as a sign of tender protection, even though she was then eight years old and he was twelve, when the Liserays and Dormiers had become neighbors at Bourg-la-Reine. The delicate and resolute little girl had reigned over her big booby of a comrade. And she still called him *my little old man*, even though he had then been beginning to be a tall young man, when Monsieur Dormier and his family had been obliged to leave Bourg-la-Reine and go to Geneva six years later.

For Jean, those childhood years at Bourg-la-Reine were the enchanted years of his life. In his memory, they always seemed to him to be accompanied by music.

Since that era, however, he had known the most seductive landscapes, all sorts of places and all sorts of skies. When his father had died, during his twentieth

142

year, he had launched himself into long-distance report-age. The profession had taken him all over the world—but every time he came back, he always found the means to see Marilène, wherever she was living. He pressed her cheerfully with questions: "Unroll your film for me."

Once, in Geneva, he learned that the Dormiers had divorced. The fact is that Monsieur Dormier, a stern functionary, could not be easy to live with from day to day. Another time, he had met Marilène in Lyon, where she was studying law. Later still he had found her in Paris, in a place of honor, attached to the staff of a Minister.

It was in Brazil that he had caught wind, with his reliable journalistic instincts, of the schism in Lausanne. He was mounting an aerial raid in mysterious Amazonia, having covered the Exhibition in Montevideo, the carnival in Buenos Aires and the Bolivian revolution. Within a wing-beat, he returned to Paris, ran to embrace his mother, still faithful to old Bourg-la-Reine, and then headed for Switzerland. At Geneva, he picked up Marilène, spending the holiday with her father, and took her to spend the day in Lausanne.

At the moment, he was enjoying a temporary respite, far from events, in that uniform calm, amid the fresh odor of the beaten water and the gilded mist, on the blue lake whose surrounding mountains, painted in a light color-wash on the horizon, seemed to isolate it from the world.

"I have to make a confession, Marilène. I've had enough of this Wandering Jew existence. I want to settle down. One doesn't always have to be searching the ends of the Earth for subjects of study; there are heaps close at hand, and enormous ones. I've run around enough—ten years. I have the right to dig the ground a little in one place. I have a name now. I have a public. People will listen to me. Don't you agree?"

"But, my little old man, if..."

"Yes, it's a stupid existence. Also, Mama has no one but me. Every time I go away I wonder of I'll find her again when I come back. This time, haven't I left it more than a year without seeing her? Then again, there's you..."

"Me?"

"Yes, you. You miss me, you know, Marilène. It's when one is far away from people that one loves them the most."

"Charming..."

"But yes. Because one measures the place they held by the gap they leave behind. Often, when I was far away, and alone, I tried to see you again, with my eyes closed. It's odd. I found your stubborn forehead, your warm gaze, your snub nose, your little beak, but it always seemed to me that you were wearing jewelry, which you never do. It's doubtless because you sparkle naturally, because you give off gleams..."

She shrugged her shoulders with a gesture of annoyance. "What are you getting at?"

"Twice, in my last voyage, I thought I was done for—an airplane crash in Amazonia, and a fire aboard ship at sea. Well, the only thing I regretted was you...Marilène, it's necessary for us not to be separate any longer. Would you like us to make a life together? Would you like me for a husband?"

"What an idea!" she cried. "You don't think so, do you?"

The tone of dry violence disconcerted him more than the words themselves. Rapidly, in any case, she apologized. She had a poor, wry smile. "I beg your pardon, my little old man...but you took me so much by surprise. It's true. You have a funny way of declaring yourself."

Already, in his indulgent heart, he was collecting himself. Yes, he knew. He knew that he had the manners of a big clumsy dog, who knocks over those he loves in testifying his tenderness and joy. He was exactly like a St. Bernard: the friendly and honest gaze, the muzzle always moist and quivering, the surly manners.

"You're right," he said, "I'm too abrupt. But you see, it's also the fault of this unique morning, in which we're so far away from everything, and simultaneously so close to one another. And then again, perhaps you're not feeling well. You seem to me so weary, all of a sudden. Not true? There's nothing wrong? In any case, don't give me an answer today. No, no. Don't discourage me. I'm not saying anything irrevocable. Take your time. Reflect..."

Chapter V
(Wednesday)

When he went into his office in the Hôtel de Ville at ten o'clock, the mayor, Monsieur Marigot, started in astonishment. Collapsed piles of telegrams, letters and printed documents covered his table. And immediately, the telephone took possession of him, gripping him by the ear and refusing to let go.

That was because, since the day before, when the ministers had suddenly met, the alert had been quietly sounded. None of the nations under arms wanted to be the first to mobilize, but none of them wanted to fall behind, so every effort was being made to ensure an advance by means of clandestine preparations, partial convocations and an entire covert concentration.

War...

Marigot was not afraid of it even though, this time, it was putting the entire country in peril. Like everyone else, he was convinced that he, personally, would escape death. The war, in fact, represented itself to him as a new opportunity for enrichment—but he put that anticipation aside, out of a kind of superstitious prudishness. No, amid all these heaps of paper, all these telephone calls, he was primarily alarmed by the initiatives and responsibilities immediately demanded—for he did not have the soul of a leader. He knew full well that he had been elected because of his fortune, and had accepted out of vanity.

But so what? Was not Jeanne Surène, the secretary of the Mairie, going to help and support him? That prospect appeased him delightfully. She was so decisive, had so much judgment and authority. In her company, he breathed an atmosphere of wellbeing and security, felt more fully alive than elsewhere.

The very sound of his secretary's voice charmed him. At that moment, as soon as the telephone gave him a moment's respite, he could hear her, because the door between their offices stood ajar, and he listened blissfully.

She was, however, using her official voice, the voice she reserved for the public, which was by no means tender. Her rigor was notorious. She knew the regulations perfectly, but she knew nothing else. At that very moment, she was scolding his administrators again. She asked one whether he could read. She sent another away because he had used blank paper instead of headed notepaper. She forbade a third to smoke.

According to legend, two travelers passing through, who had come in search of information, had been surprised by her strict and curt manner. As they drew away, one had said to the other ironically, and rather loudly: "It's astonishing what a pleasant manner that young woman has." To which she had replied, in her most cutting tone: "I'm not required to be pleasant."

Marigot secretly approved. After all, she was right; she wasn't required to be pleasant. The mayor saw no inconvenience in her leading the town by the collar, provided that she led it straight. In sum, she was the incarnation of an old French tradition, which requires a functionary to display a surly arrogance toward an obedient and resigned public. Administration has remained feudal; the counter has replaced the drawbridge.

Finally, Marigot was flattered to hear Jeanne Surène change her voice as soon as she addressed him alone. Certainly, she maintained, even in private, a dark moodiness, something of the wasp, always quick to believe that she was being attacked and to unsheath her sting, but they took as much pleasure as one another from their encounters.

Come on, no false modesty. Why should he not please Jeanne Surène, a single woman in the bloom of youth, well turned-out, who was reputed to be intelligent, who knew that he was rich and that the best families in Briolle dreamed of annexing him?

Fundamentally, they ought to have married one another, but she was too proud to declare her feelings and he refused to marry a woman who had no money. Yes, he knew it, and blushed over it; he was held back by his avarice—for he was a miser, a classic miser.

It was said that his parents, rich farmers, had sowed wheat over the tomb of grandfather Marigot and carefully harvested that single square meter of crop. On bad years they had said: "Grandfather's yielded poorly." He was a miser, he immediately knew the price of the meanest object placed before his eyes: a cigarette, a piece of candy, a flower. For him, everything had a price-label attached. He employed incredible ruses to obtain a rebate, a reduced tariff or a "good price." He suffered physically from paying, from parting with his money, as if he were having to tear away and part with a little of his own substance. For him, every purchase was a torture and every saving a sensual experience.

Marigot pricked up his ears, however; there was no sound in the next room; Jeanne Surène was alone. He moved to join her, tasting in advance the delicate pleasure of seeing her, hearing her, of being proud of her.

Suddenly, however, alarm immobilized him. Might not war suspend payments, prevent creditors from claiming their due? He had lent rather large sums, as much out of political calculation as natural cupidity; he helped the electors at high interest. Some were behind. Were those arrears going to escape him? That wasn't possible. He had only one anguish: "My money!"

He felt dizzy. Then he exhorted himself to pull himself together. He would act to recover the sums while the town was still ignorant of all those orders from Paris that were assailing him, all those preparations for mobilization. As soon as they heard about them, his debtors would glimpse the imminent possibility of not paying.

For a second, he swayed. Would not Jeanne, in the circumstances, give him good advice? But no, no. Time was pressing.

And, leaving the mail, the telephone and the secretary herself, he ran outside.

148

Cutting across the square, he headed straight for Truchard's shop. It was the merchant of talking and seeing machines who had borrowed he largest sums and owed him the most arrears of interest.

Marigot had had his reasons for not pressing him. For one thing, Truchard's shop, where people came to obtain news at the end of the day, was an excellent arena of electoral propaganda. Then again, the mayor had faith in the constructor's skill; one day, he would discover some fortunate improvement that would make him a fortune and enable him to recompense his creditors handsomely. Finally, he could not help feeling a sort of pitying admiration for the man, who, going from one physician to another, spent so much money in vain for his wife. He was, moreover, no more fortunate as a father than as a husband. His son was reputed to be an idler, an abnormal, and a deviant. But it was no longer a matter of going soft over Truchard's misfortunes. War and the moratorium were approaching...

The constructor worked alone, in the back of the shop, in an odor of gutta-percha. His hair and eyes were discolored, his features fixed and washed out by misfortune. His gray skin distilled droplets of oily sweat. With the back of his blackened hand he often moved back a stray wisp of hair the barred his forehead. The mayor's features, bronzed and dry, fine and cunning, contrasted curiously with those of the man annealed by grief.

"You can guess why I'm here, can't you, Truchard? You're terribly behind, my friend. You aren't able to pay me?"

Truchard shook his head, and pushed back the wisp of hair with the back of his hand. He cited his wife's condition, yet again. A specialist, recently summoned from Paris, had charged him very dearly. Penetrated by the respect that titles inspire, especially in people who do not know what they mean, he repeated: "A professor, you understand, Monsieur Marigot—a professor..."

"Yes, yes—but I have me expenses too, Truchard. "And he reminded him that his trade as a stockbroker obliged him to pay out large advances.

"Oh, Truchard, I hate being forced to seem exacting, ferocious, in spite of your misfortune, but, I repeat, I have expenses. Make your arrangements..."

He was maddened by the thought that his money might escape him, thanks to the war. His dark gaze, charged with an anxious fury, swept the entire shop. "It's necessary to bend every bow. You have stock here. You can liquidate it."

"They're machines on deposit," said Truchard, humbly.

"Increase your production then!" Margit almost shouted. "Make more sets. You work well, but too slowly. You're too finicky. And then, damn it, your son Emile could help you, if only as a salesman. He could extend your market. Where is he? What is he doing, right now?"

Truchard's face fell further. A drop of sweat condensed at the point of his chin. He wiped it away with the back of his hand.

"Monsieur Marigot, if you hadn't come to the shop this morning I would have come to see you in your office. I'm worried about Emile. Since yesterday, I've been afraid..."

"What? What? What's happened?"

"Well, this is it: yesterday evening, at about nine o'clock, Emile and I were alone in the shop. I'd tuned into Radio France when François Thibault read his appeal in favor of peace. You didn't hear it?"

"No."

"Naturally, one could see and hear him as if he were in the room. At one time, he begged the men and women of the entire world to band together against war. Emile, who hadn't said anything until then, uttered a sort of furious roar. He waved his fist at the screen. He spat out threats. It was as if he'd gone mad. Then, without waiting for the end, without saying good bye to us, he leapt into the last bus to Paris. I'm afraid, Monsieur Marigot. You know how excited Emile gets...and then, he's subject to the influence of his friends, his reading..."

What? The life of François Thibault was under threat? François Thibault, the pride of the town, the greatest glory in the world? Marigot shared Truchard's anxiety. For an instant, it made him forget his avarice.

"You were right to speak, Truchard. I'll give it some thought." And he slowly made his way back to the Hôtel de Ville.

Chapter VI
(Wednesday)

Pierre Arnage went back to his Ministry in the Place Vendôme on foot after having eaten lunch at his Club in the Champs-Élysées. Under the beautiful sky, the vellum of blue silk that had been hanging for three days, in a derisory manner, over a Europe that was tearing itself apart, he missed Briolle, his pleasant and compact park, its tender verdure, the resurrection of spring, the upsurge of sap that extends even to the hearts of men. But he could not leave Paris. The ministers abruptly recalled to the Élysée the day before had met again that morning had had adjourned until the afternoon: a true permanence.

Interminable and vain palaver, in which so many chatterboxes salivated like snails—and yet, destiny was becoming more aggravated with every passing hour. Pacts, ententes, protocols, alliances, federations, all those nets thrown over the war to hold it captive, had come apart successively. Were not the bonds holding them together too new, too frail? What was certain is that at the sight of the unchained beast, all the apparent masters of the world remained hypnotized, as if struck with stupor.

The diplomatic notes that had been read again that morning in the Council reminded him ironically, by virtue of their anxious prudence, their compassionate uncertainty and their nebulous circumlocutions, of the letter he had written to Marilène the previous evening. There was the same embarrassment, the same indecision, the same ambiguity, the same fear before the threat of the future. For he had wanted to send her a sign of affection right away, to avoid her feeling abandoned out there—in the midst of an ordeal for which he was, in sum, responsible—in the company of a rigorous father. But while exhorting her to patience, courage and hope, he had been obliged incessantly to dissimulate and to constrain himself, for he could not tell her that he would take back his liberty, would divorce in order to marry her; he did not even know that himself.

So, he was taking his cares for a walk, through the crowds. He was astonished that, in these glorious avenues, it looked almost exactly the same as usual, that there was scarcely any evidence of anxiety or fever. Sometimes, however, a newspaper crier ploughed through it, head down, paper in hand, shouting the title in a catastrophic voice, without even taking the time to reel off his spiel.

The accursed newspapers...

Evidently, the evening paper would make the same clamors heard as the morning editions. They would fulminate against the authorization given to François Thibault the previous day to speak at the Radio France station. They would rail indignantly against the exhortation to peace that he had issued to the world.

The affair had been hotly debated at the Council. It had taken up half the session. With Fontange, the Minister of the Interior, retrenching pitifully behind him, Arnage had been forced to stand up to all his colleagues, anxious about the unleashing of the press. Yes, François Thibault had approached him to intercede on his behalf with Fontange. He had done so. Were they not compatriots, and neighbors? But a man of that status had no need of trickery. He could perfectly well have addressed himself directly to the Minister of the Interior, who would certainly not have refused the authorization. To which Fontange, with the approval of the entire Council, had replied that, at any rate, having learned the lesson of the previous day's scandal, he would not be granting it a second time.

To tell the truth, there was, in the Council, an unhealthy fear of the opposition press. It was not a matter of revolutionary opposition, which was closely monitored, but of conformist opposition: that which supported itself on the most ancient traditions, the ones with the richest patina of custom, the most glittering; that which defended leaders who were doubtless excessive and cruel, but were served by talent and fêted by the salons. Such concern was defensible. When one governs, what point is there in preoccupying oneself with the majority, that calm sea? It is necessary to keep an eye on the reefs, which never cease to foam and thunder.

Was the national press, as had been claimed for thirty years, in the pocket of industrial finance? In untiringly stoking up chauvinism, hatred and violence by means that were alternately gross and subtle, flattering the basest instincts of their readers, was the papers consciously serving those powerful individuals who wanted, not war itself, but incessant and profitable preparations for war?

Doubtless the question was not so simple. Arnage confessed that he was incapable of answering it. But what did it matter whether the newspapers were fabricating popular opinion or simply reflecting it? In either case, that opinion existed. It was even, for the moment, white hot, raised to the temperature of an electric furnace. And damn it, a government is obliged to take account of it, if it wants to live.

Ah, power! It exercises such an attraction. What a magnet! When one holds it, one can no longer let it go, and not just for the money, certainly—a stockbroker earns more than a minister—but for all the enjoyments it procures: the prodigiously facilitated, clean-swept life, in which all doors open; in which, as one advances, a carpet rolls out beneath one's feet, between two hedges of bowed heads; in which one has the best seat everywhere, attentions, cares, flatteries, tributes, and even the smiles of women, because one is the State...

At a street corner a few paces from the Ministry, Pierre Arnage stopped. He interrogated himself. In good faith, was it really to stay in power that he and his colleagues were following public opinion today in its march to war? No, a hundred times no. The conflict appeared to them to be inevitable, like a natural scourge. Had they talked less, they would not have been able to act more.

They had been overtaken by events. Their chatter masked their impotence.

He admitted it: they did not want war, but they had *accepted* it. Although it was illegal, they still considered it as a means, almost an institution, not as filthy or stupid butchery. It did not make them vomit. They were resigned to it, without even being able to imagine it exactly. For thirty years, in al speeches, from all lips, war had been disparaged—but in the depths of the heart, the deification of warriors continued.

As he passed under the porch of the Ministry, the porter, sweeping the air with a great swing of his helmet, announced to him that Madame Arnage had just arrived.

His wife? What did she want? The day before, sending the car back to Briolle, he had warned her via the chauffeur that he was retained in Paris. She had not been planning an imminent trip. He was not expecting her. He went straight up to the private apartments. He found her in the bedroom, where she was emptying a small valise on to the bed.

"What's the matter?"

Straight and stiff, her lips thin, her eyes wide, she was the very image of reproach. She pointed with her chin at an envelope placed on the quilt.

"That was in the letter-box this morning."

He read the anonymous letter. Who could be so well-informed? His suspicion floated over the servants, without settling. He threw the piece of paper on to the bed.

"What a dirty..."

"Is it true?" she demanded.

He was tempted to deny it, but it would have been necessary to make up a story, to be cunning. He had

155

enough on his mind. He got out of it with a single word: "Yes."

"Do I know her?"

"No."

Why had she come to interrogate him? She knew full well that he had mistresses. Ordinarily, she turned a blind eye. Doubtless she had been afraid, this time, because of the child. She was anxious about the future.

Indeed, she demanded: "What are you going to do?"

Already, he was irritated. He was suffering, in his pride, from having made a mistake, from being diminished, from seeming guilty before her. He replied, testily: "How do I know?"

He strode back and forth in the large room, whose banal furniture-store luxury struck him for the first time. His wife remained standing by the bed. Suddenly, he saw that she was weeping. She simply lowered her head to hide her tears.

At the sight of those girlish shoulders shaken by sobs, a tender pity plunged through him like a dagger, attaining depths to which he had never descended. It seemed to him that a spring of generosity welled up within him. He wanted to set himself free, but the words would not come out.

Horrified by the tears, he simply said: "Oh, please, I beg you..."

Someone knocked. He ran to open the door. An usher gave him a piece of paper. His chief of staff, alerted to his presence, was sending him the list of people who were waiting to see him. He read, in a whisper: "President...of the Bar...Appeal Court..." Then, to the usher, he said: "All right—I'm coming."

Chapter VII
(Thursday)

Three days had passed since the Schism of Lausanne. Late in the afternoon, François Thibault came out of his laboratory at Bellevue, traversed the gardens with an anxious tread and joined his family in the residence. His wife Marianne, his son Claude and Pierre Contal were together in the living room. He immediately went to the wireless set and set the dial to Radio France. Animated images were projected on the screen. A speaker was commenting on the views, taken all over the world. There were processions, bellicose crowds that opened passage for fanatical crowds; there were hostile assemblies outside shops kept by foreigners, in front of consulates and embassies.

Pierre Contal sighed. "It really is the end."

At the first alarm he had left his property in Burgundy. He had come to his daughter in Bellevue in order to be at the source of news. For that great zealot of the Past, war retained its aureole. He dreaded it, in the sense that a believer dreads a redoubtable divinity, while François Thibault simply execrated it. Thus, it haunted both men, who nourished opposed sentiments in its regard, to the same degree. For both of them, it filled the entire horizon.

"And to think," said François Thibault, "that a hundred paces away from those brawls, life must be continuing placidly—but reporters, by means of images as well as words—always present events in the most alarming aspect. They seem to have given themselves the task of maddening the masses, of breathing anxiety and panic into them. One would think they experienced satisfaction, even sensuality, in predicting fatal war, war tomorrow. Are they obeying their instinct, or some instruction? Both, undoubtedly. In any case, the objective is attained. The sky's getting darker by the hour. Yesterday, it was the closure of the Lausanne Congress, recourse to the Tribunal at The Hague. A grave indication: today, all the Stock Exchanges went down, collapsing completely."

He tuned in to foreign stations. He understood the majority of their communications. In the epoch when he had launched the Starter in America, he had suffered so much from his ignorance of foreign languages that he had sworn to learn the principal ones. Thanks to the most ingenious methods, and sojourns in England, Russia, Germany and Italy, he had kept his promise as soon as his success had won him independence.

He clucked his tongue in irritation.

"What is it now?" Pierre Contal asked.

"Naturally, people in all the big cities in every land think they can see foreign airplanes flying overhead..."

"On the eve of a war, people always think they can see the enemy everywhere," said Pierre Contal, sententiously. A man of tradition, he was satisfied to observe that all wars have common features, areas of resemblance. He was one of those who reel off the irritating adage: "There's nothing new under the sun!" He was already intent on fitting into the framework of ancient wars the monstrous conflict in which Europe would perish, turned into a desert of gravel, which only the stink of four hundred million cadavers would protect against a yellow invasion.

The news items visibly enervated François Thibault; nevertheless, he continued to collect them. He imagined those furious cries for vengeance, those appeals to force, those provocations, al that bravado, all those messages of hated borne by the air-waves, which were intersecting, striating space, flowing into every hearth, bursting through speakers, more dangerous than lightning.

He was glad to think that, on the contrary, he had been able to make those same crowds hear the peaceful language of reason. Alas, on that occasion too he had been able to measure the pitch of excitement to which minds had been heated. The next morning, it was not only the orthodox newspapers that had been slavering with indignant rage, but five hundred letters he had received. The majority had been basely, sometimes excrementally, insulting. They had called him a coward and a contemptible wretch. He was "in a funk." He had diarrhea. Or else he had sold out to the enemy. He deserved death. And on that dung-heap, only a few delightful flowers grew: fraternal spirits encouraging him. They understood that he was obedient to the concern, not of fleeing the gunfire, but of sparing others from it. In sum, brides and mothers thanks him, kissed his hands...

The telephone bell rang. Claude rang to pick it up in the study.

"It's for you, Papa, on behalf of Monsieur Arnage."

"Indeed, I asked him to call me at seven o'clock. I'm coming."

On his return, he did not hide his chagrin. He let himself fall into an armchair with all his forceful mass. Sometimes wringing his hands, sometimes running his palm through the thicket of his hair, he said: "It's incredible! I wanted to speak on Radio France again. For form's sake, I asked Arnage to tell the Minister of the Interior. I thought I was authorized once and for all. Not at all. It appears that the Council of Ministers was alarmed by my first communication, or by its consequences, and that it has decided to forbid me to speak again. Even Arnage seemed to me to be under pressure, summary and constrained. He's obviously disavowing me himself.

"But I only said simple things…that peace is the natural state, that people aspire to it under every roof in the world; that war, on the contrary, resolves nothing, ruins everything, for a long time, and only enriches despicable parasites…and finally, that humans are masters of their lives at least as much as their other wealth, and that they should not be dispossessed of it without consulting them.

"It appears that one does not have the right to proclaim these humble verities of common sense. It seems that there is still shame in celebrating peace, and glory in celebrating war. I've been gagged, stifled…and at what a moment!"

He stood up. "To be unable to alert those crowds that we have left in ignorance, who are wandering in the dark, on the edge of the abyss... To be unable to warn them of the peril, to enlighten them, to make reason glow over their heads, like a rocket..."

He meditated.

Suddenly, he said: "Well, no. I won't resolve myself to it. It's necessary to run the final risk..."

Braced on his strong legs, he had stopped in front of his wife, who was sitting next to Claude on a sofa. He consulted her with his gaze. Beneath a damascened headband, her admirable brown eyes were still resplendent. She remained "the silent darling" who only ever inserted a single decisive remark into a conversation.

"Yes," she said. "Do it."

The inventor's powerful and tender visage lit up.

"You really think the moment has come to risk the experiment, reckless as it seems? That it's necessary to force people to see clearly?"

"Yes," she repeated. "Do it."

"You too, Claude?"

"Yes, Papa."

From the depths of an ancient armchair, Pierre Contal raised his voice. In the faint shadows of the twilight, his white hair and beard seemed shot through with light.

"I'd really like to know what the three of you are plotting."

François Thibault turned toward him. "It's a matter of a discovery. Excuse us for having kept it secret until now. You shall know all about it—but it's Claude who took the initiative in this research; it's only just that he should do the honors."

Placid and gracious, the young man remarked: "You know very well, Papa, that without you, I wouldn't have found anything."

"Explain anyway."

In truth, Claude was about to find in Pierre Contal a deplorable listener. Like all adversaries of progress, he made considerable use of it. It did not displease him that, thanks to the most modern methods, his books were printed, and then advertised and distributed throughout the world. He appreciated the comfort of a home that was well-heated in winter and well-ventilated in summer. When ill, he demanded the most recent serum. When in a hurry, he confided himself to the fastest vehicle. But he avenged himself on that science, whose services he accepted, by maintaining in its regard a magnificent ignorance, the ignorance of a society lady or a child in the cradle.

"Well, this is it. You know, grandfather, that air contains a mixture of oxygen and nitrogen, and that by combining those two gases—which is to say, causing them to react with one another—one can obtain several compounds..."

The author of *Génie antique*, opening frightened eyes, raised his hands as if to request mercy. In his placid voice, Claude continued.

"So, one of them, nitric oxide, gives off reddish fumes known as rutilant vapors. Another, nitrous oxide, has been used as an anesthetic under the name of laughing gas, because it seems to intoxicate the patient and provoke fits of laughter. Well, Papa and I have discovered a third compound of oxygen and nitrogen, which presents new properties."

Pierre Contal interrupted in a sulky tone. Irritation was evidently causing him to exaggerate the dryness of his remark: "I don't understand any of this jargon."

"Yes, yes," Claude continued, tranquilly. "You understand it very well. By means of a special process of electrification, therefore, we combine the oxygen and nitrogen in the air and we obtain this new gas, which we call pink gas, because we have reason to believe that in great density it appears to be pink, as the air appears to be blue..."

François Thibault judged that the moment had come to take over from his son. "Our laboratory experiments are conclusive. First we carried them out on ourselves, in order to assure ourselves that the pink gas wasn't toxic, and then on our assistants, whom we hadn't warned about the expected effects. They all experienced identical impressions. It's a sort of expansion, of euphoria. One feels indulgent, more lucid, better. One rises above oneself. One sees clearly and far. Everything becomes simplified: barriers are lowered, base instincts buried, the finer ones exalted. All human possibilities appear in finite perspectives; one feels oneself becoming god-like..."

"But it's a drug like opium, your pink gas!" exclaimed Pierre Contal.

"Not at all," the inventor replied. It's not a matter of sleeping or dreaming. It's in a state of wakefulness that one experiences the generous exaltation, observes the flood of potency. It's a very healthy sensation. It's reminiscent of the glorious wellbeing that one aspires on high mountains, in the crystalline air rich in ozone that has passed over a snowfield. Isn't it logical that tonic gases exist, just as there are toxic gases, gases that vivify as well as gases that kill? The great law of equilibrium that rules the world demands that compensation."

"But I don't see the connection between your medicine and the imminent war," said Pierre Contal.

"Don't you understand that we want to share that generous inebriation with all human beings for a few hours, in order to open their eyes, in order that they might see clearly, and become aware of their stupidity?"

Slapping the arm of his chair with his hand, Pierre Contal cried: "Marianne, your son and your husband are mad!"

"Less so than the warmongers," she replied.

"No, Father," François Thibault went on, "the enterprise isn't mad. By combining a small fraction of the oxygen in the air with the nitrogen, we can make the pink gas appear in the atmosphere. We've developed powerful broad-beam electric generators, which provoke the combination, rather like wireless stations that broadcast their waves into the air. As soon as the first threat of war emerged, four of those transmitters were sent by airplane to four of our Sidereal Energy stations, which can furnish them with the enormous power they require: Ottawa, Tokyo, Tomsk and our factory at Fraicourt, near Mantes. They're ready to function simultaneously, at our signal. The experiment will last one day."

"Madness, madness," repeated Pierre Contal.

"No. It's no more inconceivable to enable everyone on Earth inhale the pink gas engendered by our stations than to enable them to hear the words propagated by radio transmission."

Pierre Contal put his hands together and tilted his head back, gazing at the ceiling. "To improve humankind, for a single day!"

"But come on, Father, don't individuals and groups attain that step toward perfection, that superior state of mind, momentarily? I'm not just talking about the slight inebriation that a glass of champagne pours into the heart, but that of lovers, fiancés, stifling their defects, expanding their sympathies, genuinely improving themselves in their desire to please. They realize, for a while, a better humanity. And at the other extreme of life, people who sense their end approaching suddenly become radiant with forbearance, altruism and grandeur. Love and death work those miracles. A generous play, a fiery speech or a noble piece of music lift the enthusiasm of an entire audience, giving it a superhuman soul. There are corners of the Earth, like our Provence, where all hearts are good, because they beat beneath a clement sky. The world of laboratories, where altruistic and disinterested scientists swarm, realize a superior humanity. Is it necessary to remind you of the historical examples—the night of August fourth,[8] the cassation of the Dreyfus affair, when centuries-old prejudices melted in an hour? Even without pink gas, waves of bounty and hope sometimes pass over the Earth..."

"And afterwards? When you've plunged humanity entire into that kind of intoxication for a few hours, what will you have gained?"

With all his massive presence looming over Pierre Contal, wagging a prophetic finger, François Thibault said to him: "Afterwards? But human beings, having glimpsed their folly in a flash of lucidity—the abyss into which they're about to hurl themselves like beasts—will step back in time, will refuse that absurd suicide. Do you remember the maxim that I forged and which has never ceased to haunt me, to sustain me in my work: *When people have seen what they might be, they will blush with shame at what they are.*"

Chapter VIII
(Thursday)

Once again, Jean Liseray returned to his old lodgings in Bourg-la-Reine. On the day after receiving a hard blow—and doubtless on the eve of leaving it forever...

The house where he had been born was perhaps a hundred years old. Miraculously, it had resisted the great urban upheavals of the last thirty years. The street had changed its name twice. The old place did not flinch. The two terracotta statuettes still stood watch in the niches of the façade, crowned with a second story under

---

[8] On 4 August 1789 the members of the French National Assembly swore to end feudalism and abandon their privileges—a key point in the Revolution.

the roof, and the skylight still remained open over the "swallows' room," where the birds were allowed to build their nests every spring. It was said that it had been constructed by an old eccentric who, naturally, had died before moving into it. The lock-plates and door handles were made of hand-fashioned copper. There was stained glass in all the windows, and paintings on the ceilings. In Jean's room, angels amid pink clouds had flown over his childish dreams.

To think that he had still been in Lausanne the previous evening. No journey had ever seemed so long to him—to him, who had been rolling around the globe for ten years...

He and Marilène had wanted to prolong the delightful isolation they had experienced on the lake for a further hour. They had eaten lunch outside the town, in a restaurant on the shore, before beginning the hunt for information. Marilène seemed to be striving to shake off the melancholy that had weighed upon her during the crossing. She almost apologized, poor thing, for being distracted, in order to appreciate the fine fare, the nice Fendant wine, dry, sparkling and as limpid as Topaz...

Finally, it had been necessary for him to resume contact with the world. His profession was demanding. And immediately, he had learned of the abrupt closure of the Congress announced an hour earlier. Since the Schismatic vote three days before, the two opposed parties had remained present, but, weary of vain negotiation, of waiting for a firm decision from the Society of Nations, they had given up. Already, amid the loud clicking of doors and portfolios, delegates were leaving the city.

Nevertheless, they would still submit the litigation to the International Court of Justice at The Hague. That was the supreme recourse. Because of the crazy mental tension, it had even been asked to issue a provisional judgment urgently—a kind of injunction.

"It's gone bad," said Jean Liseray. The peoples, overexcited and duped, would not have the patience to await the verdict, or would not submit to it. The conflict now seemed to him to be unavoidable.

Out of professional conscience, he resolved to remain in Lausanne until the evening, in order to interrogate the laggards, while Marilène took the boat back to Geneva, where her father was expecting her. They had granted one another one last break, arms linked, along the flowery quays of Lausanne-Ouchy, which is one of the most sumptuous and enchanting promenades in the world.

It really was the last break, for Jean Liseray was certain of being conscripted. Of course, the war would be aerial, chemical, microbial and electric, but the General Staff, by virtue of instinct and self-interest. They would mobilize the young men, oppose them to one another breast to breast, as in the good old days—or they would imprison them in those profound bunkers that mine the frontiers. Had they not concreted, at great expense, the redundant coal-mines of the Flemish and Lorraine valleys?

Yes, for him, that promenade had carried a strong risk of having no tomorrow. So he would have liked to know his friend's intentions. To be sure, that very morning he had asked her to reflect, but the circumstances had changed. The storm gathering on the horizon was now overhead, ready to burst. In words, he had pressed her as gently and tenderly as he was squeezing her arm—but she remained obstinately silent. Then he stopped, to look her in the face. Was she upset by the alarming news, abruptly brought down from the pleasant intoxication of the meal? She seemed worn out. Beneath her profound brows, her eyes were ringed as if they had burned their lids.

And suddenly, she made up her mind. The words had emerged with difficulty from her mouth, tightened like a flower in bud. "Listen, Jean…I can't be your wife…I wouldn't be able to hide the truth from you for long… I'm going to have…I'm expecting a child…"

He had been stunned, as if he had been hit on the head with a sledgehammer. He wondered where he was. But he had pulled himself together rapidly. He loved Marilène enough to think of her first.

He did not ask the name of the man. He cut straight to the heart of the matter.

"Why doesn't he marry you?"

"He's married."

"Do you still love him?"

"Yes."

In the distance, the calm beating of paddle-wheels was audible in the calm air. Mechanically, they retraced their steps back to the landing-stage. Jean fell silent in his turn. He imagined Marilène being obliged to confess the truth to her father, a hard traditionalist, a rigid conformist, one of those blind partisans of repopulation who believed in honoring the mother while dishonoring the unmarried mother. To what excess would he not abandon himself? She was heading straight for catastrophe. He alone could still spare her. Her pregnancy, still invisible, must be recent. Under the threat of war, the formalities of marriage would doubtless be abridged. The instinct of the St. Bernard drowned out all other voices in him.

"Marilène, let me marry you... You'll remain free, but you'll be saved."

She sketched a poor smile. "How good you are..." Her burning eyes volatilized her tears.

The boat was coming closer. Jean had not wanted to leave her at such a moment. He had offered to go with her to Geneva, but she refused.

"No, no, Jean. Stay in Lausanne for your investigation. In my turn, I ask you to reflect. In any case, we'll see one another again very soon."

And, her step light in spite of everything, she had gone along the gangway.

Now, on the threshold of the little house in Bourg-la-Reine, which he had quit the day before yesterday, he wondered what his mother would think of that attempted rescue. She had known Marilène since the time when the Dormiers and the Liserays had been neighbors. She treated the girl benevolently—but he did not feel very reassured.

Although it was still early, Madame Liseray was already weeding the paths in the garden behind the house. At the sight of her grown-up son she stood up swiftly in her unbleached smock, seemed tall and thin, going gray, imperious in her features and her bearing. She uttered a dry of surprise: "Already!"

While embracing her, he joked: "Thanks!"

She explained, awkwardly: "I only mean that I didn't expect you so soon, and I don't have anything ready for your breakfast."

Thus, for what would soon be thirty years, misunderstandings had arisen perpetually between them. The mother and the son undoubtedly loved one another, but they were not very good at it.

He reassured her. When he got out of the airplane at Longchamp early that morning, he had eaten in the canteen at the aerodrome. While they sat down on a bench nestling in the lilacs at the far end of the garden he added: "I'm coming back sooner than I thought myself. Yesterday, in Lausanne, everything fell apart. There's certain to be war, without much delay."

Putting her hands together, her first lament was for herself. "Is it possible? To think that I'll have lived long enough to see war twice..." Then, abruptly: "But what about you?"

"Oh! Obviously, mobilization is imminent. It'll be necessary to go."

She had always deplored his choice of an errant life. She sighed. "I would have seen you leave anyway..."

"This departure," he added, "will hasten many plans. So, me...you know that I've always had a great deal of affection for Marilène. Well, I've decided to marry her..."

"And to think that you've never said a word to me..."

She as more offended than surprised. She had always wanted to know about her son's love life. She made allusions to it that irritated him, and made him secretive. This time, would he open up fully?

He had reflected a great deal during his nocturnal journey by airplane. Should he tell his mother about Marilène's condition? For the time being, he would be able to hide it from her. But when he was gone, mobilized, the two women would have an interest in communicating with one another. And the day when Madame Liseray realized that she had been duped, she would take out her annoyance on Marilène, at the moment when the poor girl would be most in need of aid and comfort. He had, therefore, resolved to speak.

"I had been thinking about the marriage in a still-confused fashion during my year in Latin America, but yesterday, in Lausanne, events moved rapidly. First there was the rupture in the Congress, the sounding of the toc-sin. Then I learned that Marilène was unhappy. Yes, she's compromised...in brief, she's given herself to a man who can't marry her..."

"Who is he?"

"I didn't ask her. Now, there's going to be a child..."

"She started on the bench and turned to her son sharply. "What? You want to cover up someone else's sin?"

"Let's say that I want to do a good deed. You can't refuse to help me."

"But my poor child, do you understand what you're asking of me? I can't oppose your plan, that's under-stood—but I disapprove of it absolutely, with all my heart. I don't want, in any way, for a single moment, by any action, to seem to be condoning it. And you're ask-ing me to associate myself with it?"

"Just think, Maman. I can save the child, merely by reaching out a hand before I leave. It's a matter of a ges-ture, a simple gesture..."

"No, my child. You're pledging your name, your life. You'll become the laughing-stock of people who know the truth—especially the man who knows, the lov-er... By introducing this disreputable person into our family, you'll be doing us incalculable harm. You can do so much better. We had such dreams for you. Oh, if your unfortunate father were alive, what chagrin he's be expe-riencing today..."

"But when all's said and done," he exclaimed, "I love Marilène!"

"Don't say another word. You'll never convince me."

"Maman...I would have liked so much to feel that you were on my side, with me..."

"I beg you...I repeat that your persistence would be futile. It would be painful for me."

To make it perfectly clear that she did not want to hear any more, she got up, and headed for the house, with a stiff tread.

He followed her briefly with his gaze. He was about to leave for The Hague without delay. Afterwards, no doubt, mobilization would take him. Those dry and curt words...this was perhaps his last conversation with his mother. He would have liked so much to touch her, to soften her—but there it was. They had never revealed the best of themselves to one another. If he died, she would never even know about the sudden surges of compassion he felt when he discerned signs of her aging, when he realized the sadness of her solitary widowhood, or the sufferings and the privations she had endured in order to bring him into the world and raise him...

In his turn, he went back to the house and went up-stairs. Exhausted by his sleepless night, he threw himself on his bed, in the room where his childhood had been laid to rest. Before sinking into oblivion, he caught a glimpse of the ceiling, where the little angels were flying among pink clouds.

Chapter IX
(A fragment of Emile Truchard's Journal)

Thursday evening. He must die. He shall die, by my hand. Henceforth, I shall attach myself to his steps. He decided his fate the day before yesterday, when he sowed the sacrilegious words to the four winds, when he exhorted people to resist the war. Unpardonable language...

Yesterday's meeting of the League confirmed my resolution. I feel that I am the chosen one, the predestined one. I shall have saved the world. I shall have prevented it from sinking into shame, into the mud. My name will shine in history among those of the martyrs and apostles, eternally.

Precisely because my action will be capital, all the circumstances that will have led me to its execution will be important. None of them must remain in shadow.

On Tuesday, I was at Briolle, in my parents' home. At seven p.m., my father gets the news from one of the sets in his shop. Ordinarily, I avoid those listening sessions, for which it's necessary to understand all languages. It's Babel in the home. I have a horror of those intruders, those barbarians who dare to slip into our hearths. On hearing them, I always experience a hateful revolt, a physical disgust. It seems to me that I'm watching an invasion. But the news had been so serious, since the previous day, that I overcame my repugnance.

Suddenly, I saw the face of François Thibault surge from the screen. I heard his voice. At the moment when all the people were getting ready, in a magnificent uprising, to defend their liberty against infamous oppressors, the wretch was clinging on in a cowardly fashion to peace! He was forbidding us war, that school of courage and grandeur, that divine era when the virtues blossom in glory. He was stealing it from us!

His craven language was slackening the springs of national energy. At the same time, he was fortifying the confidence of the adversary, giving him to believe that we weren't ready, that we would shirk the combat. Thus, he was playing the enemy's game twice over. It was at that moment that I made a vow to annihilate that baneful influence.

In front of the apparatus I howled: "Enough!" I brandished my fist, as if he could see me.

He was speaking from the Radio France studio. He was in Paris. Instinctively, I wanted to get close to him without delay, to get on the track as soon as possible. In the square, the last bus was about to leave. I heard its signal-horn. I went upstairs. I got my automatic pistol. My mother was asleep. I didn't wake her. As I went through the shop I sent my father a vague word of farewell. I leapt into the vehicle.

In the room in which I live in Paris, I would have liked to go to sleep immediately, in order to be lucid and strong in the hours to come, but I couldn't sleep. I was too excited by my resolution. For a long time, with my lamp lit, I reread the admirable maxims of that perfect hero who was both a great soldier and a great scientist, René Quinton[9]—the maxims that I had copied in capital letters on pieces of paper and pinned to the wall.

---

[9] René Quinton (1866-1925) is nowadays remembered as a biologist, who made significant contributions to physiology and evolutionary theory, and as an aviation pioneer, but he also served a colonel in the Artillery during the Great War, in which he volunteered for service in spite of his age; he was wounded eight times, and was awarded the Croix de Guerre.

As I write, they're before my eyes. It seems to me that they light up my room, that they're inscribed in letters of fire, like the *Mene Tekel Upharsin* of legend.

Pacifism is an outrage against honor. Man has but one majesty, which is to know how to die. Pacifism denies him that.

Hatred is the great affair of life. Sages who no longer hate are ripe for sterility and death.

Peoples who love war are virile peoples.

The days that end wars are days of mourning for the brave.

Nature has endowed men with virtues, but they are only deployed in war.

Whoever does not know war does not know man. Mediocre in everyday existence, man his beautiful in war, because his virtues are warrior.

War is the noble mode of human activity. Men are brothers therein. War is the Golden Age.

One of the joys of war is that it returns man to primitive existence.

War brings peace to the heart.

Men who make war sense that they are doing good.

Great combats sanctify. Those who do not fight are to be pitied.

Action, for the honest man, is only possible in war.

Not having gone to sleep until morning, I woke up very late. My resolution had not changed. My fury had not abated. I looked in the mirror, with a kind of fervor,

---

The quotations reproduced here are reproduced from the posthumously-published *Maximes sur la guerre* (1930; tr. as *Soldier's Testament*.)

at my face, that would soon be engraved in everyone's memory. We had a meeting that afternoon of the Section of the League. I found my comrades seething with excitement. Our newspapers, which I hadn't yet read, proudly accepted the risks of war, and they were fulminating against François Thibault's appeal. They were covering the wretch with insults that I can still see, and which, by their abundance and their repetition, imposed themselves on the mind: scoundrel, criminal, traitor, hireling, parricide.

An article was passed around that I have kept to reread: "There is talk of war, but the lambs are bleating and will perhaps frustrate us of the glorious adventure. To avoid that defeat, it is important to drown out their voices—or, better, to stifle that of their shepherd. There are, in that latter intention, the elements of a magnificent project. Has the man capable of realizing it not been born? Raised up by our admiration, he will attain the summit of History." I felt that I have been designated.

Our words, our speeches were merely commentaries inflamed by that appeal. They reaffirmed my decision. I was tempted to cry out: "Yes, that man has been born! It is me!" But I constrained myself to silence, for the filthy party has spies everywhere. Enemy ears were certainly listening to us. The traitor would have been put on his guard against me. I kept quiet. Silently, I savored the pride of knowing, and being alone in knowing, that I was going to realize the wishes of that elite. Dusk was falling when we separated.

Outside of his sojourns in Briolle and facts of public notoriety, I knew nothing about François Thibault's private life—I couldn't have said whether he lived in Paris or Bellevue—because our two families had quarreled. It was so long ago that I don't know exactly why.

It was, I think, a matter of a rivalry of municipal councilors between my grandfather Truchard, who was a violin-maker, and François Thibault's father. Curiously enough, that Thibault had resigned his commission in the navy to look after his vineyard. To abandon the glorious career of arms to sell wine…what sacrilege! François Thibault takes after him.

I swear to God that that old quarrel has no influence on my resolution. We don't speak to one another; we ignore one another when we pass in the street. It's become a sort of habit, a tradition, that's all. I ought to mention, however, that that unpleasantness had had indirect consequences for us. Even at the most critical moments, my father, a modest inventor on a small scale, has never asked for help from the powerful François Thibault, greatly enriched by the discovery of the Starter. For his part, the latter has been easily able to ignore his neighbor's difficulties. That's why we have had to put ourselves in the hands of the mayor, Marigot, in spite of his miserly cunning.

No, no, no base jealousy guides me. I've always heard my father praise the genius of François Thibault, whom he considers to be a great man. And I had no animosity against him myself until the recent day when, in a speech at a prize-giving in Briolle, he showed that pernicious utopian spirit, which has now become criminal and intolerable.

This morning, therefore, I went to Bellevue. It's definitely there that François Thibault lives. A warden gave me the information. His laboratory and his residence are built in a sort of public garden on the edge of the famous terrace that overlooks Paris. The small detached house where the inventor was living when he discovered the Starter still exists, but it's no longer anything but a guest-house, eclipsed by a sumptuous villa that he constructed as his fortune grew.

Every day François Thibault works in his laboratory at the Study Center. Every day, at the same times, he follows the same paths to return to his home. It's there that, hidden behind a bush, I'll shoot the traitor. For it is written: *Pacifism is an outrage against honor.*

Chapter X
(Thursday)

Nine o'clock in the evening. Pierre Arnage was anxious, worn out. Sometimes, he leapt up from his armchair, as if the springs in the seat had suddenly unwound. Then he walked back and forth in the ample and solemn study of the Ministry. The raw light of the electric chandelier struck the wallpaper and the old furniture, created under softer lit and made for it, too harshly. He opened a book, a file, scanned a page without taking any of it in, and then slumped again into a chair at his desk.

That same morning, his wife had gone back to Briolle. Offended by her husband's curt and gruff manner, by his determination not to explain himself or apologize—the fact is that it would have been odious to him—she had beaten a retreat. Without recriminations, patient and proud at the same time, she had ceded the ground to him, and left him disconcerted, in the dark regarding his intentions.

Then Marilène had come back to Paris. He was expecting her now. She had telephoned him during the day to notify him of her arrival and her visit. Prudently, she had adopted the tone of a petty employee talking to the big boss. Entering into the game, he had remained very "high and mighty" on the phone, to such an extent that he had known nothing about the reasons for her abrupt return—but it had not augured anything good.

Another worry. It would doubtless be necessary for him to leave, the day after tomorrow, for The Hague. All the States of the European Union had resolved, the previous day, to submit their litigation urgently to the International Court of Justice. Given the unprecedented importance of the conflict, they had all decided to delegate to The Hague their Ministers of Foreign Affairs and Ministers of Justice.

Arnage deplored the necessity of accompanying Ducros, that megalomaniac gnome who, dreaming of cuts and bruises for others, had allowed his jubilation to burst forth three days ago. He disapproved, for, deep down, he remained human. Like all politicians, he affected a blasé, mocking, integral skepticism, but for him, as for the majority, it was merely a suit of armor, a ceremonial clothing, like an officer's dress uniform or an academician's green gown. They would have been embarrassed to seem sensible. They hid their hearts as one hides one's sexual organs.

Had it not cost him, on that excessively heavy day, to relay the Council's decision to François Thibault? Obviously, he was only a messenger. The chore had only fallen to him because the inventor had come to him, but it was no less disagreeable for that. Personally, he thought that the great man—the very great man—had talked sense. He knew full well that the warmongers were fabricating public opinion, that they were imprinting it in minds thanks to their press, which they were patiently prepared to convince the crowd of the unavoidable necessity of war. And he was secretly enraged to feel that he and his colleagues had fallen victim in their turn to those suggested hatreds.

Having simply knocked, Marilène came in. No usher was accompanying her; she was one of the family. Emotional and valiant, she smiled. Arnage locked the door, even though his mind was scarcely turned in the direction of pleasure. They exchanged awkward caresses and stumbling words, which did not connect up. Then he made her sit down and asked her, without further delay: "What's happened?"

"A silly story. Yesterday, I spent the day in Lausanne. I came back to Geneva late. My father was waiting for me. He was impatient with anxiety. We quarreled. Things got heated. He finished up voicing his suspicions."

Arnage glimpsed an immediate scandal: the functionary standing up against a sitting minister. Life ebbed within him. In a hoarse voice, he enquired: "What? He knows?"

"His maidservant, who is devoted to him—too devoted—detests me. She must have been spying on me, noticing signs, sickness..."

She fell silent momentarily. Even before the man to whom she has refused nothing, a woman is reluctant to talk about the indignities that nature imposes upon her. She went on: "I didn't want to deny it. What good would it do? He'd still have found out. Naturally, I didn't name you. He was even more irritated by that. He's a man of another age. To have a child outside marriage still seems like a crime to him. In brief, he was so hard, so abominable, that I left the room, and decided to come back this morning."

Arnage was silent in his turn. He wanted to persuade himself that all this was impossible, that he was having a bad dream. He sought in vain to pull himself together, to get a grip.

She said to him, softly: "Don't be sad. I don't want you to worry about me. You don't have to..."

Furious at putting on such a poor show, Arnage experienced an unhealthy need to retreat, to be alone. He appealed to hazard to put an end to the conversation. He was astonished that the organism was capable of such contradictions, that one could wish, almost with identical force, for both the arrival and the departure of a beloved woman.

It was Marilène who broke the silence. She put a hand on the desk and said, slowly: "Pierre, do you believe that one can love two people simultaneously?"

He thought that she was asking about him. Doubtless she wanted to know whether he was simultaneously experiencing tender feelings for his wife and for her. He replied, in a grave and penetrating tone: "Yes, I believe it's possible."

She seemed relieved, and said, swiftly: "Isn't it? I think so too. You know what you are to me...what I think of you...such a superior man...a demigod. Well, I've met an old friend, who, naturally, doesn't exist by comparison with you, but who has shown himself so good, so tender, so affectionate, and so attentive, that he's truly touched me. Oh—you know the name. He's a reporter...Jean Liseray."

"That petty journalist!" he grated.

She did not react to the hurtful intention. He understood that she did not want to say anything for the moment, but that in reality, she had faith in Jean Liseray's talent.

"Yesterday," she continued, "I went to Lausanne with him..."

The Minister got up. "What?"

"Yes. Every time he returns to France he comes to see me. This time, he was coming back from a long voyage to South America. First he told me that he wanted to marry me and asked me to think about it, but when we learned that the news had got worse, that war seemed imminent, he became more pressing. He wanted a reply."

She smiled weakly. "It was definitely a day for confessions, for I thought it honest to tell him why I couldn't accept. I didn't tell him your name either. Anyway, he didn't ask me. And as he's very good, very chic, he maintained his proposal. He offered to marry me, without asking for anything in return, as a passport in life for my child and myself."

Arnage was striding back and forth, head down, his hands behind his back. What he had heard left him incredulous. More than ever, he hoped that he was dreaming. He sniggered. "Yes, yes. Familiar, the blank marriage. No one holds to it."

Then, standing in front of her, he said, in a concentrated voice: "In sum, do you love him?"

"I'm more than grateful to him. Besides, didn't you agree yourself that one can love two people at the same time.

He exploded. "Did I know what I was saying? I thought you were talking hypothetically, in the void—or that you were setting a trap for me. No, no. It's not possible. You're not envisaging being someone else's..."

He thought he was watching an atrocious film. A man, someone other than him, younger and more virile, was substituting himself for him with Marilène, striking the same attitudes, enjoying the same liberties, the same kindnesses... That burned his eyes like a handful of pepper. He thought he was going to cry. But he was suffer-

182

ing at least as much from pride as jealousy. What? The woman who adored him like a god—she had said so a moment ago—had been able to listen to another man, to welcome him, to give him a place in her heart? She dared to give him a rival—him, Pierre Arnage!

He repeated: "No, it's not possible."

"But Pierre, I don't know myself what I'm going to do."

He became suddenly humble. "Marilène, if this is a test you're subjecting me through, you can admit it now. It's succeeded. Yes, I see it now. I don't love anyone but you."

He was sincere. He told himself, to justify his volte-face in his own eyes, that he was playing a part, that he was attempting to reconquer her by vanity, to tear her away from the other, but in reality, she had become dearer to him since he had been threatened with losing her.

He discovered her. Never had he found her as radiant. A splendor. Everything about her became precious to him, necessary to him: her tight little mouth, her profound and brilliant eyes, her scintillating grace.

The desire obsessed him to accompany her to Billancourt, to the dwelling that had sheltered their encounters for two years. He leaned toward her: "Let's leave together. Let's go home. I'll be good. Just to be close to you...to feel you beside me..."

She refused with a slow movement of the head. Since two men were soliciting her, she no longer wanted to yield to either of them. She was reserving herself.

Arnage was maddened by that resistance.

"And what if I free myself? What if I get a divorce? You'd no longer have any need for anyone else's help, for this passport, as you call it..."

183

She stood up. "No, no. I don't want that. Your wife hasn't done anything. You don't have the right to abandon her."

"In sum," he cried, "you've really decided to marry that scribbler? That's what you've come to tell me?"

She repeated, in a weary tone, as she headed for the door. "No! I came to confide in you...my worry, my embarrassment..."

He was no longer listening. Again, the implacable film unrolled before his eyes. No, he did not want her to be another's. He would prevent it, at any price. Yes, rather a catastrophe that would shatter and annihilate all his plans. Let war break out, let the planet blow up. But not this film, not this film...

Chapter XI
(Friday)

The day after making his decision, at seven o'clock in the morning in Paris, François Thibault sent the agreed signal to the four stations at Fraicourt, Ottawa, Tokyo and Tomsk. They were the words that, four years before, on the anniversary of Briand's[10] death, the children of all nations pronounced, as they threw flowers on the tomb of the great human being who had been able to incarnate the universal hope: "For world peace."

---

[10] Aristide Briand (1862-1932) served eleven terms as President of the Council, including one term during the Great War; he was one of the originators of the proposal for a European Economic Union and a tireless campaigner for disarmament—he was a joint winner of the 1926 Nobel Peace Prize.

PART TWO
(Which unfolds on Friday in its entirety)

Chapter I

The limpid morning was still scintillating with dew. The nacre of the dawn seemed to be lingering in the sky. In the garden on the terrace at Bellevue, Emile Truchard was crouched behind a lilac bush. In the right had pocket of his jacket, his hand as clutching the butt of his revolver. He was lying in wait for François Thibault, who was pass close by as he went from his house to his laboratory.

He was ready to kill him, but he did not feel completely in possession of himself. The perfume of the lilacs, the clusters of which were brushing his cheeks, must have dazed and intoxicated him. Without taking his eyes off the threshold of the villa, he strove to pull himself together, to get a grip.

But François Thibault appeared at the top of the front steps. His son was with him. Emile Truchard had not anticipated that complication. Bah! It wouldn't prevent anything.

The two men came down the steps and then advanced at a tranquil pace. Their vices, animated and cordial, resonated in the crystalline air.

Emile Truchard brought his weapon out of his pocket. He raised it to the height of his eyes, for practice. It was trembling slightly. But François Thibault was still twenty meters away. There was no urgency. He let his arm fall back, in order not to tire it needlessly.

For the first time in his life, he heard his heart beating with dull thuds, which echoed all the way to his throat. The thought went through him of the *other* heart—the one that would soon cease to beat. It compelled him to imagine that man full of vigor, haloed in glory, who was advancing defenselessly toward death— who, in a moment, would collapse, would be no more than a heap of flesh in a pool of blood.

That vision frightened him.

Immediately, he invoked his reasons for hatred, but they fled his memory...

He tried to appeal to his rescue those whose faith he shared, those who had given it to him, his comrades and his gods—all those, in sum, who were waiting for him to act, all those whose wish he was about to grant, whose suffrage he was about to merit, whose delight he was about to unleash...but he could not find their faces. He could no longer hear them. The link that bound them to him seemed to have broken...

A new and unexpected circumstance presented itself: the two men, leaving the path to the Laboratory, were heading toward the terrace; they would not go past the lilac bush.

Emile Truchard felt relieved. It would always be easy for him to get close to François Thibault, and this respite accorded him by change would permit him to get a grip on himself. Inhaling deeply, he drew air into the depths of his lungs, in order to ignite a more ardent life there. The more he breathed, however, the more he had a sensation of being detached from himself and uplifted. He emerged into a new world, as clear, as luminous and as crystalline as the marvelous morning.

François Thibault and his son had stopped at the stone parapet overlooking Paris. Their silhouettes, similar in height, the one massive and powerful, the other slim and lithe, stood out against that singular sky, in which the dawn still seemed to be smiling.

At that moment, the father put his arm around his son's shoulders. That simple gesture moved Emile Truchard. Great man as he might be, the inventor was a man like any other. He had a wife and children. They were attached to him and would suffer if he died...

Emile did not blush at that human compassion. He did not consider it to be fairy-tale sentimentality. He became inebriated by it as a natural wine, honest in taste, and new to him. He took delight in it. Yes, François Thibault was a man like others, a man like him. They both had the same organs, the same needs, the same penchants, the same weaknesses. They had doubtless shared in the admiration of the same masterpieces. They must be taking equal delight in that marvelous morning, in which the sky seemed to be made of a single rose petal traversed by light.

And they undoubtedly had the same good faith. Emile, sat that moment, looked down on their opposed doctrines as one sees cities from the height of an aircraft. He compared them. One loved the city of the past, where force triumphed, the other the city of the future, where mildness would reign. And both were extending their arms toward their ideal with the same sincere impulse.

Clouds split, revealing new perspectives to his eyes. How could anyone suspect François Thibault of betraying his country? Thanks to him, was not his fatherland the cradle of the most prodigious discovery, with infinite consequences?

Obviously, the inventor wanted to prevent the war. Since Emile had escaped himself, however, since he believed that he was more alive, and living an improved life in an increased light, the maxims pinned to the wall of his room had come to seem outdated, like the inscriptions engraved on the lintel of a ruin. Their author was indicating, in fact, that war served the genius of the species, that it was the rude preface of love, that it revealed the strongest, the most virile, and the most masculine, like the nuptial flight of bees. Perhaps that had been true in the days of hand-to-hand fighting. But modern warfare, on the contrary, sacrificing youth and preserving old men, was an inverse selection.

Meanwhile, François Thibault drew away from the parapet. He retracted his steps. Doubtless he would go to the laboratory, past the clump of lilac bushes. Again, Emile perceived the muffled explosions of his heart. Momentarily, the inventor passed so close that he might have heard them. Keeping his weapon at the end of his lowered arm, however, Emile Truchard did not shoot...

And he felt immediately uplifted by joy. He repeated to himself: "I have not killed...I have not killed..."

It seemed to him that he had just escaped death himself. It appeared to him that the first rule of life really was respect for life. He would have liked to confess the frightful temptation, to obtain absolution, to proclaim his delight and his deliverance. He had wings.

Then, shoving the useless weapon back in his pocket, he launched himself toward the terrace where Claude Thibault, left alone, seemed to be studying the nacreous sky. He almost shouted at him: "You're Claude Thibault, aren't you? I'm Emile Truchard. We've never done more than catch glimpses of one another at Briolle. Our families have been at odds for such a long time that I no longer know why. You don't either, do you? Would you like to put an end to it?"

He held out his hands.

Claude seized them, and said: "I should think so!"

He did not seem unduly surprised by that action. He welcomed it with an amused smile, as if he had expected it. Without further consultation, they began to walk along the terrace together.

They talked abundantly about their families, filling in the gap. "Me, my father..." said Emile. "Me, Papa..." said Claude. For they were both very proud of their fathers.

Emile revealed the difficulties and vicissitudes that his own had encountered, and he delighted in those confessions. He tasted the profound joy of reconciliation, the gladness of making up for lost time, of resuscitating the past, of making the present...the gladness of forgiving and being forgiven...the gladness of vanquishing the malice of fate, the traps that destiny sets for us.

Even under the dominion of that clear frankness, however, the two men retained secret corners within them. Emile Truchard did not tell Claude that he had left his room at dawn and traversed the Bois on foot, driven by the obsession of killing his father. And Claude did not admit to his companion that he was his first "subject," the first creature in which the miracle of the pink sky was being accomplished before his eyes.

Chapter II

That same morning, the ministers, reunited in Council at the Élysée, had to determine the role of their two delegates to The Hague.

Although the combination of circumstances was grave, the session opened in an atmosphere of confidence and hope. The Head of State, the austere Crépin, started speaking in a tone that was almost affable to the

President of the Council, Martory. A half-smile human-ized his granite face.

It was soon perceptible that the prime minister's manner had also changed. He had dropped his noncha-lant and disillusioned mannerisms. Instead of slumping sideways, on one buttock, in the depths of his armchair, he was sitting up straight, his elbows by his sides. His forearms were resting on the table. With a very simple gesture, he drew them apart, as one opens a fan, and he said: "My dear President, my dear colleagues, everyone here desires, don't we, to avoid war?"

Ordinarily, such a declaration would have seemed shocking. One did not simply admit one's love of peace, especially before a threat of conflict. One dressed it up, took detours. There was, however, such benevolence in the air that no one gave evidence of astonishment or res-ervations. The approval was unanimous. One could feel it pass by, like a warm breath.

"Well," Martory went on, "I'm of the opinion that our two representatives at The Hague should speak straightforwardly, as their hearts bids them to—that they say what they think, quite frankly: what everyone here thinks; what the immense majority in all countries think."

Pierre Arnage, who was due to depart for The Hague, pronounced in a penetrating voice: "Obviously."

He had just spent the most atrocious night of his life. He had almost summoned the worldwide catastro-phe that would prevent Marilène from belonging to someone else. Undoubtedly, however, like the prime minister, he had been touched by grace. He was not at all surprised to approve and applaud his courageous sinceri-ty.

Martory continued: "For after all, we're ministers, which is to say that we're here, as our name indicates, to administer the interests of our fellow citizens. Now, the immense majority in the country—in all countries—wants peace. Under every roof, around every hearth, the same dream of tranquil happiness is nourished. Do you know how many people are appealing, more or less secretly, for war? About one per cent. Yes, from the most powerful armaments manufacturer to the smallest shopkeeper, the people who will make a profit from the slaughter represent scarcely a hundredth part of the mass. The others can expect nothing from war but anguish, mourning, ruination, martyrdom or death. Well, I say that we ought to speak, and ought to act, not on behalf of the hundredth person but on behalf of the other ninety-nine!"

"That's perfectly evident," said Arnage, again.

To tell the truth, Martory, who had deplored and then prohibited François Thibault's speech before the microphone, maintained an analogous position in the presence of his colleagues, but Arnage felt in his heart such a need for generosity and frankness that he was not astonished by this conversion.

"Then again," Martory continued, "it's necessary to have the courage to say it: war resolves nothing. The final treaty doesn't conclude it; it prolongs it. It encloses deadly germs in the bandaged wound. War ruins both those one continues to call victors and those one considers defeated. All our misfortunes are the consequences of war. Forty years after the last conflict, we're still expiating it. Imagine that, of every five francs of tax, two francs go to pay for the last war and two to prepare for the next. Only the last franc goes to the endeavors of life: education, public works, public hygiene, science, the arts and solidarity."

"It's crazy," said the Ministry of Finance, "but it's true."

"Since war ruins everyone and resolves nothing, it's necessary to avoid it. We can. I shout it out loud: there is no inevitable war. It's necessary to howl it at every horizon. Oh, I know. Someone will object that in some cases, prestige or honor demands combat. But when two individuals submit their litigation to the law, do they suffer any loss of dignity? Less, at any rate, than if they settled their quarrel with their fists like two drunken ragpickers. Well, the Nations are now sufficient grown-up to offer themselves the luxury of an arbiter.

"Someone else will say to us: there are predator nations; there are others that dream of revenge. If we are attacked, should we allow ourselves to be invaded? To begin with, let us mistrust the accusations that represent our neighbors as bloodthirsty. They have been leveled at us; we know, therefore, that they can be unjust. And then again, between ourselves, don't we know how conflict is born? The peoples, I repeat, are composed of people who want nothing but happiness in peace. They do not hurl themselves against one another; they are hurled."

All around the table, voices approved: "Of course... Very true…, Bravo!"

And Martory concluded: "in brief, everything comes down to unmasking, in every country, the men who drive the others—and we know them well; we, the ministers, know them well, all those who, coveting commands and markets, besiege us, needle us an oppress us…all those who, seconded by the impatience of military men, the impotence of diplomats and the frenzy of fanatics, mobilize their banks, their press, their loudspeakers, first alarming and then inflaming universal opinion, attempting to put the authorities at the service of their appetites and govern the government...

"It is necessary not to hold it against them. They don't know. It has been said: they are inhuman. They would blow up the planet to preserve their profit. But it is against them that we ought to struggle, against them that we ought to put the crowd on the alert. Here, in The Hague, in all the capitals, we ought to denounce them. We ought to track them to their lairs, shine the searchlights of clarity upon them, keep watch on them, frustrate their maneuvers, and prevent them from doing harm."

Was that frankness contagious? Henceforth, all the ministers in the Council spoke in a tone of confidence, effusively, as at the end of a generous repast. They searched the table instinctively for half-full cups and bottles, cigars that were smoking by themselves in the notches in ash-trays.

Ducros, the Minister of Foreign Affairs, confessed that it was, in fact, necessary not to count on diplomats to prevent the conflict. Some of them, in circumstances that had not yet been forgotten, had exposed the country to mortal risks: amateurs who had sinned out of ignorance and sadists who had slaked their cruelty. But most of them were, in the main, victims of their upbringing. Strangers to the century, pretentious and superannuated, they lost their footing in a tempest, carried away by the first gust like little paper manikins.

And Ducros started to read the latest diplomatic notes: "We ought to associate ourselves with all efforts in favor of peace compatible with our engagements, but it is important to leave responsibilities where they are...

"In a conversation of the highest importance we have long envisaged the redoubtable difficulties presented with an equal good will to adapt them to reciprocally acceptable solutions...

"It is appropriate to dispute whether certain accommodations are compatible with the dignity and prestige for which the States have an equal concern..."

He did not go any further. In contrast with the gigantic events that were looming over the horizon, the frightful platitude of the formulas became obvious. The body of ministers at the table burst into laughter, with a certain nervousness, as people who have just escaped a great danger laugh. To think that it had been possible to confide the future of the world to such weak hands, such puppets...what madness! Fortunately, the peril had been discovered in time.

In his turn, Barbier, the Minister of War, agreed that the impatience of military professionals unwittingly served the designs of the great feudal lords of industry.

"They're honest, disinterested, often ascetic men, but an incredible thirst for advancement devours them—and one never advanced in rank as rapidly as in wartime. They always want to 'form a column,' as the colonials put it. It's damnable difficult to hold them back. Oh, the swine aren't easy to manage. For a start, they're bitter; they're serving a regime they execrate. Think of it—in the armies of the Republic, there's not a single Republican. Then again, they're spoiled children. They're treated as gods. Even though, in modern warfare, the danger is equal for everyone, they alone seem to wear the aureole of sacrifice. As they form a closed caste, regulated by ancient laws, they ignore or despise the rest of society.

"But what renders them particularly redoubtable is that they never consent to being reduced. On the contrary, they always tend to increase. If you give them an airfield they build a city. They're very enthusiastic to adopt new weapons, but without abandoning the old ones. The cavalry has never been as numerous as it is now that it's unnecessary. I'm sure that they wouldn't let me abolish the warden of a battery even if it dated back to Vauban.[11] They put out branches, I tell you, they pullulate. And as no country will allow itself to be overtaken, you can see that the armaments manufacturers have free play..."

Florentin, the Air Minister, interrupted. A former pilot, he had a dreamy gaze, romantic hair, and a voice as profound and musical as a cello. "Leave your military men in peace," he said to Barbier. "In general, they don't talk much, and that's a good thing. It's us, most of all, who play the game of the big metallurgists, with our inflammatory speeches. They only have to blow on the coals that we've lighted.

"Of course, it's natural to love one's country. One is attached to it, like a plant to the soil. It's a prolongation of ourselves. But what connection is there, I ask you, between that love and the hateful chauvinism that sets the tone today, that species of aggressive and furious monster, that bogey-man which spits bile and farts fire, which bristles with spikes, puffs itself up, wants to be the first in everything, to have the biggest paw, the highest crest, the longest tail?

"That overheated nationalism can't be very old, though. It didn't animate the great ministers of the sev-

---

[11] The Maréchal de France Sébastien La Pretre, Seigneur de Vauban (1633-1707) was the foremost military engineer of his era.

enteenth century or the great thinkers of the eighteenth. One can find no trace of it in their speeches or their writings. It must date from the Revolution, from the Empire. Scarcely two centuries! And yet it only requires the clash of a cymbal, an emblem, a word, to excite it in us. I've given in to it like others, but I was using a conventional language that wasn't in accord with my profound sentiments—and I reproach myself today before you all for having done wrong."

In his turn, Gabrillon, the Minister of Public Education, took the floor. He was a sensitive, emaciated, nervous man. He sat up straight, as white as a bust, and said, in an excited voice: "Yes, yet, we have our share of the responsibility. Let's admit it. We didn't do anything to combat the great supporters of war, against those who protect it and who live it. We didn't warn the crowd against them. We didn't put them in a state to resist their abominable influence.

"It's them, we know full well, who are advertising, or having advertised on their behalf, the fatal war, the inevitable war, the imminent war, tomorrow's war. It's them who are incessantly spreading, or having spread, alarming news and slyly concealing all the signs of détente, all the reasons for hope. Well, we don't enlighten the crowd about these maneuvers, we don't give it the judgment, wisdom, self-confidence and investigative spirit that would permit it to avoid panic.

"Nor do we combat the resignation to war that renders war possible. We let the mothers and sons murmur 'Since it's necessary,' lowering their heads. How can they look up, then, and perceive above them, in the tempest, the unleashing of great mercantile appetites?

"We don't act by means of education, which can do anything, and could in a generation bring about a metamorphosis of the world. In our textbooks, war is still the framework of history, the capital source of heroism and glory. We don't fight war itself. We still admit it in its language, its mores and its exploit. We don't yet commit it to execration. We don't yet put it to shame, as we put all the actions from which we want to deter people...

"Finally, the international organizations, like the Society of Nations and the European Union, have never opposed either war, or resignation to war. They couldn't. They wouldn't. We've created an International Bureau of Employment; we haven't created an International Bureau of Education. And yet, salvation is there. We haven't yet undertaken the great international crusade to the cry of 'Shame upon War!' We continue to live in convention, in deceit, in darkness. It's now time to react, and preach by example......"

The austere Crépin stood up, and pronounced the words that the sovereigns whose portraits decorated the walls had never heard;

"Yes, my friends, let's tell the truth..."

Chapter III

Sprawling in his armchair, head tilted back, chin held high, legs apart, Marigot, in his office in the Hôtel de Ville, is listening to the carillon that precedes the chimes of noon. He has knotted his fingers over his belly, as if he were giving himself a cordial handshake. He is smiling blissfully. Above him, the notes take flight from the bell-tower like little airborne ballerinas. Soon, the hour itself, that star dancer, will make her entrance on tiptoe, her arms rounded.

But the carillon has fallen silent, and the mayor is still smiling. That is because he is not only listening to the genteel ballet of the bells. From time to time, in the next room, from which he is only separated by a stood that stands ajar, he can hear another music, even more enchanting: the laughter of Jeanne Surène. A laughter fresher than that of a child, purer than the sound of a little waterfall, an arbor full of birdsong, of pearls shaken in a crystal cup.

Yes, the laughter of Jeanne Surène. All morning, she received enquiries with a good grace, a cheerful patience. She elucidated every matter briskly, and explained it abundantly. After she had spoken, everything seemed clear and simple. The good people who had approached the caustic secretary cautiously, were ecstatic, melting in gestures of thanks. She interrupted them with polite remarks, which punctuated her pearly laughter: "Not at all... It's quite natural... That's what I'm here for... It's necessary to be helpful..."

Marigot, who was no longer astonished by anything that morning, thought he knew the secret of that metamorphosis, and he abandoned himself to his pleasant dream. Oh, if smiling words could be exchanged in that manner across all counters, how much more pleasant life would be, without it costing anyone anything...

The public, the poor public, would no longer confront, with quailing hearts, shrewish employees...and the work would be less ingrate, and the functionaries more human. How sunny the day would be, by the grace of a smile...

In all the offices in the world, a hint of cordiality, of good humor, would change the taste of life.

Marigot could not know that his dream was being realized at that very moment, that the miracle was being accomplished every where on Earth that it way daylight.

For him, it was very simple: Jeanne Surène was amiable because she knew that she was beloved.

Yes, he had declared himself, an hour earlier. He had asked her to marry him. It was an event so unexpected that he sometimes wondered himself how it had come about.

It is true that he had woken up unusually cheerful. The weather was beautiful, as fresh as a rose. Outside, his steps bounced on the esplanade. In his office, he was tempted to sweep away with a gesture all the military papers that continued to pile up there. "What's the point! There can't be a war in weather like this!"

Reckless words, evidently. He knew full well that the beauty of the sky does not appease the stupidity of human beings, and that the World War had been unleashed in the splendor of the month of August. But it was so bright and so mild what one could, so to speak, breathe in confidence in the future. And he nursed the hope that the lesson of the past had not gone to waste; forty years after the last conflict, the planet had suffered enough, and it would perish from a relapse.

In accordance with his custom, he had taken advantage of a moment when Jeanne Surène was alone to join her in her office in order to bring himself up to date with the day's business. With him, she always seemed to be in a good mood; she reserved her surliness for the public. This morning, however, he had found her particularly agreeable. Momentarily, the list of marriage banns had fallen under his eyes. They had increased since the rumors of war had begun to circulate. Future spouses were complaining to the secretary that the delays had not yet been reduced in the face of the threat. Marigot had ventured to Jean Surène: "And you calmed them down?"

"I told them that we don't have any instructions."

"You asked them to be patient?"

"A little."

"So you believe in marriage?"

"Why not? Those people won't be alone; they have a chance of being happy."

She had smiled softly at those last words. He had noticed then that she had the most appetizing smile, with teeth like fresh almonds. And a secret voice had cried out to him: "Marry her, then, you old skinflint. Marry her. See how pleasant she is, as soon as she wants to be. What? She has no money? But what does that have to do with it? You're rich enough for two. At least let your hoard serve for something. This is an opportunity to cure yourself of your filthy avarice, to extirpate it in your entrails. You sense that she loves you, this young woman, and is only hiding it out of pride. Be generous, for the first time in your life. You'll see how content one is, how joyful one is, when one has made a nice gesture. Come on, surpass yourself. Be superior to yourself. Have wings. Consent to happiness. Try it."

He had tried. He had picked up the list of banns in two fingers, and in a falsely light tone he had said: "What if the two of us were to be inscribed here? What do you think?"

Oh, with what fervor she had thrown herself into the arms he had opened to her. What rewards, what treasures of tenderness he had glimpsed. How well she had sealed the pact with the magnificent signet of her lips...

And since he had been obliged to return to his office, he had heard, thanks to the gap in the doorway, the sound of her happiness passing into Jeanne's voice and laughter...

Outside, he walked with a lighter step. He had wings. He felt truly liberated from his avarice. Why should he not be cured of it? Human defects are not necessarily eternal. One could therefore get rid of them, as one could now get rid of a useless or dangerous organ. Wasn't the appendix taken out, for the greater profit of the entire being?

He had always blushed secretly at the vice with which he knew himself to be afflicted. But now that he had extirpated it and had held it up to the light before his eyes, he perceived all its hideousness.

Amassing money—what a dirty and stupid folly! Was it not, fundamentally, that of the false paupers found dead of starvation in their mansards on mattresses stuffed with bills and bonds, crawling with vermin? One accumulates wealth of which a revolution, or even a change of regime or a crisis might dispossess us, which an unexpected death might prevent us from enjoying.

Miserliness...what base acts it constrains us to commit, how much pain, anguish and sweat it costs us, what privations it imposes upon us. Except for the solitary pleasure of avarice, it constrains us to ignore all the joys of life, from the humblest to the most delicate, and especially the supreme joy, which is that of giving.

At the sight of Truchard's shop, Marigot reproached himself for having pressed and pestered that unfortunate man, who was already struggling amid the worst difficulties. Behold the faults of stinginess, which constrain you to be inhuman!

He resolved to grant the small-scale manufacturer delays and facilities, in order to appease his remorse and make someone happy. With a great surge of generosity that lifted him off the ground, he would have liked to share his joy with the entire world.

But Truchard, who was repairing a set, was already displaying a radiant visage. Joy was particular touching in that man, who seemed doomed to misfortune. One sensed that his large sad features were not in the habit of expressing joy. It appeared there as a stranger.

"Ah, Monsieur Marigot! We've very happy. Emile has made peace with the Thibault son. He met him at Bellevue this morning. They talked—and he came back right away to tell us the good news. He's here. He kissed his mother."

This was a new source of satisfaction for the mayor. Since he had found out about the obscure threats made by Emile Truchard against François Thibault, he had been hesitating, torn between reluctance to denounce the constructor's son and the fear of abetting a crime by his silence. This reconciliation got him out of the difficulty.

"Yes," continued Truchard, who seemed very excited, "I'm very happy. Emile has shown me the example; I shall do likewise. When François Thibault and I meet, we pretend not to see one another, and we don't even know why any longer. I, who admire him so much...for he's a very great man, you know. Often, I've wanted to tell him that, when our paths crossed—but no; I've turned my head. But now, I'll no longer hold back."

"Well, everything's perfect," said Marigot. "And look: good news comes in series. I came in just now to tell you that I've reflected since the other evening. Take your time to settle our arrangement. There's no hurry. Concentrate on your work. No, no, it's not as meritorious as that. I've seen things clearly, that's all. It isn't by knocking you down that I'd have permitted you to get back on your feet." And to cut short Truchard's thanks, he asked: "And how is your wife?"

"Well, imagine that, she feels better this morning. She's a woman, you see, who had no desire to get better. She was letting herself go. Now, she's hanging on again; she's recovered her appetite for life. Since waking up this morning, I've felt hopeful myself, with courage in my heart. Perhaps I've given it to her. After all, panic is infectious, isn't it? Why shouldn't confidence be infectious too? Well, there it is."

His son was the same. Both of them seemed transfigured. While the mayor shook hands with Emile, Truchard, having finished his repair, tried the set. An organ concert emitted by a northern capital emerged through the speaker. The interior of a cathedral appeared on the screen. The sounds, sometimes powerful and full, sometimes delicate and tenuous, seemed to be coming from the nave, as profound as a gigantic conch-shell.

All four of them listened silently. They felt, gladly, that they had escaped, one from illness, the second hatred, the third misfortune, the fourth avarice, and they all displayed luminous faces. Borne away on the wings of the music, they rose above their misery.

Chapter IV

At Billancourt, on the site of the old Renault factory, which had been relocated to the environs of Creil, smart villas had flowered, all decked out with verdure. The abundance and lightning rapidity of public transport had favored the spread of such pleasant and meticulous parks, of which the allotments consecutive to the world war had only been pitiful sketches. Every evening, for thirty kilometers around, guided by the aerial rails, bolides and transport rockets dispersed the population of offices, shops and workshops. As François Thibault had said: "It's time that projectiles finally served some useful purpose."

The afternoon was beginning when Pierre Arnage, having got out of his car at the entrance to the Billancourt park, headed toward the shady house where Marilène lived. During his brief meal after the Council session ended he had telephoned to ask her to see him. He was leaving the next day for The Hague and he had resolved not to leave her under the impression of their painful argument of the day before—all the more so because he had changed so much, made such progress, since their quarrel in his office at the Ministry.

Oh, how could a man give rise to such contradictory thoughts with respect to the same object? Was it conceivable that the same envelope of flesh, the same epidermis, could, so t speak, enclose beings so different, like a bottle that contained, alternately, the most troubled liquid and the clearest essence?

He had spent an atrocious night.

After Marilène's departure, he had not wanted to stay in his office any longer, in the atmosphere and location of their quarrel, nor to go immediately into the large cold apartments in which one had no companions but his reflection in mirrors. He had gone out, aimlessly.

Where should be go? He no longer had any friends, because he had not wanted to confide his liaison with Marilène to anyone in the world. He had closed the doors of his life to others two years ago—and today, when he would have liked to pour out his pain, he was alone.

He had gone through the Tuileries, crossed the Seine and lunged into the first street that opened before him. Along the closed facades he had fled his obsession—Marilène in another's arms—with long strides. He strove to drive away that vision, which seems obscene to us as soon as we are no longer actors. At times he was almost running, uplifted by rage.

He astonished himself with the violence of his transports. He had previously thought that novelists were forcing the tone when they depicted the maddening effects of jealousy—but no. If he had perceived he couple on the other pavement he would have run across the road, leaped upon him, and insulted him verbally, fist raised, like a brute.

Suddenly, he stopped. His instinct had led him to the windows of the Ministry of Public Education, where he had met Marilène.

Two years...and yet, he had not understood the young woman's charm immediately. At first, she had seemed to him to be stiff and tense. How much time had been lost...

In order to discover her, it had required that trip into the Dauphinoise Alps...ah! On returning, the décor of the Ministry had become so welcoming, simply because she animated it and enchanted it with her presence. The slightest corners had shielded their audacious mischief—like the hidden corridor that permitted the Minister direct access to his office, so narrow that one was obliged to embrace in order to pass along it two abreast.

Avid to be together, taking advantage of the most trivial reception, they had also met up in all the other Ministries Together, they had savored the color and the beauty of those palaces of State: the truly regal salons of Finance, whose windows overlook the floral carpet of the Carrousel; the colonnade of Marine, overlooking the never-ending circulation of automobiles around the square that had accommodated, two centuries before, the scaffold of the king, the queen and Charlotte Corday; the small town-house of the Minister of War, juxtaposed with the Ministry like an outhouse, so harshly ornamented with panoplies and somber military paintings; the gardens of Agriculture and Commerce, which meet up and overlapped behind the facades, like lovers at a rendezvous; Foreign Affairs, whose reflection is carried away by the course of the Seine; and the distant social Ministries that had swarmed at Grenelle; and Air, which had taken flight as far as La Muette...

He had resumed his walk though the nocturnal streets. In all the houses filled with slumber, dreams and love, existences overlapped, adapting to one another, like the stones in a wall—and at the foot of those walls warm with humanity, he ran and fled, chilled by rage and despair.

Well, yes. He admitted it. He needed Marilène. She was essential to him. She was precious to him because she admired him, because she gave him confidence in himself. She was precious to him because she had a spangled wit, simultaneously mischievous and profound, because she communicated an incomparable savor to life. She was precious to him because she was undoubtedly his supreme conquest, because after her, his amorous career would be finished. Finally, she was precious to him because she was going away, because she was going to someone else, someone more attentive, more affectionate, younger...

And he was going to let her be carried away and yield her treasures? He was going to shirk the contest? He was going to accept the insult—him, a man of his stripe and importance, was going to give in to this journalist? Get away! Never. He would fight, he would keep her, by any means possible. He would prevent her from going to this Jean Liseray.

But what if he failed, though? And it was then that a voice had whispered to him, in a breath of death: "But if there's war, all these plans will be disrupted. Marilène won't be taken from you." Yes, such was his delirium that he had not closed his ears to that atrocious suggestion. Obscurely, he had desired the cataclysm: that the gases, the microbes, the lightning, all the toxins, all the bombs and all the radiations should annihilate the planet, in order that Marilène should not belong to another...

Having not gone to sleep until it was almost dawn, he woke up late, just in time to go to the Council. At first he had had the impression of emerging from a nightmare. Had he really been wandering half the night, furious and desperate, through the deserted streets? Had he really wanted war, in order that Marilène might be no one's but his? He was horrified. As the minutes went by, he extracted himself from that bad dream, purifying himself.

His generous excitement had increased further during the Council, where it truly seemed to have infected all his colleagues and caused them to rise above themselves. And, showing him the way, dictating his attitude, it had driven him to Marilène's home with an invincible surge.

They sat down side by side on the veranda, facing the garden whose tender foliage isolated it from the neighboring houses. There, leaning forward, his elbows on his knees, he said to her: "We parted on bad terms yesterday evening, Marilène. I'm leaving for The Hague tomorrow. I didn't want us to remain with that memory. I've reflected a great deal since that last meeting. I'm no longer the same. I've changed, especially since this morning. Yesterday, when I became aggressive, I was certainly obedient to my affection for you, but to its less noble aspect. I was obedient to jealousy, to pride. Last night, they inspired the worst thoughts in me. Oh, it wasn't pretty! But now, I blush at it, I'm denouncing myself for it, in your presence..."

She too seemed to have been infected with forbearance. "Pierre, it doesn't matter. Let's forget it. I was harsh too..."

"It's necessary that I speak. Yesterday, Marilène, I loved you, even when I was angry. But I loved you badly. This morning, I feel that I know how to love you better. You're going to be a mother. I ought to be able to marry you, to give you the place by my side that you deserve, but I can't abandon Annette. You recognized that; you said it yourself: she hasn't done anything."

"That's true..."

"Only one means remains for me to contribute to your happiness, and that's not to shackle you. It's to efface myself, to bow down."

She put her hands together, in a gesture miming gratitude. "Pierre..."

"I have no great merit, my poor love. In reality, I can't prevent you from following your destiny. I have no right to do that. All that I'm bringing you is a promise not to put obstacles in your path, not to try to turn you aside—a promise not to compete for you with another, not to recriminate, and to help you as much as possible..."

This time she murmured: "How good you are, Pierre..."

"Marry Jean Liseray. I've been unjust toward him. Forget what I said. And above all, don't think that, knowing myself beaten in advance, I'm merely covering my retreat with an appearance of generosity, nor that I want to flee from my responsibilities and pass them on to someone else. Such calculations are unworthy of me."

"I'm certain of that, Pierre."

"It's costly for a man of my age to renounce a woman like you without a fight, especially if she isn't yet entirely detached from him. It's hard. But I promise you not to importune you with my plaints. I'll find the strength to stifle them. I feel that. But why, today, is it the best of me that's speaking the loudest? It seems that, since this morning, I have a clearer vision of the world, a simplified sense of things."

"Me too," she said. "I'd like to rise above myself, show myself worthy of you, Pierre, you're so generous, so exquisite... I'm hesitant... I'm afraid, whatever route I take, of doing harm, of being cruel. Oh, it would be necessary to have two lives! You must forgive me, Pierre."

"Forgive you! But you'd only be cruel to me if I threw myself in your path and you stepped over me. I'm effacing myself, adapting myself: you won't crush me. Forgive you! But you've given me the greatest gift that one being can give another: you've given me your youth. And as for me, I've only ever given you a life unworthy of you, in the shadow of mine. But everything balances out, in the end. It's me who, in my turn, will play an obscure role, a hidden role, in your existence—because to the child who will be born, whose father I shall be, I shall never be anything but an unknown..."

"Pierre..."

"Bah! That's justice. The true parents of a child are those who form him, not those who make him."

He had risen to his feet. While she accompanied him to his car, they only exchanged a few rare words, full of tenderness and serenity.

"You will be the most beautiful memory of my life, Marilène."

"And I shall continue to admire you, Pierre, and follow your career with emotion."

"I would like us to think of one another with gratitude."

As they were saying their farewells, he made an allusion to his departure for The Hague, for the great litigation. But the light that seemed to be descending from the sky showed him war as it really was: ruinous, inhuman and stupid. It had never settled a conflict; it always laid the groundwork for another. The planet would take centuries to expiate it, if it did not perish immediately. The most imperfect of arbitrations was a hundred times more preferable.

Thus, Arnage was able to finish reassuring Marilène about her future and that of her fiancé. As he climbed into the automobile he said to her, in good faith: "Don't worry; there isn't going to be a war."

Chapter V

In the morning, Noblemain, the stout garage-owner of Briolle, paused in surprise at an article in his newspaper: *The Starter's Silver Wedding*. François Thibault's discovery had, indeed, been made twenty-five years ago. So, various organizations, including the Center for Studies in Physics at Bellevue, where the apparatus had been born, and the factories at Fraicourt, where it had been mass-produced, had decided to celebrate the anniversary of the prodigious invention.

Ordinarily, the happiness of others oppressed the envious Noblemain. Every time he learned about a recompense, a distinction, or any success whatsoever, he was hurt by it. The glory of François Thibault, so vast and so close at hand, was particularly crushing. He had even taken revenge on his genius. In the great man's garden, on the edge of the square, stood a rustic summer-house in which he liked to sit. In two indigent lines, traced one night on a shutter, Noblemain had affirmed that the inventor had run out of inspiration. He had a weakness for couplets:

> *The great François Thibault once sat here*
> *Striving in vain to get his brain into gear.*

Now, on that rosy morning in May, an incredible phenomenon occurred. Not only did the news of that anniversary celebration not depress Nobleman, but it even suggested to him the plan of associating Briolle with it. Why should the town of the inventor's birth not celebrate the invention of the Starter too? Immediately, the garage-owner imagined a local committee, of which he would be the driving force. In sum, he would take care of the electricity and the mechanics himself. He was very popular in Briolle. Everything designated him as the man to take such an initiative.

What, one might say—that jealous individual proposing to serve the glory of François Thibault after having tried in a cowardly fashion to soil it? Well, yes, that was how it was. On waking up he had felt, so to speak, liberated from his infirmity, which constrained him to such wretched gestures. He had been purged of the bile that had poisoned him: a veritable puncture had drained it, purifying him, cleaned him out. He had recovered the soul to go with his face—an open and generous soul.

He retained nothing but shame and remorse for his baseness. Impelled by an imperious need for redemption,

211

he wanted to undo all the effects of his villainy. What would he not have given to efface those two poor lines written on the Thibaults' summer house? At least, he would repair it. He would furbish the glory that he had tried to tarnish.

Obviously, it was a bad time for an apotheosis; there was the dread of war—but was the alarm really warranted? Noblemain doubted it, on such a beautiful morning. No one wanted to fight. And if no one wants war, who will make it?

In sum, the obsession to serve the glory of François Thibault racked him so forcefully all morning that he finally had to give in to it. When he had eaten lunch, he left his garage and went to the Hôtel de Ville.

The mayor, Marigot, was not there. Enthused by his plan, the garage-owner revealed it to the secretary, Jeanne Surène—not without a certain apprehension. She was so ill-tempered...

But the project earned him a smile, for she welcomed it with an unprecedented good grace. "Certainly, Monsieur Noblemain...an excellent idea, Monsieur Noblemain...no one is better qualified than you, Monsieur Noblemain..." She offered to draw up a list of the notable people worthy to serve on the committee, and she promised to submit it without delay to the mayor, who ought to be just finishing his lunch.

The fat garage-owner went down the stone steps of the Hôtel de Ville briskly. Light and lithe, he bounced from step to step like a rubber balloon. He was no more astonished to have encountered Jeanne Surène humanized than to find himself agile and fit.

There was certainly a benevolence and delight in the air. He had observed other signs of it during the morning. Two opposed streams of cars ran incessantly past his garage, because Briolle is traversed by a major road. Usually, some of them were traveling like bolides, but since he had woken up, those insensate speeds had not been evident. Every driver seemed to have understood the folly of risking his life, and those of his passengers or pedestrians, in order to gain a few seconds in the overall journey-time. Everyone had admitted that such a slender advantage was not worth the risk of death, injury or dragging the remorse of a murder around as long as he might live. Some of them even stopped gallantly to let a woman cross the road—and she would thank him with a smile, in which the promise of a new world shone. Yes, a better world, a realizable world. For after all, what imbecile necessity prevented people from ever putting a little good grace into their dealings with one another?

From the threshold of his garage he had noticed other changes. For instance, every morning, maidservants beat carpets noisily at the windows of the Hôtel Moderne, above the tables of the café. Proud of carrying out a duty, confident in following a tradition, they sent into the customers' glasses all the human residues and wastes that a stay in a hotel room can conceal. Now, today that bombardment had not taken place. What mysterious voice, then, could have revealed the incongruity of the custom to them?

Meditating on these metamorphoses, he had gone to see Marigot. The mayor had changed too. Ordinarily, his eyes suspicious, his skin jaundiced and his moustache bristling, he received visitors meanly, even if, like Noblemain, they had their ears to the ground. In order to clink glasses with them he poured them a frightful vitriol that scoured the teeth, gums and throat, which the townspeople nicknamed "the client-deterrent." This time, by contrast, his gaze starry, his complexion clear and his manner conquering, he seemed magnificent. He offered the garage-owner a cigar as long as a forearm and an authentic brandy, warm and spirited. He waxed ecstatic about Noblemain's project, approved Mademoiselle Surène's list and subscribed a regal sum.

Excited by this triumphant beginning, Noblemain went on to visit his committee members. The majority lived around the square, including the pharmacist Mirot, the pâtissier Mousseron and the bookseller Lacreté. Everywhere, the garage-owner extolled the glory of François Thibault impetuously. Previously, in public, he had commiserated with poverty and thundered against injustice, but he had never pronounced words of praise. He had been unable to do so. So they had, for him, a new and delightful taste, which intoxicated him.

His step buoyant, he took his inflamed eloquence from one doorstep to the next. He paused momentarily in front of Truchard's shop. The quarrel between the Thibaults and the Truchards was notorious in Briolle, even though its origins had been forgotten. The very difficult of the enterprise excited Noblemain, however. It would be all the more meritorious to triumph. He did not even have to fight, thought. He had before him luminous faces, mouths split from ear to ear. The children of the two families had been reconciled that very morning—and when Truchard heard about the garage-owner's plan, he grabbed the opportunity to imitate his son, and get into François Thibault's good graces, with both hands.

Noblemain resumed his route. He was definitely encountering the same relaxed and benevolent atmosphere everywhere. All the rivalries that collided between the four walls of the square like fish in a pond seemed to have eased. The aquarium became clear. One might have thought that the town, having agreed to celebrate its hero, was getting into a party mood already. Instinctively, Noblemain looked for Venetian lanterns in the trees, garlands of flowers strung across the streets.

Everyone seemed, like himself, to be liberated from their moral flaws, entirely given over to the joy of putting on a new skin. Fundamentally, why should people not be thus liberated someday? Since the discovery of anesthetics, which had led to the triumph of surgery, the flesh could be stripped of all that vitiated and corrupted it. Why should it not be possible one day to clean out and purify the mind? Life would seem so much more pleasant, so much easier, if it were cured of its defects. Poisoned by envy, Noblemain had suffered from all successes; since he had been liberated, he rejoiced in every one.

No, he was not alone in feeling the benefits of such a cure. All the merchants in the square seemed to have been racked by scruples, gripped by an appetite for probity. Having become expansive, they were confessing candidly that they had been taking advantage. They were moderating their impatience and their prices. They were changed their price-labels. One of them had made a striking statement: "If I were not honest by nature, I would be out of self-interest."

How true that was. And Noblemain was astonished that all the fairy tales, all the naively rose-tinted literary works that exalted virtue had only praised it for its own sake. They had not built their morality on a terrestrial platform; they had left it floating in mid-air. They had not dared to proclaim and demonstrate that we obtain advantages, that we have an interest, in being honest.

Meanwhile, the garage-owner had arrived at the little door to the park. He would have liked to flee from the memory of that letter, addressed to Madame Arnage, that he had recently slipped into the letter-box. What a shadow over that radiant day...

He did not know the results of his villainy, and feared their discovery. He would have liked to recoil momentarily from a visit that was nevertheless unavoidable, for Pierre Arnage was designated as the president of his committee.

Just as he opened the door, an automobile stopped behind him. Arnage got out briskly. He took the garage-owner's arm.

"Are you coming to see me, Noblemain?"

He seemed full of energy, his forehead and gaze cheerful. Noblemain breathed out, relieved. His infamous piece of paper must not have provoked any drama. He began to explain his project.

Pierre Arnage cut him off, casually and cordially. "For François Thibault, anything you wish. Except that I'm leaving for The Hague tomorrow. I wanted to call in at Briolle, but I don't have a moment to spare. You can explain your scheme to me in detail when I get back. You'll excuse me, won't you, my good friend? Until then..."

He took the path to the château. Turning round, he waved his hand to bid farewell, and repeated, warmly: "For François Thibault, whatever you wish."

He was almost running, light and nimble—and Noblemain watched him draw away under the arch of foliage, like the living symbol of the delight that reigned over the town and in his own heart.

Chapter VI

When Jean Liseray went into the little house in Bourg-la-Reine at four o'clock he found that there was no one there. But his mother could not be far away, for her embroidery seemed to be waiting for her, simply set down on a table nearly the window in her room. Her sewing-box was still open. Jean recognized, in the pell-mell of pincushions of every color the favorite play-things of his early childhood: the wooden egg that was inserted into stockings in order to repair them; the sculpted cases that contained needles; the three pairs of scissors tucked into a leather sheath; the metal thimble that retained the warmth of a finger for such a long time...

That morning, he had seen the editor of the *Bonjour*, the paper that published his reportage—a momentous occasion, for he was one of those modern Mikados so absorbed by their immense business affairs that they have to time to see anyone, that they are practically invisible. In reality, he spent entire afternoons playing backgammon with his mistress, a cinema starlet. O miracle! This morning, the Mikado was humanized. His subjects had been able to contemplate him face to face. He had given Jean Liseray not merely time, but also praise, and those were two commodities with which he was equally miserly. He had congratulated him on his recent reportage, in terms so just and warm that Jeans had felt his heart melt.

On going into the editorial office, he had been firmly determined to abandon his profession as a globe-trotter. In particular, he did not want to be too far away from Marilène. But the boss had asked him to leave for The Hague, in order to describe the great assizes in which the fate of the world would be settled. Still swooning under the delightful weight of eulogies, he had not had the strength to resist.

Except that, before leaving, he wanted to plead Marilène's case once again to his mother, to bring the two women together. He refused to let the previous day's curt and painful conversation be the end of the matter. He must have gone about it the wrong way. He would do better today. He had a joyful presentiment in his heart. And as he was to see Marilène again later that afternoon, he retained the hope of announcing the success of his mission to her.

Madame Liseray came back in. More animated than usual, a little color in her cheeks, she told him that she had just obtained the latest news from the neighbors' radio. It was excellent. A genuine volte-face had been produced since the day before. Everyone seemed inclined in advance to accept the verdict of The Hague.

And Jean understood that she was primarily fearful for him. She had been afraid that her grown-up son would be taken from her. But she had always hidden from him that she went to the neighbors for news like that. Undoubtedly, she had only confessed it to him because she had been taken by surprise, on finding him in her room, leaning over her sewing-kit. Oh, that prudery of tenderness......

Sitting down at the window, she resumed her embroidery. The work was mounted on a square of green waxed canvas. Every time she tugged the needle, there was a little dry click. Jean sat down beside her, on a low chair.

"I'm confident too," he told her. "Everyone's beginning to take account of the stupidity of war. Arbitration will save us from it. But after all, if it fails, there'll be general mobilization. I'll be caught up in it as soon as I get back."

"It's not possible!" she said, sharply. "It's not possible."

"It is, in fact, improbable—but in any case, I'd leave for The Hague more tranquil if you were to promise me to be kind to Marilène, if I were sure that she could, if necessary, take refuge with you. Yes, I've come back to that. I have the impression that we lost control yesterday, that we ran into the buffers..."

In a pensive and affectionate tone, she said: "That's true..."

She stopped working. The little dry click of the needle on the waxed cloth was no longer audible.

"Let's not argue," he went on, "as to whether I'm right or wrong to marry a young woman in Marilène's situation. For fifty years, heaps of plays and novels have stirred up the question without resolving it. Besides which, no one has ever convinced anyone. And I don't have any intention of trying you make to abandon your ideas. No, no. What I'm asking, Maman, is for you to set your ideas aside, to by-pass them, for me, in order to permit me to leave reassured. Something tells me that you'd like that."

Without bitterness, with a kind of resigned bonhomie, she confessed: "It's true that I have old-fashioned ideas—but what do you expect? One has the ideas of one's era. One has old ideas, just as one has old cheeks. One can't do much about it. You have to put yourself in my place, to think about everything that troubles me, everything that disconcerts me, about your decision. You mustn't hold it against me."

"Hold it against you! Oh, Maman..."

"But that doesn't prevent me, you know, from sensing how good and generous you're being to Marilène."

"It's so good to be good. And I'm rescuing her. And then again, I love her..."

"And you also know that I'd do anything to make you happy, that I'd do anything not to lose you..."

"Then...you'll be good to her too...spare her, take her in, if I have to go away...in sum, adopt her?"

"I'll try."

"Oh! Thank you, Maman."

Getting up, he threw his arms around her neck. Ordinarily, a kind of timidity, restrained his gestures; he only gave his mother awkward and furtive kisses. Then he sat down again close to her, at her feet. He marveled at the fact that, by virtue of a sudden metamorphosis, she had found in her tenderness the strength to stifle her prejudices. How he had misjudged her...

He no longer had anything but gratitude and contrition. "If you knew, Maman, how much pleasure you're giving me...and I've so often caused you pain. Oh, I've kept count. I held it against myself. Only, I didn't tell you. Look, that birthday, when you had asked me to come to dinner...I'd promised...and you waited for me, alone, at the table...I'd forgotten... And again, last year, didn't I reproach you, stupidly, for having deprived me of comradeship, of scholarly discipline, because you had the admirable patience to educate me yourself in order to keep me out of school until I was twelve? And so many others, so many other intolerable memories. When they came back to me, when they stabbed my conscience, during my travels, I tried to get rid of them. I couldn't. Then I would have liked to escape from myself, as one jumps out of an airplane..."

"My little Jean..."

"Oh, everything that one keeps within oneself...and what's atrocious, absurd about it is that, while sometimes showing myself so hard and so secretive, I felt sorry for you. I know how sad your life had become, in this house that you knew when it was animated, alive, where you had been happy, and where you had to remain alone, always alone. And I wasn't just compassionate, I was grateful—but I still kept quiet. I know how much I've cost you, since you brought me into the world, the anxiety, the insomnia, and time, and money. Oh, it's true—I hadn't asked to be born; that's not important. I know that a child gives more pain than pleasure, that it represents a complete and harsh sacrifice. Yes, I've thought all that, but I never told you. If you knew how happy I am to feel liberated, to be able to speak. Maman, I beg your pardon for everything..."

"My big...but I too, couldn't speak. And yet, I had so many things to say to you, every time I saw you again. Oh, it's just, you see, that I was a little afraid of you..."

"Of me?"

"Yes. It's funny, isn't it? I made you, carried you, nursed you, taught you the A B C of everything—and yet you scare me slightly. In your presence, I become anxious, I lose my head."

"Maman! But that's impossible."

"But yes, yes—and then, as if I had a gag in my mouth, I keep quiet, I choke. Or worse, I say exactly what I shouldn't. I feel it coming; I try to stop it; I can't. It comes out. And there you are, offended, discontented. And me, so sorry..."

"But now it's all explained, it won't happen anymore."

"Yes, it's finished, isn't it? And since we're confessing, I might as well tell you that I haven't always handled you very cleverly. Oh, I know. For example, in my letters, I complain about the length of your absences. When you come back, I complain that you don't come to see me often enough. I was wrong. You did what you could. It must have irritated you. But I didn't know, since I didn't know you until today; I often imagined that you didn't love me..."

"Oh, Maman..."

"Then too, I've been jealous, cautious about your life. I've wanted to know everything. I've employed all sorts of petty means, that must also have indisposed you toward me. But you have to forgive me. You understand, now; it was tenderness again, such great tenderness..."

Then, their hearts mysteriously blossoming, they strove to dissipate, gradually, the most tragic of all misunderstandings: that which arises between a mother and the creature that has emerged from her.

Chapter VII

From the first moment of his prodigious experiment, François Thibault, became slightly feverish, in spite of his robust optimism. Would it succeed?

Obviously, it was too soon to be certain. He saw that the sky retained, even after sunrise, the nuances of the dawn. He knew by courtesy of messages that the transmitters—whose operators did not know the exactly what they were doing—were functioning normally in the four Sidereal Energy stations. Finally, he observed in himself and the members of his family the lucid wellbeing and glad excitement that were raising them above themselves.

But was the whole Earth enveloped by the pink gas? And were all human beings experiencing that benevolent inebriation? Only his wireless set could furnish him with precise symptoms and permit him to take the planet's pulse. Throughout the morning, however, he was unable to obtain any truly significant indication.

Thus, he wandered impatiently, somewhat at a loss, around his petty kingdom at Bellevue. Sometimes he stood on the edge of the terrace, overlooking the stone ocean of the city, on the lookout for rumors. Sometimes he took refuge in his laboratory at the Center of Studies. There, as was his habit, he strove to forget his preoccupations in some new research. This time, however, he could not succeed in escaping them.

Eventually, he gave up. As he came out, he scrutinized the gigantic globe that ornamented the vestibule. Instinctively, he looked around it for the pink veil that ought to be surrounding the world. He went back to his villa, and switched on his wireless set again.

It was not until the early afternoon, at about two o'clock, that he began to collect evident signs of a metamorphosis.

At that time, it was six o'clock in the morning in San Francisco, ten o'clock in the evening in Peking. America was only just beginning its day, Asia was finishing its own. Most of all, it was Europe that could be heard. When a speaker was using a foreign language, François Thibault translated the gist of what he was saying for those grouped with him around the screen. All the speeches presented the same new feature.

Previously, no chronicler had ever failed to proclaim, in respect of anything whatsoever, that his country was the foremost in the world for the intelligence and taste of its inhabitants, the genius of its inventors, the beauty of its monuments and locations, the excellence of its products, the perfection of its industry and the glory of its armaments. At the same time, none ever missed any opportunity to mock and denigrate neighboring countries, slyly delivering slaps in passing. Now, they had all abandoned that tone of peevish chauvinism, as if they had suddenly discovered that the waves carried their words beyond national boundaries, where their painful impropriety must become obvious.

Another feature: the majority of the speeches gave evidence of an unaccustomed boldness. Ordinarily, in all countries, texts were carefully checked before being read in front of a microphone. Today, however, the speakers, doubtless carried away in mid-course by generous impulses, were giving free rein to their thoughts, speaking from the heart. And one could see their faces lighting up on the screen as they directed their attention toward the future.

The wireless set hurled all those cries of hope, transmitted by the waves, into the room, from the most modest wish to the most ambition adjuration.

For the good of the race, women and children, one voice proclaimed consenting maternity. Another preached solidarity "We are dependent on one another. In a crowd, a public vehicle, everyone breathes into his lungs the air exhaled by the lungs of others. Since that solidarity exists, let us be conscious of it, utilize its strength. Let us be the cells of one vast organism."

A doctor demanded the preventative cure of the half-mad, which would permit so many dramas of power to be avoided. A league proposed the abolition of the egotistical and stupid habit of abandoning broken glass and fat Sunday papers in the suburban woods.

Someone thundered against social iniquity. "It's necessary that it ceases to seem natural to us. It ought to offend us and be intolerable. Let us work toward leveling upwards. It can be realized; the example of people's palaces and museums proves it. And when we see a dazed drunk, a dirty or boastful worker, let's blame ourselves, for it's our responsibility to remove them from ignorance and fifth."

A professor spoke out against examinations, in which only memory triumphs. He denounced the excessive duration of education. Thanks to the cinema, it could be reduced by nine-tenths. The schools were often merely internment camps. It was necessary to provide youth with abundant leisure and play. It ought to remain, in our memories, the garden of life.

Someone deplored the faults of import and export duties, the imbecile pretention of certain peoples to sell to everyone and not to buy from anyone, to live on their own produce like Robinson Crusoe on his island. "It's necessary to put an end to a regime in which an abundant harvest is considered a calamity, where wheat, coffee and cotton are burned when so many people elsewhere lack nourishment and clothing. We erect barriers between individuals, between castes, between peoples, between races, and then we fight over them. It's necessary to lower them. The planet is a living being, which technology has endowed with an admirable nervous system. It's up to us to unify it, harmonize it, to make it a superior organism. As Elie Faure predicted thirty years ago,[12] it's a matter of passing from an individual civiliza-

---

[12] The reference is to *D'autres Terres en vue* (1932) by the art historian Elie Faure.

tion to a symphonic civilization, a matter of *orchestrating the Earth*."

Finally, with regard to the war, all the orators gave free voice to the common sense view that the people in power had forbidden François Thibault to voice two days earlier. No one any longer wanted these armaments and engineering works that only profited their entrepreneurs. No more subterranean fortresses whose defenders would perish asphyxiated by gases; no more billion-franc ironclads at the mercy of a floating mine, which, during the four years of the World War, had only confronted one another once, in an indecisive battle, had had not even succeeded in forcing the Dardanelles.

Untiringly, they evoked the motives and consequences of war: on the one hand, the profit of a few thousand parasites; on the other, millions of innocent victims, and a series of crises, convulsions and miseries that force humankind to expiate its folly for even long than it would mourn its dead.

During a gap, François Thibault, his face illuminated, said to his son: "And yet, the radio doesn't register everything. Many signs are escaping us. Thus, undoubtedly, at this moment, thousands of reconciliations are taking place like the one that brought you and Emile Truchard together this morning. That's the precise emblem in miniature of the rapprochements that must one day take place between classes, nations and races. It's the triumph of the heart and reason over or meanest motives. For vanity, self-interest and tolerance are the origin of all vexations. It's the sweetest flower of progress."

"Yes," said Claude. "When I saw Emile Truchard coming toward me on the terrace, holding out his hand, I had the same impression as just now, before the wireless set: that of being transported into better times." And he added maliciously, turning to Pierre Contal: "All this doesn't modify your opinions slightly, Grandfather?"

The author of *Génie antique* was sitting down, his head slightly tilted back, his wide beard spread out. His elbows were leaning on the arms of his chair. His fine hands were touching, at the extremities of his splayed fingers. It was a familiar attitude. In a voice that was both emotional and cheerful, he said: "But I'm not far from thinking like you, my dear Claude. Well, yes, deep down, I like the progress of science. Why deny it, since I profit from it? When I have to go abroad to visit a museum, an excavation or a monument, I like the airplane that saves me time. In an automobile with the windows down, I like the wind that strikes my cheeks with the speed of my travel. When I'm far away from all of you, it's good to hear your voices and see your faces over the telephone. I appreciate comfort and I'm glad to see it extending. And when I'm anxious about your health or mine, it's good to think that the curative arts are improving every day..."

François Thibault was not surprised by that conversion. Pierre Contal was too intelligent not to have taken note of the advantages of progress. Faithful to his attitude as a man of the past, however, he had been obliged to keep his observations secret, to bury them within himself. Today, under the pink sky, these confessions were emerging from the depths of his soul.

Even in the course of his audacious experiment, though, the inventor was still haunted by his great dream: the immortality of the Earth and the human race, which would permit human beings to attain divinity. Thus, he asked: "In that case, Father, you're no longer denying that humans are capable of improvement?"

Pierre Contal curled up in his armchair, without separating his delicate white hands. "Well, this is how I see things. Three stalks emerge from the human stock; they represent art, science and morality. Art has quickly attained its full stature and is no longer growing. Science has grown vastly in the last hundred years. All things considered, it's possible that morality, much slower to grow, might catch up with the others."

"Marvelous!" said Claude, gaily.

"Here," Pierre Contal went on. "I'll give you an example of the progress in mores—which is to say, moral progress. Today, you see, it's me who's showing you the way. You know about the circus games; you know that gladiators fought to the death. It's true that, most of the time, they were condemned criminals or prisoners of war—but still, they were men. Now, I'm weary of saying that in present day boxing matches, the vanquished must go to the land of dreams for ten seconds. Well, that's the progress accomplished in two thousand years: on the one hand, definitive, eternal death; on the other, apparent death, for ten seconds."

"That's true," said François Thibault, pensively.

"Fundamentally," Pierre Contal concluded, "I don't despair of human beings or their possibilities. But what I reprove and detest, of course, is excess. I like moderation. Note in passing that I'm not one of those fake ascetics who, without depriving himself of anything, goes about shouting everywhere that it's important to restrict the needs of humankind. I don't know of any gesture more deplorable than that of Diogenes breaking his superfluous bowl. Such pruning would lead us rapidly to the condition of the fakir, spending years laid out in a coffin—one might as well have the complete death that robs us of all our needs. No, no. But I repeat, I don't like the excessive speed, excessive production, excessive ambition and excessive avidity that presently harasses us."

"It's only temporary," said François Thibault.

"I know that. It's just a temporary fever, a fad. People thought of themselves as Corneillians in the time of *Le Cid*, libertines under the Regency, Romantics with Lamartine and ferocious since the World War. They're still human. To discern the future, it's necessary not to be hypnotized by the present. It's necessary to take a step back, to have a sense of duration, to be able to juggle with centuries, with hundreds of centuries. Our fashions, our successive ways of being, are merely waves, as rapid as those of the wireless. The important thing is to grasp the song that they produce, to know whether it's a ritornelle that is finishing, or a song that will rise up and never end."

Chapter VIII

Scarcely had he escaped from Noblemain than Pierre Arnage went through the little iron gate and heard it click behind him. He went rapidly through the park on the path to the château.

He was in haste to appease Annette—for she must still be angry with him. When she had left Paris she was justly offended by the curt admissions that she had extracted from him, which he had not even been able to soften with remorse. Although he had told her that he was coming to Briolle, she did not know yet that he was coming back repentant and liberated.

At an intersection of paths, he saw her slender silhouette. She was coming toward him.

She said to him, simply: "I heard the automobile but I didn't see anyone. Were you held up? A voter?"

"And a weighty one! Noblemain. He wants to apotheosize François Thibault. He's right, of course—but it was a bad time. I scarcely listened to his speech. We have so many things to say to one another, Annette. Shall we go for a walk?"

She agreed without stiffness: "Let's go for a walk."

He felt that she was ready to be indulgent, and rejoiced in being worthy of it. They wandered along the paths at random. The park was the true luxury of the château, a corner of the forest isolated in the town. The tender shoots of spring were spreading a green mist there. To the west, the branches were outlined in black against a ruby-red sky.

In broad strokes, Arnage indicated how he had been raised above himself. Resolved not to divorce, he could not be sure of Marilène's fate, but, by virtue of the instinct of a jealous male, he would have been capable of competing for her with the man who had offered to marry her. He had found the strength within himself to renounce her, to resume the straight path.

"It's over, then?" she asked, timidly.

He nodded his head gravely. "It's over."

They sat down on a stone bench in front of a narrow and deep basin that was known as the Fontaine de la Marquise. A spring filled it with water so pure that it was invisible; only its ripples revealed its presence.

"I've been so upset," she confessed.

Those simple words devastated him. He would have liked to get down on his knees. "You mustn't be upset any longer. I repeat, it's over. There's only you in my life. You're the only one who counts. Fundamentally, there's never been anyone but you. The others...oh, I was obedient to an imbecilic desire to collect adventures, not to let any opportunity that presented itself pass me by—for they did offer themselves. Come on, it's necessary to confess: as soon as one is a star, especially in government, one is incessantly ambushed, solicited, tempted. Most of the time, it's the women who seek out the men, while persuading them that it's the other way around. Out of vanity, one doesn't dare to run away; one lets oneself go, allows oneself to be caught. Oh, it will be necessary to watch over me, Annette, to protect me, to defend me. I confide myself to you. No one but you can save me from myself and others."

She murmured: "Why didn't you speak sooner, Pierre."

"Yes, I should have—but I couldn't. I was retained by some imbecile prudery. Deep down, you see, the whole world is timid. The audacious are perhaps even more so than the others, for they only use excessive words to make their anxieties. One always holds back one's most tender impulses, those that depart from the most profound regions of being. One never speaks sufficiently in accordance with one's heart."

"That's true."

"In the twenty years that we've been married, how many times I've wanted to, and should have, given you thanks. But no, I kept quiet. If you knew how often I admired your courage and your miracles of economy, in the hard times of our early days, when neither of us was rich, how I raged at not being able to ornament you, dress you as I would have wished... I remember a little mantle, so thin. When I saw you put it on, cheerfully, in winter, I felt a chill all the way to my heart; I could have wept. But I didn't say anything..."

"I don't regret those times," she said.

"Me neither. Outside of our money worries, they've left me an enchanted memory, which often comes back to mind in gusts, like a fresh and new perfume."

"I bore the deprivation every well, in secret. I only had one dread, one regret. I was afraid of not being able to please you with my four-sou dresses, of not seeming pretty enough to you. And then, think of the recompenses you offered me. When I attended a session at which the entire Chamber gave you a standing ovation, I whispered to myself: "That's my man." It wouldn't have taken much to make me shout it to my neighbors on the benches. But that evening, I too said nothing. I didn't know how to tell you how proud I was of you."

"I sensed it, though. I remember how, in very difficult circumstances, you advised me, supported me..."

"Not enough, not enough. I should have told you more often how much I admired your intelligence and your talent. I shouldn't have left that care to others. Oh, it's so difficult to pay compliments!"

"Almost as difficult as to give thanks. Just think, Annette—in twenty years I haven't thanked you once for your patience with me. And I'm not easy, I know that. At times, I'm damnable pig-headed. And although I'm not above reproach, not once did I ever thank you, in words, for being such a faithful wife..."

She smiled. "Bah! Since you no longer have anything for which to reproach yourself..."

"That's good. I'm very happy that this evening, by some miracle, we've been able to say something of what's in our hearts. Now that we know the defects of silence, we won't mistrust one another any longer, will we? Communication is established. Let's keep it."

A pink gleam lit up the crystal of the spring. The birds, returning to their roosts as dusk approached, filled the park with their sweet racket, as at dawn. Under the influence of a mysterious exaltation, Pierre affirmed his faith in his marriage. In a flash he had fathomed destiny. Certainly, the marriage would last and improve. Every man, after having desired all women, only wants one wife. And the story of one man reflects, in miniature, the story of humankind. After the promiscuity of early ages, the apotheosis of the couple slowly emerged. In the distant future, Arnage glimpsed the union in which tenderness would be molded by esteem, gratitude, common memories and mutual indulgence, in which the felicities of habit and pride in duration could be savored, in which the games of pleasure would be added to the enchantments of amity.

But what an effort of frankness such a tight entente demanded...it would often be necessary to let his heart speak, finally to let his most tender impulses and his most cherished thoughts take flight. For we continue to resemble the sea, from which all life emerged, from which we emerged ourselves; in our depths repose the excellent and the worst, just as mud and pearls repose on the sea bed. Those exquisite spheres must rise up from the abyss and finally make their way into the light.

Chapter IX

Marilène and Jean Liseray, arm in arm, slowly went along the Champs-Élysées. They allowed themselves to be carried along by the great current that was heading toward the Étoile.

At the end of that day, on the eve of the assizes at The Hague, which would decide the fate of the world, everywhere, in every town and every city, people were gathering instinctively around monuments to the dead.

The memory of the men who believed that they were putting an end to war was evoked. People were inspired to take inspiration from their example, to grant their supreme wish.

In Paris, it was around the tomb of the Unknown Soldier that the crowd gathered. It was meditative, but it was not sad. One sensed that its conscience was strong, proud of its unanimous desire, glad to be able to assure itself of salvation. All faces were radiating benevolence, a cordial mildness.

"I've seen a lot of crowds," said Jean Liseray, "I've seen them in all colors, under all skies, but I've only ever seen one crowd analogous to this one. It was on a Sunday in spring, at the Roseraie de Bagatelle.[13] I don't know whether the beauty and the purity of the flowers inspired a sort of respect and reserve in the visitors, or whether they were slightly intoxicated by their perfume, but as they walked slowly under the flowery aches, they had the same discreet and courteous stride, the same air of serenity, of polite good humor that's evident today. There's benevolence in the air, and delight, and love…don't you think so? I believe I can see the reflection of my own joy in all the faces, all the eyes. It seems to me that all these people have come here to celebrate our engagement."

For it really was their engagement celebration. All resistance to their union had abruptly given way. As soon as they had met up that afternoon, Jean had told Marilène that he had won his mother to their cause. She would welcome the young woman with open arms, hands extended, without dwelling on the past. In her

---

[13] The rose-garden in the Parc de Bagatelle in the Bois de Boulogne, the site of an annual competitive show.

turn, Marilène told Jean that she had just received a long radiogram from her father in Geneva. He regretted having provoked his daughter's departure by his violence and harshness. He wanted her to come back. One might have thought that in response to a signal from some mysterious voice, his eyes and his heart had opened, that he had come to understand the rigor, the narrowness and the archaism of his prejudices.

Was a breath of indulgence passing over the Earth? It seemed to be animating the crowd around Marilène and Jean. Comical spectacle could be seen on street corners. People were smiling at things that might have irritated them. People were mildly amused when a soldier, his arm as rigid as a gallows, his hand at the corner of a bulging eye, snapped a salute at an officer who returned it negligently, as if handing out alms. It was realized that the army, in recognizing inferiors and superiors, was perpetuating inequality between men, at the very moment when universal efforts were being made to reduce it. People were covertly amused by such customs, as obsolete as the chastity belts that they went to see at Cluny.

More discreet smiles greeted a cortege of automobiles coming back from some official ceremony at the Étoile: plumed bicorns, jackets embroidered with gold thread or verdure, scarlet robes, toques like cake-molds, breasts spangled with decorations like choir banners. In the crowd, women masked their hilarity by putting their fingers to their lips, in order not to offend those important individuals, who seemed pitiful and uncomfortable enough in their fancy dress.

Jean Liseray held on to his companion's arm tightly.

"I feel so courageous, so resolute, Marilène. Is it you who's communicating all this valor to me? You were missing, you see, like a part of myself, but we've come together again. Imagine the joy of an amputee who wakes up to find himself complete…how well we march in step, the two of us. How facile and simple the directive appear to me: respect human life, celebrate those who embellish or ameliorate it; realize the advantages of probity, limiting one's happiness to that of one's neighbor, sensing solidarity, causing the least pain, knowing by one's own example that one is laboring a little for the future…"

They reached the Place de l'Étoile. The stone arch loomed up like an enormous pachyderm standing on its four feet in the human pond. Not far away, a man was passing by amid a murmur of surprise, compassion and mockery. He was wearing a gas mask.

At the sight of the sky that had retained the tints of dawn all day, the rumor had begun to spread that the composition of the air must have been modified. One individual, more mistrustful and more timorous than the rest, had put his mask on just in case. Behind the glass goggles, anxiety and fear could be read in his eyes. Two large annealed tubes rose up from his snout, connected to a reservoir strapped over his stomach. One might have thought that he had brought his esophagus and trachea out into the light, and was wandering through the crowd like a monstrous anatomical specimen.

That man scarcely suspected that among the two billion inhabitants of the Earth, he was the only one to have escaped the pink gas. Behind his mask, he alone was breathing the previous day's air from his reservoir.

Astray in that crowd, whose light intoxication was bearing its members into the future, he was a man of the past.

He belonged to the age of the innumerable intermediary and stupid tipping, the age of murderous customs duties and odious passports, the age of blast furnaces and large companies.

He was a man who delighted in the clamors of the Bourse and military fanfares; a man whose ideal was to administer the work of others; a man who believed in tortuous and subterranean schemes; a man who coveted wealth as if he had a hundred stomachs and a hundred sexual organs to satisfy, when he only had precisely one; a man who did not have time to live; a man, in sum, who, limiting the universe to himself, enclosed in his hard shell, was unaware of the pleasure of mingling, of giving himself, of entering as a merry dancer into the human round-dance and feeling the warmth of other hands in his...

But a name rose up from the crowd:

"François Thibault...François Thibault..."

At home, on the screen of his wireless set, among the processions that were streaming toward the monuments to the dead in every city in the world, he had seen the people of Paris assembling around the Arc de Triomphe. He had not hesitated. "My place is there."

Accompanied by his son Claude he had come. Mounted on the stone step that circles the foot of the edifice, he emerged. His massive torso could be distinguished, his forceful and tender features, his hair as bushy as the edge of a forest.

He raised his hand. Paris fell silent. Megaphones distributed around the plaza repeated his words.

His rapid speech was uninterrupted. Only the sympathy of the gazes that were directed at him, a meditative attention and an occasional frisson that ran through the crowd marked its approval.

"What do we want?" he said. "We want our representatives, who are ready to leave for The Hague, to know what we think, so that they can carry it there. I shall therefore express that thought—for I know that I am in communion with you. It's simple. We want Peace. We want Peace via Arbitration. And I want to add immediately that the same appeal is rising up and reaching us from every city on Earth. We want Peace because it appears to us to be the key to all good, the normal state of being, the condition of life. We want it because we know now how wars are made.

"That peace depends on us, since it is with us that wars are made, with our lives, with all our lives...

"Oh, I know! People say to you: 'But what if there is a people that wants war?' Well, you reply that, in its immense majority, a people that wants war is composed of people who want peace! A handful of warmongers, whose mouthpieces are unconsciously playing the game of silent manipulators, drives the inert and credulous masses to their death. It is up to us to unmask them, to denounce those forgers of war untiringly. You will be surprised by their small number. And besides, if a nation is a victim of real injustice, will it not be the first to submit its case to the Law?

"People will also say to you: 'War is a scourge inherent in humanity.' Well, no. Incurable war is as false as necessary suffering. It's with such formulas that resignation is exploited. And even if it were true, even if the instinct of war were rooted in human nature, would that be a reason not to rip it out? The history of humankind is exactly that of the incessant struggle against our own defects, against the evils that assail us, against the scourges that surround us.

"No, no, let us not weaken in our resolution; and to affirm it further, let us repeat that modern warfare, between armed nations, destroys everything, resolves nothing, and unleashes in its wake endless repercussions, as painful and as stupid as itself.

"On the eve of the Arbitration, therefore, let us affirm our pacific determination, at the very foot of this edifice at celebrates the glory of military conquests. Let us not declare anathema. Let us take delight in, and be proud of, the moment when human beings, rising above themselves, finally becoming conscious of their power, have decided to live.

"Let us spare ourselves this. Let this be for us a vestige of a vanished era, a monument to the past. Let us meditate upon it as upon ruins. Let us simply think about the eight million dead that the names of the hundred victories inscribed on these walls represent. Let us think about the man whose symbolic tomb is celebrated by this arch. He believed that he was dying in order to vanquish war forever. Let us remain faithful to his ideal. Let us bring him the most beautiful palm, the olive branch. Let us swear Peace before him. Yes, let it be from this place, the star on the forehead of Paris, that it radiates over the world."

Supported by his son's arm, François Thibault got down from the stone step. He was eager to return to his listening-post in Bellevue, but he had to go through the crowd in order to get back to his car, and he was immediately enveloped. People rendered him thanks with stammered phrases and gazes full of affection. Some, with timid gestures, brushed his clothing with a caress. People took his hands, shook them, covered them with kisses. The certainty penetrated him of being in intimate communion with that crowd, of being its emanation, of being its soul.

And when the car finally drew away, Claude was frightened by that very fervor. What would happen tomorrow, when the exaltation had subsided, the experiment having been concluded?

But François Thibault reassured him. "Remember what I said to Pierre Contal: when people have seen what they might be, they will blush with shame at what they are."

WINGS OF FLAME

With a brief surge, the airplane took off. Immediately recovering from her initial emotion, Claire, sitting in the narrow seat beside Lucien Chatel, savored the delights of the unfamiliar sensation. Farewell to the jolts of the road, the trepidation of the railway, the rolling and pitching of the sea, the splash of the river. Even the gliding of skates over ice seemed rude and coarse by comparison with aerial travel. Surprised and cowed by the abrupt attack of extended wings, the air became the most reliable slave, and carried the enormous machine at an even and fast speed over the innumerable routes of the sky. Infused with confidence, wellbeing and pride, Claire wanted to cry out her joy at escaping the earth.

She felt liberated. And the delight of that escape was confused within her with the certainty of escaping the odious man whose name she had been obliged to bear for five years. Even the law had rendered her the liberty that she had reconquered in fact, breaking the final link by a judgment of divorce in her favor.

Free, free—she was free! And soaring into the blue sky symbolized her freedom. It seemed to be carrying her forward in life, marching into the future.

The future…for her it was in the hands of the same man who was taking her on such a prodigious flight. She was about to forget the bad dream, recommence her life beside the dear companion of her adolescence that she had finally rediscovered. She would be his wife…

She contemplated his space-filled eyes and tenacious profile, beneath the fur-lined helmet that his portraits had rendered legendary during the past year. Every time she exclaimed her delight aloud, he lit up with a lovely smile, youthful and charming. *Everything about him pleases me*, she thought.

The large mahogany joystick acquired the majesty of a scepter beneath his nervous fingers. Was he not a young sovereign, recognized and acclaimed, of the realm of the air, in this triumphal chariot that he seemed to be guiding toward some apotheosis? Oh, how she loved him, how she loved him...

He rose up, describing a large spiral around the airfield. Leaning over, Claire distinguished the glazed roofs of the Chatel workshops sparkling in the sunlight, and the foliage of the Bois de Vincennes, spread out like a giant carpet of moss. They were still climbing. The tranquility increased at these heights. One could no longer hear anything but the silky purr of the propeller and, from time to time, some echo of life—an automobile horn, a firework at some country fair, the barking of a dog...

And, realizing thus the most ancient human dream, of escaping the laws of nature and the rumors of the earth, climbing in a glorious spiral toward the blue infinity, in that pure crystalline air, amid that solemn peace, the feeling that she was alone beside someone she adored, on the very day that she could promise herself to him, was for Claire an unprecedented, amazing betrothal in mid-air.

As they touched down, the crowd, breaking through the barriers, came running from all directions, surrounding them with a confused clamor, a circle of extended hands, camera lenses, open mouths and raised foreheads. And suddenly, among all those faces, Claire was only able to see one face: that of Villeret, her former husband.

She shivered. Her worst memories rose up vividly before her. Behind that neat and glossy beard, he divined the jaw of a shark, enormous, massive and full of insults. She knew how quickly that tender gaze could be imbued with hatred and charged with cruelty, how quickly the honeyed voice could be embittered.

How she had suffered before unmasking him! He had been introduced to her as a respected engineer, an administrator of important industrial enterprises—but she had gradually discovered, too late, an entire past of expedients, varying between mines at the Cape and in the Caucasus, a hundred shady enterprises in quest of the money necessary to his vices. Married, he had continued to slide down the slope until the fall: a vile story of gold mixed with sand to falsify the assay of an African deposit. That day, Claire had been obliged to use her inheritance to buy the silence of her husband's dupes.

Undoubtedly, if Villeret had only been a poor wretch disarmed against temptation, she would have continued to help him, out of pity—but he was as brutal as he was cowardly, as jealous as he was debauched, as cruel as he was criminal, and without a trace of love to excuse his violence. The day after the scandal she had separated from him, resolved to earn her living.

She had a considerable talent for drawing. She especially liked painting birds, so she produced small pictures of that sort, which gradually found buyers. Villeret badgered her. His appearance was usually sordid, but sometimes, he was impeccable and magnificent. He pressed her to resume their life together. She could not determine the proportions in which jealousy, poverty and an obscure need for tyranny drove him to those attempts, but she refused obstinately, getting rid of him with a little money.

That ambiguous life had been going on for a year when Claire met Lucien Chatel again. They had known and loved one another in adolescence, but there could not be any question of marriage between them. Unite two children of the same age, especially when the young man has no fortune? Villeret had been preferred. But such first loves are like initials carved in the bark of young trees. Far from effacing them, the years enlarge them and hollow out their traces. And when Lucien, already rich and famous before the age of thirty, found Claire alone and unhappy, they perceived that their hearts had not changed. Their life resumed where it had left off...

Since then, Chatel had pleaded with his friend incessantly to recover her liberty completely. Villeret had committed too many sins against her for him to dare to oppose it. In fact, stifling his rage, he had allowed the divorce petition to go forward without protest. For two months, she had not seen him. What did he want?

Oh, the flight in the open sky, the blue intermission, had not lasted. As soon as she touched the ground, she felt anxious again. Villeret's eyes were fixed upon her. As soon as their gazes met, he sketched a brief signal of summons. So be it. She consented, inasmuch as she feared a conflict between the two men, who knew one another by sight. She would have a decisive conversation with Villeret. It would be the last. In sum, he was nothing to her any longer.

Anxiously, she went to the edge of the wood and took a path vaulted with foliage, where Villeret soon joined her. Immediately, she attacked.

"What do you want?"

He laughed, his voice amiable. "I wanted to congratulate you. It's was charming, that escape *à deux*. The life of bees…the nuptial flight—for you're going to marry, naturally?"

"Yes."

Villeret stopped. His mask had fallen. Hideous with hate, his fists clenched, he cried: "Well, I don't want that—you hear, I don't want that!"

She shrugged her shoulders, fortified by the courage that love brings.

He became exasperated. "Yes, yes, I know—I have no right to oppose this marriage. You're forced me to divorce. It's finalized today. And you're triumphant. But I don't care about the law; I…"

She cut in ironically, making allusion to his shady deals: "Yes, I know…"

But he was not listening. "Admit," he went on, "that you never stopped seeing that man, that you've let me sink, ruined me, in order to get rid of me!"

She protested. "I swear to you that I never saw Lucien during our marriage."

"In any case, you've got what you wanted, both of you. You're free—you think you're free. But I repeat that I don't want you to profit from your liberty. I wanted to see that flight…I was in the crowd; I heard everything people were saying about him, about you, about both of you. Oh, how I suffered…how I wanted to strangle the people around me… So, I don't want it to go on. I don't want to spend my life watching your apotheosis.

It's not possible. I'll stop you. I'll…give it up, Claire—believe me, you'll do well. Give it up."

He was respiring such cruelty, such perfidy, such suffering that she was afraid. What could he do against them? Murder? No, he was too cowardly. Some sly treason? But Lucien, forewarned, would be on his guard. What if he succeeded in carrying out his threat, though? Then what? Was it necessary, in order to avoid the danger, to renounce her cherished future? No. They would suffer too much, both of them.

She shook her head. "There is nothing more between us now. I won't do as you say. Leave me alone, once and for all."

Already she was retracing her steps toward the workshops. He touched her shoulder with a feverish hand. "You shan't belong to another. You shan't marry that man."

She declared, firmly: "We're engaged this very day. I'll marry him."

Then, overcome by rage, he grated: "All right. I wanted to warn you. I wanted to avoid misfortune. You've no one to blame but yourself for what happens."

It was advertised widely that the following Sunday, Lucien Chatel would fly over Paris at high altitude, from the Bois de Vincennes to the Bois de Boulogne. He proposed to fly straight and high, to trace an invisible rainbow over the city.

He scarcely suspected, in deciding on that experiment, that he was signing his death-warrant—for Villeret was determined. That flight over Paris seemed to him to be a sign from destiny. On that day, Lucien Chatel must die.

In that brain degraded by vice and corroded by hatred, the idea of murder had gradually been sown, had taken root and blossomed. Now it had invaded his entire being.

Having condemned his rival to death, Villeret prepared the execution with ferocious care. He needed, on the eve of the attempt, to work secretly for an hour on the apparatus that would take the hero aloft. All his ingenuity and cunning was concentrated on that goal.

Who would be on guard, when night fell, in the annex to the workshops where the great white birds rested? Villeret soon discovered the watchman in whom Chatel placed his confidence. Was there one man who performed the Herculean task of bringing an airplane on to the field? That was Lanoix. Who, then, brought the cans of fuel at a trot, and the water-sprinkler? Lanoix again. Who excelled at keeping curiosity-seekers behind the barriers, without prevarication? Still Lanoix. At every moment, one heard the firm voice of Lucien Chatel and the more excited voices of clients sitting at the joystick for the first time calling: "Lanoix! Lanoix!"

He was both the guard-dog and the sheep-dog rolled into one. But what a mastiff! A giant, tall and broad, massive, his upper body molded in a blue-and-white striped jersey, his legs lost in immense brown velvet trousers, his knees, fists and chin always jutting forwards, as if ready to fight—and with all that, bright eyes and fine full lips, in which, beneath the bushy moustache, an eternal cigarette was perched.

The proprietor of a nearby drinking den completed Villeret's information. Lanoix was a former wastrel from the Marne. In those times, when he had been drinking, he was terrible. After one brawl—perhaps he had drunk too much absinthe—he had got a year in prison. When he came out, Monsieur Chatel had had the bizarre idea of hiring him. He had domesticated him, rendered him as gentle as a demoiselle. Lanoix no longer drank. That would last as long as it lasted. Deep down, the tavern-keeper remained skeptical, and somewhat scornful, with regard to the man who refused a little tot. But Monsieur Chatel had faith in him. The proof was that he had confided the guard of his machines to Lanoix. The former wastrel had built himself a kind of cabin in a corner of the hangar in which he ate and slept, with a large revolver within arm's reach. Oh, it wasn't a good idea to rub him up the wrong way—for Lanoix was trigger-happy.

On the Friday before the flight over Paris, Villeret waited for the moment when the machines had been put away, Chatel had gone and the crowd had begun to disperse. Accosting Lanoix, who was closing the gates of the forecourt, he said: "*Bonjour, mon brave*. Not long before bedtime, eh? Would you like a little aperitif first, just over there?" And he pointed to the nearby tavern.

Lanoix spat out his cigarette and swallowed his saliva—but if he was agitated by a desire, he quickly stifled it. Shaking his head, he refused flatly.

Villeret feared that he might give himself away by persisting too strongly. He gave up, searching for another line of attack. "It's too late to visit the workshops today, I suppose?"

Lanoix chopped the air with his enormous hand, like the blade of a guillotine. "Closed." Not prolix, the wastrel.

"That's a pity," said Villeret, regretfully. "I'm a friend and admirer of Monsieur Chatel."

Ah! Monsieur Chatel certainly had no more fervent admirer than Lanoix himself. He was his god. The guardian remained inflexible, however. He rolled another cigarette with a single glide of his palm over his thigh.

"Talk to him." And he closed the gate.

Villeret shrugged his shoulders. He could not reckon with the brute by means of a frontal assault. It was necessary to use cunning, and quickly, for time was pressing.

The next day, Saturday, the eve of the exploit, when all eyes were on Lucien Chatel, who was flying at a great height, Villeret, summoning up his audacity, introduced himself cautiously into the courtyard and went into the deserted garage. There he paused momentarily. Along one wall, immense packing-crates were lined up, which served to send airplanes over long distances, draped with tarpaulins. Villeret threw himself into that hiding-place...

An hour later, when the trials had finished, Lanoix closed the door, locking the enemy inside.

Through the gaps in the tarpaulins, Villeret had watched the reentry of the great white birds. In particular, he had taken careful note of Chatel's apparatus. He did not take his eyes off it. Damn! He must not make a mistake—but no error was possible. Once it was in place, the young inventor had carried out a detailed inspection. It was definitely the one that he would employ the following day.

Now Villeret remained alone in the immense hall. Undoubtedly, Lanoix had gone in search of his meal at the nearby tavern. It was necessary to profit from his absence. Villeret had quickly discovered the watchman's cabin in the corner opposite his hiding place. He ran to it and took an inventory with a glance: a little bed with a brown coverlet in a pine frame, a small beside table on which there was an old magazine, a candle in a tray and an enormous revolver.

Rapidly, he took from one of his pockets a bottle wrapped in silver paper stamped with a Cross of Geneva, placed it clearly in view on the floor and ran back to his refuge.

Two minutes later, Lanoix came back.

Villeret waited for two hours in darkness. He chewed over his hatred, ruminating his plan. Oh, he had thought about it carefully, rejecting many possibilities. Obviously, he could have taken a file to the propeller-tree or some part of the engine, but everyone knew that a Chatel apparatus, deprived of means of propulsion, glided gently through the aerial strata to land softly. No, it was necessary that the fabric of the wings, the taut canvas that maintained the machine in the air, should suddenly disappear, be annihilated... Then nothing would remain but a heavy carcass, five hundred kilos of metal, which would collapse, plummeting to the ground...

Of course! It wasn't sorcery. It was sufficient to think of it. He would coat the canvas with a phosphoric solution of his own manufacture. At rest, it would remain quiescent; nothing would betray its presence, but when the air struck the wings at a hundred kilometers an hour it would evaporate, and the phosphorus, struck like a match, would catch fire. In the wind of its velocity, the varnished and rubberized fabric would burn like lamp-oil, like a firework.

In order to do his work well, however, Villeret needed Lanoix to fall asleep, stunned by drunkenness. Would he empty the bottle of absinthe set before his eyes as a temptation? After his long abstinence, would he throw himself upon the delicious poison?

Suddenly, the door opened and the giant appeared, his face illuminated from below by the light of the candle he was holding in one hand. In the other, he was clutching his revolver. On the threshold, he stumbled heavily. Then he came out, lurching. He was drunk.

Doubtless moved by an instinct surviving the disaster, Lanoix was making his round as usual: a terrifying spectacle. At a slow pace, his head and shoulders swaying with a circular motion, his revolver in one hand and candle-tray in the other, the colossus advanced between the great white birds. Sometimes his moving shadow was projected sharply on stretched canvas, sometimes it spread out enormously over the walls and the ceiling. His head bumped into the stays, became entangled in the wires. His face was hollowed out be a bleak fury. At times, he pursued an imaginary enemy with unspeakable insults. At others, he gurgled filthy refrains. Then there was silence.

For a moment, he brushed past Villeret, crouching down as low as possible behind the tarpaulins, but already he had passed on, belching vague words, stumbling here and bumping into something there, still clutching his weapon and his candle. It was a miracle that he did not set fire to anything. Instinct guided him, however, and as he continued his march, the great white wings rose up in the darkness and the fuselages stood out like antediluvian skeletons, a whole fantastic herd waking up, whose mobile shadows fused on the walls with that of the watchman.

Then, one last oath burst forth, and the light went out. The brute collapsed in his den to sleep off his drunkenness.

Five minutes later, in the absolute calm, Villeret heard deep and regular breathing—the respiration of sleep. Then, suppressing his terror, but with his heart in his mouth, his hands reaching forwards in the darkness, with a stealthy tread, Villeret headed with infinite pre-

caution for Chatel's airplane. When he had finally recognized it and felt it, he began his deadly work with
careful and tender strokes.

The crowd covered the former drill-field, and
throughout the city, millions of gazes we about to follow
the aircraft, support it is its course. The weather was
splendid. The sky, palpitating and silky, seemed a great
canopy suspended from the golden nail of the sun and
stretched over the fête.

Claire was watching all her fiancé's movements
from a distance. She was afraid. Villeret's threats were
haunting her. If she had dared, she would have run to
Lucien and begged him not to go, but she did not dare.
Then again, Paris was expectant.

With his helmet pulled down over his eyes, Chatel
shakes hands, allows himself to be buttonholed by a
journalist, by a friend, surveys the sky, returns to his apparatus, checks the propeller and the wires once more.
He takes out his watch. Nearly time. Lucien heads toward Claire. In front of the crowd, for the sake of respect, they content themselves with a handshake—but
who can tell how much consolation, hope and love might
have passed between the two gripping hands...

Already, Chatel is at the joystick. He raises his arm,
to tell everyone to stand clear. The engine starts, the
propeller turns—and while the pilot, with a customary
gesture, adjusts his helmet, the bird begins to move,
skimming the soil, leaves the ground and abruptly takes
flight.

Instinctively, the crowd is rushing behind him, but
Claire is incapable of moving forward, and is left alone.
All her life is up there. She feels a great dolorous void
within her. She has difficulty breathing. How rapidly he

is climbing. It will take him a quarter of an hour to describe his curve over Paris. How long a quarter of an hour is!

Suddenly, a snigger burst out behind her. She turns round. Villeret...him again! And he is transfigured by such an unholy joy that apprehension immediately takes hold of Claire, choking her. She is certain that something bad is about to happen. What trap has he set? Her entire being asks the question.

Oh, Villeret cannot contain himself. He wants all his pleasure—and the best of his vengeance is not the sudden death of Chatel; it's the torture of Claire, who will know, who will wait, who will live through seconds of unparalleled horror.

In a few words, he relishes his secret—and it is indeed an unparalleled torture. No one who has not been in love can comprehend it. Thus, perhaps in a second, perhaps in five interminable minutes, that small white thing up there, which is carrying her life, will burst into flame, collapse, plunge down like a falling stone. Lucien! Lucien!

And there is nothing she can do. It is her impotence, more than anything else, that enrages her. Not to be able to do anything...

She would like to scream, to howl, she would like her voice to carry all the way to that tiny dot shining in the sunlight: "Come down! Come down, quickly!" But there is nothing she can do...

Ah! Villeret has chosen his moment to speak very well: soon enough to watch for the inevitable, too late to prevent it...

Claire stammers a few inconsequential words. It seems to her that she is shrinking, becoming a little girl again. She would like to weep, to fall to her knees, no

253

longer to se, to die. Her vision becomes blurred. Sparks dance before her eyes. Is that the little white dot catching fire? Yes? No, not yet.

And to stay there, to stay there...

Suddenly, behind her, a great clamor goes up. Ah! This time, it's the end. But Villeret spits out a furious cruse. She turns her head, to behold a dream-like spectacle...

In front of the workshops, a man, all by himself, a colossus, is hauling a burning airplane behind him, launching himself on to the drill-square. The wind of his prodigious run excites the fire and deploys enormous wings of flame behind his back.

He stops. Claire dares not hope yet, but Villeret has already pulled himself together. Has he mistaken the apparatus in the dark, in his confusion? Has Chatel, suspicious, chosen another at the last moment? What does it matter? He has to start again.

Saved! Lucien is saved! And while, in the distance, the little white dot continues to describe its glorious curve westwards, Claire thinks she might faint in the exquisite relief, the abrupt passage from agony to ecstasy.

Meanwhile, the giant abandons the airplane, which completes its consumption. He has broken the circle of curiosity-seekers. He comes closer. His hair and moustache are charred. His blackened face is swollen with fury. One would think that he were searching for someone.

He has recognized Villeret—and fragments of words collide in his mouth, still thickened by drunkenness...

That's him—that's the man who tried to buy him. It was him who put the bottle of absinthe in his cabin. He suspected as much. If he had not, when scarcely awake, still drunk, thrown his lit cigarette at the canvas of an apparatus, he would never have known—but now he understands everything. That bandit wanted to kill Monsieur Chatel. Kill Monsieur Chatel, his god! But he's caught, the swine...he won't try again...

And before anyone can stop him, Lanoix, crazed by absinthe and indignation, brings his revolver out of his trouser pocket and fires six shots at Villeret, killing him like a dangerous animal.

SF & FANTASY

Henri Allorge. *The Great Cataclysm*
Guy d'Armen. *Doc Ardan: The City of Gold and Lepers*
G.-J. Arnaud. *The Ice Company*
Charles Asselineau. *The Double Life*
Cyprien Bérard. *The Vampire Lord Ruthwen*
Aloysius Bertrand. *Gaspard de la Nuit*
Richard Bessière. *The Gardens of the Apocalypse*
Albert Bleunard. *Ever Smaller*
Félix Bodin. *The Novel of the Future*
Louis Boussenard. *Monsieur Synthesis*
Alphonse Brown. *City of Glass; The Conquest of the Air*
Emile Calvet. *In a Thousand Years*
André Caroff. *The Terror of Madame Atomos; Miss Atomos; The Return of Madame Atomos; The Mistake of Madame Atomos; The Monsters of Madame Atomos; The Revenge of Madame Atomos; The Resurrection of Madame Atomos*
Félicien Champsaur. *The Human Arrow; Ouha, King of the Apes; Pharaoh's Wife*
Didier de Chousy. *Ignis*
Michel Corday. *The Eternal Flame*
Captain Danrit. *Undersea Odyssey*
C. I. Defontenay. *Star (Psi Cassiopeia)*
Charles Derennes. *The People of the Pole*
Georges Dodds (anthologist). *The Missing Link*
Harry Dickson. *The Heir of Dracula*
Jules Dornay. *Lord Ruthven Begins*
Alfred Driou. *The Adventures of a Parisian Aeronaut*
Sâr Dubnotal *vs. Jack the Ripper*
Alexandre Dumas. *The Return of Lord Ruthven*
Renée Dunan. *Baal*
J.-C. Dunyach. *The Night Orchid; The Thieves of Silence*
Henri Duvernois. *The Man Who Found Himself*
Achille Eyraud. *Voyage to Venus*
Henri Falk. *The Age of Lead*
Paul Féval. *Anne of the Isles; Knightshade; Revenants; Vampire City; The Vampire Countess; The Wandering Jew's Daughter*
Paul Féval, *fils. Felifax, the Tiger-Man*
Charles de Fieux. *Lamékis*

Arnould Galopin. *Doctor Omega*; *Doctor Omega and the Shadowmen* (anthology)
Judith Gautier. *Isoline and the Serpent-Flower*
Léon Gozlan. *The Vampire of the Val-de-Grâce*
G.L. Gick. *Harry Dickson and the Werewolf of Rutherford Grange*
Edmond Haraucourt. *Illusions of Immortality*
Nathalie Henneberg. *The Green Gods*
V. Hugo, P. Foucher & P. Meurice. *The Hunchback of Notre-Dame*
Romain d'Huissier. *Hexagon: Dark Matter*
Michel Jeury. *Chronolysis*
Gustave Kahn. *The Tale of Gold and Silence*
Gérard Klein. *The Mote in Time's Eye*
Fernand Kolney. *Love in 5000 Years*
Louis-Guillaume de La Follie. *The Unpretentious Philosopher*
Jean de La Hire. *Enter the Nyctalope; The Nyctalope on Mars; The Nyctalope vs. Lucifer; The Nyctalope Steps In; Night of the Nyctalope*
Etienne-Léon de Lamothe-Langon. *The Virgin Vampire*
André Laurie. *Spiridon*
Gabriel de Lautrec. *The Vengeance of the Oval Portrait*
Alain le Drimeur. *The Future City*
Georges Le Faure & Henri de Graffigny. *The Extraordinary Adventures of a Russian Scientist Across the Solar System* (2 vols.)
Gustave Le Rouge. *The Vampires of Mars; The Dominion of the World* (w/Gustave Guitton) (4 vols.)
Jules Lermina. *Mysteryville; Panic in Paris; To-Ho and the Gold Destroyers; The Secret of Zippelius*
André Lichtenberger. *The Centaurs*
Jean-Marc & Randy Lofficier. *Edgar Allan Poe on Mars; The Katrina Protocol; Pacifica; Robonocchio; Tales of the Shadowmen 1-9*
Xavier Mauméjean. *The League of Heroes*
Joseph Méry. *The Tower of Destiny*
Hippolyte Mettais. *The Year 5865*
Louise Michel. *The Human Microbes; The New World*
Tony Moilin. *Paris in the Year 2000*
José Moselli. *Illa's End*
John-Antoine Nau. *Enemy Force*
Marie Nizet. *Captain Vampire*
C. Nodier, A. Beraud & Toussaint-Merle. *Frankenstein*
Henri de Parville. *An Inhabitant of the Planet Mars*
Gaston de Pawlowski. *Journey to the Land of the 4th Dimension*
Georges Pellerin. *The World in 2000 Years*

Ernest Pérochon. *The Frenetic People*
Pierre Pelot. *The Child Who Walked on the Sky*
J. Polidori, C. Nodier, E. Scribe. *Lord Ruthven the Vampire*
P.-A. Ponson du Terrail. *The Vampire and the Devil's Son; The Immortal Woman*
Henri de Régnier. *A Surfeit of Mirrors*
Maurice Renard. *The Blue Peril; Doctor Lerne; The Doctored Man; A Man Among the Microbes; The Master of Light*
Jean Richepin. *The Wing; The Crazy Corner*
Albert Robida. *The Adventures of Saturnin Farandoul; The Clock of the Centuries; Chalet in the Sky; The Electric Life*
J.-H. Rosny Aîné. *Helgvor of the Blue River; The Givreuse Enigma; The Mysterious Force; The Navigators of Space; Vamireh; The World of the Variants; The Young Vampire*
Marcel Rouff. *Journey to the Inverted World*
Han Ryner. *The Superhumans*
Brian Stableford. *The New Faust at the Tragicomique;The Empire of the Necromancers (The Shadow of Frankenstein; Frankenstein and the Vampire Countess; Frankenstein in London); Sherlock Holmes & The Vampires of Eternity; The Stones of Camelot; The Wayward Muse.* (anthologist) *The Germans on Venus; News from the Moon; The Supreme Progress; The World Above the World; Nemoville; Investigations of the Future*
Jacques Spitz. *The Eye of Purgatory*
Kurt Steiner. *Ortog*
Eugène Thébault. *Radio-Terror*
C.-F. Tiphaigne de La Roche. *Amilec*
Théo Varlet. *The Golden Rock. The Xenobiotic Invasion; The Castaways of Eros; Timeslip Troopers* (w/André Blandin); *The Martian Epic* (w/Octave Joncquel)
Paul Vibert. *The Mysterious Fluid*
Villiers de l'Isle-Adam. *The Scaffold; The Vampire Soul*
Philippe Ward. *Artahe*
Philippe Ward & Sylvie Miller. *The Song of Montségur*

MYSTERIES & THRILLERS

M. Allain & P. Souvestre. *The Daughter of Fantômas*
A. Anicet-Bourgeois, Lucien Dabril. *Rocambole*
A. Bernède. *Belphegor; Judex* (w/Louis Feuillade); *The Return of Judex* (w/Louis Feuillade); *The Shadow of Judex*

A. Bisson & G. Livet. *Nick Carter vs. Fantômas*
V. Darlay & H. de Gorsse. *Arsène Lupin vs. Sherlock Holmes: The Stage Play*
Séamas Duffy. *Sherlock Holmes in Paris*
Paul Féval. *Gentlemen of the Night; John Devil; The Black Coats ('Salem Street; The Invisible Weapon; The Parisian Jungle; The Companions of the Treasure; Heart of Steel; The Cadet Gang; The Sword-Swallower)*
Emile Gaboriau. *Monsieur Lecoq*
Goron & Emile Gautier. *Spawn of the Penitentiary*
Steve Leadley. *Sherlock Holmes: The Circle of Blood*
Maurice Leblanc. *Arsène Lupin vs. Countess Cagliostro; Arsène Lupin vs. Sherlock Holmes (The Blonde Phantom; The Hollow Needle); The Many Faces of Arsène Lupin*
Gaston Leroux. *Chéri-Bibi; The Phantom of the Opera; Rouletabille & the Mystery of the Yellow Room; Rouletabille at Krupp's*
Richard Marsh. *The Complete Adventures of Judith Lee*
William Patrick Maynard. *The Terror of Fu Manchu; The Destiny of Fu Manchu*
Frank J. Morlock. *Sherlock Holmes: The Grand Horizontals; Sherlock Holmes vs Jack the Ripper*
Antonin Reschal. *The Adventures of Miss Boston*
P. de Wattyne & Y. Walter. *Sherlock Holmes vs. Fantômas*
David White. *Fantômas in America*
Pierre Yrondy. *The Adventures of Thérèse Arnaud*

SCREENPLAYS

Mike Baron. *The Iron Triangle*
Emma Bull & Will Shetterly. *Nightspeeder; War for the Oaks*
Gerry Conway & Roy Thomas. *Doc Dynamo*
Steve Englehart. *Majorca*
James Hudnall. *The Devastator*
Jean-Marc & Randy Lofficier. *Royal Flush*
J.-M. & R. Lofficier & Marc Agapit. *Despair*
J.-M. & R. Lofficier & Joël Houssin. *City*
Andrew Paquette. *Peripheral Vision*
Robert L. Robinson, Jr. *Judex*
R. Thomas, J. Hendler & L. Sprague de Camp. *Rivers of Time*